ALL GOOD CHILDREN

ALL GOOD CHILDREN

CATHERINE AUSTEN

ORCA BOOK PUBLISHERS

Library and Archives Canada Cataloguing in Publication

Austen, Catherine, 1965-
All good children / Catherine Austen.

Issued also in electronic formats.
ISBN 978-1-55469-824-0

I. Title.
PS8601.U785A64 2011   jc813'.6   C2011-903488-3

First published in the United States, 2011
Library of Congress Control Number: 2011929259

Summary: In the not-too-distant future, Max tries to maintain his identity in a world where the only way to survive is to conform and obey.

MIX
Paper from
responsible sources
FSC
www.fsc.org   FSC® C016245

Orca Book Publishers is dedicated to preserving the environment and has printed this book on Forest Stewardship Council® certified paper.

Orca Book Publishers gratefully acknowledges the support for its publishing programs provided by the following agencies: the Government of Canada through the Canada Book Fund and the Canada Council for the Arts, and the Province of British Columbia through the BC Arts Council and the Book Publishing Tax Credit.

Design by Teresa Bubela
Cover photography by Getty Images

ORCA BOOK PUBLISHERS
PO Box 5626, Stn. B
Victoria, BC Canada
V8R 6S4

ORCA BOOK PUBLISHERS
PO Box 468
CUSTER, WA USA
98240-0468

www.orcabook.com
Printed and bound in Canada.

15 14 13 12 • 5 4 3 2

To Sawyer and Daimon,
who are not in this one,
and to a boy named Pierre,
who haunts these pages as Xavier.

When the children have been good,
That is, be it understood,
Good at meal-times, good at play,
Good all night and good all day—
They shall have the pretty things
Merry Christmas always brings.

Naughty, romping girls and boys
Tear their clothes and make a noise,
Spoil their pinafores and frocks,
And deserve no Christmas-box.
Such as these shall never look
At this pretty Picture-Book.

From Heinrich Hoffmann's
Struwwelpeter: Merry Stories and Funny Pictures
(1845)

PART ONE
TREATMENT

ONE

The airport security guard is not amused when I drop my pants in front of her. Actually, they fall down when I remove my belt. I don't want to look like a recall, so I play along: fold the pants, strip off my T-shirt, cue my charming adolescent smile. "I'm ready for my pat-down now."

The guard stares at me, blank and bored, hands planted on her fat hips. Broken body scanners, delayed flights, exhausted travelers, near-naked teens—they all blend in her muddy eyes. "Are you carrying any liquids or electronics?" she asks.

Beside me, my sister Ally giggles through her own pat-down. She runs across the room to find her shoes and teddy bear. Our mother shields her from the sight of me.

"Lady, I'm almost naked," I say. I point to my shorts and add, "I could take these off, too, if it'll get me through faster. I know it looks like I might be hiding something."

The guard frowns, blinks, reaches her gloved hands up to my neck as if she's going to throttle me. She probably hears that joke twice a day. "Did you place your electronics in the bin?" she asks. Her fat fingers scurry over my bare shoulders, down my breastbone, around my back, as if contraband could be hiding beneath my skin.

My mother's voice booms across the room. "Why is that woman touching my child's body? Is she blind? He is fifteen years old. He's a citizen—" And on and on until every traveler stares at me and my molester.

I pretend this is a normal encounter. I nod to passersby. "My mother confiscated my electronics last week," I tell the guard as she strokes my naked thighs. "I'm grounded. Actually, I'm about to be airborne. But metaphorically I'm grounded. I was a bad boy."

She groans to her feet, pats my ass none too gently and motions me onward. I dress in front of a thousand eyes that glitter like glass under the terminal lights.

I follow my angry mother to the boarding gate. New chairs, same wait. Same blend of stale gum and subtitled news: New York City is still drowning; Phoenix is still parched; transnational corporations are still profiting from disaster. I withstand it all.

I would strip again if it got me home faster, but we're stuck for another hour. Five hundred heads lean into five hundred projections: reading, playing, messaging, leering. Not me. My RIG lies at the bottom of Mom's purse, a Realtime Integrated Gateway to a world my mother won't let me access.

Mom and Ally chant together face to face—"Rock! Paper! Scissors!" and "Wild Wild West!"—feeble finger-plays Mom learned on the bus to kindergarten when she was young. Now and then she glances at me and asks, "What were you thinking?" as if she really wants to know.

Our flight is called at last. I grab the window seat as a reward for withstanding so royally. My heart pounds in anticipation. This will be the second flight of my life, and it'll be even better than last week's, because it's taking me home.

A giddy sense of freedom washed over me when that first plane lifted off the ground. I held my RIG to the window and watched dead grass and pavement recede into an abstract of greens and browns scarred by rivers and roads. Ally squeezed my leg and squealed, "It's like we're riding a pterosaur!" Even our mother smiled.

My world was shining then, as we blazed toward Aunt Sylvia's funeral, all expenses paid. I didn't pretend to be sad—I barely knew my aunt. I was ecstatic, literally on top of the world. I flew away from the first week of school, left my dull gray uniform in New Middletown and rose above a planet that looked like God's own palette.

It was glorious until cruising altitude, when Mom received a notice about a prank bomb threat sent to my school from our apartment complex that morning. She snatched the RIG right out of my hand. "You logged in as Lucas?" she shrieked.

"What makes you think it was me?" I asked.

She rolled her eyes and huffed, as if no other child would break a rule.

"It was a joke," I told her. "He left his RIG in the lobby. His password is *Lucas1*."

"You used to be that boy's friend!"

I shrugged. "He's a throwaway."

I shouldn't have said that. It's what all the academic students call the trade kids, but I would have gotten my RIG back last week if I'd just held my tongue. Mom dragged me through funeral homes and legal offices, down the unguarded streets of an ungated city, with my RIG bouncing blindly in her handbag, recording nothing.

Atlanta was the first city I'd ever visited outside of New Middletown. It was beautiful in its crazy patchwork sprawl, but seriously marred by poverty. Winds whipped down the avenues into alleyways where people lived in paper boxes. Beggars and thieves lurked around corners or banged on the windows of limousines jammed in traffic until police officers dragged them away. It was hostile and hopeless and deeply unnerving.

But behind the cars and crowds was the most amazing graffiti I've ever seen—huge, vibrant, angry. Ally snuck me her RIG so I could record a few images: a tidal wave crashing into a lopsided skyline, a line of prisoners with empty eye sockets, a salt flat littered with honeybee carcasses.

One day I'll paint a piece like that.

My mother took her time burying her sister. By the third day, not even the art could make the noise and dirt and stink bearable. My cousin Rebecca should have settled everything, but she immigrated to Canada ten years ago and wasn't allowed back. She inherited a small fortune from her mother, but the government seized it. They gave Mom nothing but funeral expenses—hence the family airplane ride, the week of hotel breakfasts, the evenings stretched out like years on Atlanta's lilac sheets.

Now we're heading home with boxes of worthless fragments from Rebecca's childhood—hand-written letters, framed photographs, report card printouts. It's like inheriting a recycling bin. But among the memorabilia were sixteen color markers packaged in plastic and three gray scrapbooks I've already filled from seam to corner with abstracts of Earth. I'll post a collage when I get my RIG back: *Out of School Withstanding on a Perilous Planet.*

Ally grips my hand when our plane takes its turn at the top of the runway. The fuselage rattles, wing flaps flutter, wheels blindly spin. We grip our armrests and fall silent. It doesn't feel close to fast enough. The plane screams and roars. It seems almost silly to try to get off the ground. But suddenly, improbably, we rise. I laugh out loud. We rise above the patchwork city into a pure white blazing light. I wish I could tell my friends, "Look up. See that silver speck slicing the sky? That's me!" But I'll have to wait until I'm home to post about it. By then, no one will care. Once you're in the past tense, you're history, and no one has time for history anymore.

There's a complimentary snack in my seat pocket. The chips taste like mold. I eat them fast, more disappointed with every crunch. Mom passes hers and I eat those, too, until I'm deeply miserable. "Can I have my RIG now?"

"No."

Ally unfolds her seat tray, lays down her chips and rests her teddy's head on them.

"Aren't you going to eat your snack?" I ask.

She grabs the bag fast as lightning and stashes it on her lap.

"I'll eat them if you don't want them," I say.

A fat man across the aisle ogles my mother and says, "Kids. They're never satisfied."

When I see men like this, I'm thankful for genetic testing. Whatever my future may hold, I'll never end up a fat bald white man. This one takes up two seats and he's still crammed tight. I point to the chips resting on his belly. "Are you going to eat those?"

"Please ignore him," Mom tells the man.

He covers his chips with his fat white hands and winks at her.

Ally taps my shoulder and asks, in a voice soft and high, "If you're not going to look out the window, can we trade places?"

"No." I fake a stretch and sneak the chips from her lap. I keep my eyes on the clouds as I crack open the bag. I dip into it languorously and pop a few in my mouth. Ally doesn't notice. "Want a chip?" I offer.

"No, thank you. I have my own." She reaches under her tray. A look of panic floods her face. She lifts her teddy, feels her legs, scans the floor, gropes the filthy carpet.

"Lost something?" I ask.

"I can't find my chips!"

"What did they look like?"

She stuffs her hand down the back of her seat. "They were in a red bag!"

I move the chips to the center of the window frame. "With white writing?"

"Yes! Did you see them?"

"Give her back her chips, Max," Mom says.

Ally looks from Mom to me to the chips in my hand.

"Here. Have these," I offer.

"Are you sure?" Ally asks. "We could do Eenie Meenie for them."

"Nah. Just take them."

She smiles at the half-eaten bag. "Thanks, Max. You're nice."

My mother sighs.

The fat man clears his throat. "Lovely children. Are they your own?"

Mom's face is five shades darker than mine and Ally's, and now it turns darker still. She looks him up and down and rolls her eyes. That should end the conversation, but the man is deeply defective. "And their father?" he asks, leering at my mother's breasts.

"Our father's dead," I say. "He died in the flu epidemic three years ago. Drowned in his own body fluids."

"Max, please," Mom says.

"So she's single now," I add.

The fat man squirms and mumbles something about being sorry.

The man in the seat beside him peeks around his gut. I groan. It's Arlington Richmond, my best friend Dallas's father. He hates me. He hates my whole family. He didn't mind us when Dad was alive, but his feelings cooled when half our income died. I salute him and turn back to the sun.

I wish I could message Dallas that his dad is surveying me at thirty thousand feet. But I can't connect with anyone without my RIG. On the upside, I can't access my homework. "We were lucky to miss the first week of school," I whisper to Ally.

She frowns. "I like school."

Mom kisses the top of her head. Ally takes Mom's face in her hands and kisses it back—her cheeks, her nose, her eyelids, over and over until the sweetness turns unsettling. "Enough, pumpkin," Mom says.

The *Freakshow* theme song rises out of the airplane chatter ahead of me. I jerk to attention and peer between the seats.

A teenage boy whips his head around and grunts. Either I have very strong chip breath or he has supreme peripheral vision. He slips in his earpiece and holds my stare. He has *ultimate* written all over him. Even sitting down, he looks like a giant. His parents must have tested a dozen eggs before they found him.

I am not an ultimate. I'm a best-of-three. Only the rich keep at it until they get a perfect embryo. There are a lot of rich people in New Middletown, so I'm used to competing with ultimates like this kid. They usually win.

Most people are freebies, conceived and birthed at home with just the barest screening for deformities. They talk about ultimates and best-of-threes like we're genetically engineered, but we're not. We're conceived in fertility clinics, but there's no splicing or even much planning involved. It's more like gambling than engineering. Parents pay for a certain number of random embryos. They don't know what they'll get until they read the genes and choose one to grow in the womb. The unhealthy are terminated and the unchosen are put in cold storage to sneak out sometime in the future when infertility reaches crisis proportions. Or maybe they're sold or experimented on or grown for parts— depending on which conspiracy theory you believe—but they're not genetically engineered.

I'm the cream of a crop of three. It's hard to get cocky about that. The kid ahead of me is the cream of a much richer crop. His eyes sparkle as he surveys me over his shoulder. "If it isn't the stripper," he says, snickering. "Nice shorts, recall."

I salute him rudely and lean back, kicking his chair out of spite. "Sorry," I say. Then I kick it again. The security guard glares from his station.

"Be good, Max," Ally says. My sister is not an ultimate or a best-of-three. She's a freebie, naturally conceived six years ago by my baffled parents. Mom says she's a gift from God. Ally has a big heart and a small brain, which suggests that God should take a good look at creation before he hands out any more gifts.

"We can't all be you," I tell her.

Dr. Richmond snickers.

Mom glances across the aisle. "Arlington? What a surprise. How are you?"

The fat man turns from Mom to Dr. Richmond as if he has a stake in their conversation.

"I'm fine, Karenna. I'm just heading back from the Global Ed Conference in Texas. I was supposed to take the speed rail, but Mexicans bombed the station. Did you hear about it? Are you coming direct from Atlanta? You have family there, don't you? It must have cost a fortune to take the kids for the weekend."

"Not at all," Mom says, not bothering to explain about the funeral or the lost week of school.

"You should take Dallas to your next conference," I say. "He'd love flying."

Dr. Richmond frowns. "They get so lippy at this age. At least you won't have to put up with it much longer."

Mom checks her watch. "Twenty minutes? That was fast."

"I mean it won't be long until we get Maxwell's behavior straightened out at school," Dr. Richmond says.

I snort but not loudly. Mom holds a stiff smile.

"The new support program's coming," he adds. "I'm sure you saw the results with your little girl last week. It provides the motivation lacking in kids like yours."

Mom's smile vanishes. "Kids like mine?"

The fat man shakes his head at Dr. Richmond and waits for an apology.

"I'm sure they're good children," Dr. Richmond says. "They're just different, aren't they?"

A recording tells us to buckle our belts, store our baggage, raise our seat trays. Dr. Richmond leans back out of view. Mom stares hard at the place where he used to be. The fat man tucks his chips in his breast pocket.

I slip my empty packages onto Ally's tray, then store my own tray, pushing it into the seat ahead of me until the ultimate growls.

"Where did these come from?" Ally asks, holding my chip bags.

I shrug. "They must be yours."

She turns them over, puzzled, before tucking them in her seat pocket. Then she leans into my chest and holds her teddy up to the window.

I kiss her head and love her like crazy, my gullible good-hearted sister.

The plane tilts in preparation for landing. I see the military escort beside us and the runway lights below. It looks like we're heading to prison. "Holiday's over," I whisper.

It's a half-hour shuttle from the Bradford Airport across the National Forest to New Middletown, but Mom still won't give me back my RIG. I'm stuck staring at the beauty of the Pennsylvania Wilds. I kick Ally's foot just for something to do.

"You will never get that RIG back if you don't stop right now," Mom says so loudly that other passengers look our way. I stare out the window like I'm not involved.

There are no cars for rent at the New Middletown station, so we take a taxi home. The driver's ID reads *Abdal-Salam Al-Fulin*. I've barely buckled up before he asks, "Did you hear about the speed-rail bombings in the southwest? Over three hundred dead. There's nowhere safe anymore."

We show a guard our IDs and drive through the gates of my glorious town. "I feel pretty safe right here," I say, but I know I'll feel a lot safer once I get out of this taxi.

Ally watches a wildlife show in the backseat beside Mom, who stares out the window. Mom was RIG-addicted before Dad died. She uploaded our lives as they happened. Now she lets the world blur by.

"I love driving in this city," the driver tells me. "Every road is a straight line."

"It's energy efficient," I tell him. "New Middletown is the most environmentally smart city in the northeast. But they chopped down ten square miles of forest to build it. We're big on irony here."

"I don't like the forest," the driver says.

I shrug. "It's beautiful." I've never actually stepped foot in the forest, but I like driving by and seeing all the different shades of green. New Middletown is monotonous. Everything in town is the same age, same style, same color. What we lack in personality we compensate for with security. Half the city is bordered by forest and the other half is walled. There are only six roads into town and all of them are guarded. We don't sprawl. We stand tall and tight. There are no beggars or thieves in New Middletown. If you don't have a place to live and work here, you don't get in. This driver probably hates the forest because he has to live there in a tent.

Over the past twenty years, Chemrose International has built six cities just like this to house the six largest geriatric centers in the world. Everyone who lives or works in New Middletown pays rent to Chemrose. The whole town revolves around New Middletown Manor Heights Geriatric Rest Home and its 32,000 beds.

"I never get lost here," the driver says as he joins a line of cars traveling north along the city spine, past hospitals, labs and office towers.

"I'm surprised you get much business," I say.

The city spines are entirely pedestrian, and each quadrant is like a self-contained village, with its own schools, clinics, gardens, rec centers, even our own hydroponics and water treatment facilities. We don't have much call for taxicabs.

"I don't get much business," the driver admits. "Mostly I take people away."

"To where?"

He shrugs. "You go to school here?"

"Sure. Academic school."

"Lucky boy. What you going to be when you're grown?"

"An architect." I don't hesitate. We pick our career paths early in academic school.

"You going to build things like that?" the driver asks me. He points to the New Middletown City Hall and Security Center, which glimmers in the distance on our left. It stands at the intersection of the city spines, in the exact center of town, rising to a point in twenty-eight staggered stories of colored glass.

"I hope so," I say.

He snorts. "I don't like it. It looks like it's made of ice." He turns onto the underpass and City Hall disappears from view.

"That's the artistic heart of town," I say.

He snorts again. "I don't see any art in this city. Never. I don't hear any music. I don't hear any stories. I don't see any theater."

"You can see all that from any room in any building," I tell him. "We have our own communications network."

He sighs. "You like living here?"

"Of course. Who wouldn't? People line up to get in here."

"Like me," he says. "I line up and wait, I come inside, I drop you off, I leave."

"Times are tough," I say.

"Not for everyone," he mutters. He drives up to ground level and heads away from the core.

Chemrose spent eight years and billions of dollars building this city just before I was born. They laid down the spines and connecting roads like a giant spider building a web. People swarmed here. But they didn't all get in. Shanties and carparks spread outside the western wall, full of hopefuls who come inside for a few hours to clean our houses or drive us home. They were hit hard by the Venezuelan flu, which wiped out half the elderly and 10 percent of everyone else in the city, including my father. The epidemic cost Chemrose a fortune in private funding and public spirit. Mom kept her nursing job, so we're fit. We moved from a four-bedroom house to a two-bedroom apartment that sits on the fringe of our old neighborhood. Ally and I are still in academic schools, so we have hope, which is a rare commodity these dangerous days. Most people are a lot more damaged.

"Maybe I will find a bed here when I am old," the driver says with another snort.

"Turn left here," I say.

We cruise through the northeast residential district, past the white estate homes where I used to live, through a maze of tan-on-beige triplexes and brown-on-tan row houses, and into our black-on-brown apartment complex. "Unit six," I say.

The driver circles the complex like a cop, slow and suspicious, passing five identical buildings before he gets to ours, the Spartan—as in the apple, not the Greeks. The apartments are memorials to fallen fruit: Liberty, Gala, Crispin, Fuji, McIntosh. "This is where you live?" the driver asks. He looks up, unimpressed.

The apartments reek of economy. No balconies, no roof gardens, no benches. Just right angles and solar panels and recycling bins. I used to mock the people who lived here. Now I withstand the mockery of others.

I hold out my hand to Mom. She stares at me curiously. "RIG," I say. She rolls her eyes but gives me what I want.

I power up, empty the trunk, drag two suitcases to the door. "Thanks for the ride," I tell Abdal. "Good luck."

"Good luck to you too," he shouts.

⸺✕⸺

Before I even cross my threshold, my neighbor, Xavier Lavigne, heads down the dirty hallway toward me. "I told Mr. Reese that our history assignment is a lie," he says, "and I showed him a report from the free media, but he said I have to go to a disciplinary committee hearing now." That's Xavier's version of *hello*. He speaks nonstop conspiracy theory to anyone who doesn't walk away, and he speaks it in seventeen languages, including binary code. He gets caught every week for illegal Internet access, but only because he posts his hacked information into his essays. His brilliant brain is defective. He thinks I'm his best friend because I'm not cruel to him, just slightly mocking. Minimal standards of friendship are part of his defect. I don't invite him in, and he doesn't hold it against me.

"Hey, Xavier. Did you sign me up for cross-country like I asked?"

He nods. "I had to forge your attendance to get you in."

"You can do that?"

He leans against the doorframe and smiles. I take a step back.

The most abnormal thing about Xavier is that he smells delicious, like a human dessert. Today it's orange marmalade. He's a compulsive bather with expensive taste in soap. He's also the best-looking guy I've ever seen. I don't mean that in a gay way, because I'm not gay. It's just a fact that still takes me by surprise. He looks like an adult. He's six feet tall, broad and sculpted from obsessive track-and-field practice. He has flawless white skin, shiny blond hair and turquoise eyes that sparkle with neurotic passion. His face is perfectly symmetrical. It's jarring against his damaged personality.

"It's easy," he says. "I forged Ally's attendance, too, to sign her up for soccer. I gave her a seventy-five in a math assessment she missed on Wednesday, and I filled out the nurse's forms for a vaccination she missed on Friday. You better tell your mom."

"Sure. Thanks."

"Did you take the speed rail? Did you see the bombings?"

"Nah. We flew."

"I heard it was the Mexicans. They sabotaged our trains because we sabotaged their desalination plants."

"That's crazy, Xavier. We *built* their desalination plants. It was a militia from Arizona that sabotaged them. They probably bombed the speed rail too."

"People are dying of thirst in Arizona."

"So they should bomb the reservoirs instead of the speed rail."

Xavier frowns. "My parents told me not to say that."

I laugh. "Afraid you'll get arrested?"

"Maybe. The state restricted the right to protest. Did you hear? You can only protest on your own land now. And they passed the universal ID."

"We already have a universal ID," I say.

"In New Middletown. Now it's coming everywhere. Faces and fingerprints."

I shake my head. "Everywhere? That'll never happen."

"Excuse us, Xavier," Mom says at the doorway. "How are you, dear?"

"They're testing pharmaceuticals on the prison population," he replies.

Mom nods, smiles, leads Ally to their bedroom to unpack.

While Xavier details the dirty deeds of Chemrose International, I filter seven hundred and thirty-five messages from my week offline. Ads, celebrity news, listserv chatter, history. I'm stunned to see a call from Pepper Cassidy. She's a member of *REAL: Reduced Electronic Activity in Life*. Her messages are rare and beautiful.

Pepper's face shines on my screen: brown eyes, pink mouth, cinnamon skin. "I need you, Max! We all need you!" The camera pans over a line of pretty pouty girls whispering, "I need you, Max." I couldn't dream it any better. Pepper leans in close, smiling. "There are only two boys in dance this term, and you know they have no rhythm. Please say you'll try out."

I save the call.

"The children in the trials are institutionalized," Xavier tells me.

"The dance trials?"

"Drug trials. Will you help me circulate a petition?"

I laugh. "I'm fifteen, Xavier. I can barely circulate peanut butter on toast."

I sort through ninety-eight messages from Dallas Richmond—that's one message for every waking hour I was offline. Ninety are single-sentence questions beginning with *Who do you think would win in a fight*. Seven are lists of names and bra sizes for the girls in each of our classes. One is a compilation of insulting names Coach Emery called me because I missed football practice. "I'm a limpdick and an asswipe," I tell Xavier.

He nods without sympathy.

"Xavier! Dad wants you!" Celeste Lavigne glides down the hallway to fetch her brother. She's a softer, curvier version of Xavier. She and I are the only people in the entire complex who have younger siblings. I think that should draw us together. She disagrees.

"Celeste!" I shout. "We're back!"

She ignores me. "Come see what I did to Dad," she tells Xavier.

I consider myself invited.

Down the hall, Mr. and Mrs. Lavigne hover inside their doorway. You have to use your imagination to see how Xavier and Celeste turned out so beautiful. The Lavignes are unusually large, white and old, like Vikings gone to seed. They're pasty and spongy and they dress in woolen cardigans buttoned into the wrong holes.

Mr. Lavigne looks especially bad today because Celeste has been working on him. His face is scored with black and pink festering flesh, like a burn victim's.

"Royal makeup," I say. Celeste is a rising star in the special-effects department at the college she attends.

"Come inside, children," Mr. Lavigne says through crispy lips. "Don't talk in the hallway." He glances at the surveillance camera in the corner. No one ever talks in our hallway except Xavier. He compensates for a world of silence.

"You're back!" Dallas shouts into his RIG. He smiles—sparkling, mature, ultimate. Dallas and I were the same size until he turned twelve and his expensive genes kicked in. Now he's the tallest kid in grade ten. He's broad and brawny, with white skin, black hair and blue eyes. His parents spent a fortune conceiving him and his brother. He's from a sperm donor, which explains why he's shining. His older brother Austin is a beast, the true spawn of Dr. Richmond. "Who do you think would win in a fight?" Dallas asks me. "Zipperhead or Juice?"

He must be talking about *Freakshow*. Kids have crazy names these days, but not that crazy. "I haven't checked out the show yet," I say. "I just got my RIG back."

"I think maybe Juice would win, if he didn't bleed to death. Zipperhead's big but slow. Tiger could probably waste them both. I voted for him." Dallas always supports the feeblest freak with the phoniest life story. He has never won the local *Freakshow* betting pool, not in all the years we've voted.

"What did I miss at school?" I ask him.

"Tyler Wilkins got in a fight."

"No way. Is he suspended?"

"No. It was off grounds. With little Wheaton Smithwick."

"Good. Not for Wheaton, but good for me." Tyler Wilkins is the school psychopath. He slapped my sister across the face last June when she grabbed at a lighter he was holding to a tent-caterpillar nest. I hit him back, of course, but he pounded the crap out of my ribs. I chased after him and tackled him on school grounds, where he wasted my face for an encore, and we both got suspended. It was embarrassing. I'm a stocky football player. Tyler is a wiry cigarette addict. But he's tall and has mania in his corner. The school took his parents to court when he was eight years old to force them to medicate him. It hasn't helped.

I gained fifteen pounds of muscle this summer and paid Dallas's brother to teach me how to fight—all so I can beat Tyler Wilkins half to death when I go back to school tomorrow. Austin is as much of a savage as Tyler, but he supplemented his savagery with Muay Thai and growth hormones. He's a supreme fighting instructor. A little light on top though—he's farting in the background right now, aiming at Dallas's head.

"I have to go," Dallas says.

Austin sticks his face in the screen and shouts, "Call's over, faggot!"

***

I sink into my leather couch and skim celebrity gossip on my RIG while Mom fries bacon for tomorrow's lunches. I love my rancid peeling home. It's cramped and flimsy and we don't belong here any more than the teak tables and oil paintings we carted over with Dad's ashes, but I am joyous to be back.

Ally stands at the living-room window, talking into her RIG. "I'm calling my best friend Melissa," she whispers.

"I thought your best friend was Peanut," I say.

She giggles. "I have lots of best friends."

I search student journals for sex and violence, but come up wanting.

Ally dissolves her screen with a frown. "They don't want me calling unless it's about school."

I shrug. "It's late. You'll see Melissa tomorrow. Eat your snack."

We take turns eating crackers with cream cheese until there's only one left. Ally points back and forth between us, chanting, "One, two, buckle my shoe. Three, four, shut the door—"

I eat the cracker.

"You didn't wait!"

"Whoever is number two is chosen in the end." I've told her this a thousand times, but she still counts out the rhyme until she's satisfied that fair is fair.

Mom slips her feet into ugly white orthopedic shoes. "I've been put on night shifts for a few weeks."

"You're going to work?" I ask. "We just got home."

She shrugs. "I'll be back in the morning. I'll sign out a car and drive you to school. Get breakfast and help Ally pack her bag, would you?"

"Fine," I say. I hate pouring breakfast and packing lunch.

I stick my head out the window and breathe in New Middletown's warm dust. It's eight o'clock at night and one hundred degrees—too hot for September. In this heat, in this apartment, it smells like rotting fruit. Down the street, a billboard announces the opening of another Chemrose hydroponics factory this winter, good times ahead, rows of young men and women in blue uniforms and pink smiles.

"Mommy's driving us to school tomorrow," Ally says. That's a thrill for her—two cars in two days. We probably can't afford the fuel.

Life is lean without a father. We could get a stepfather easily—with sperm so feeble after years of herpes, hormones and heavy metals, the useless men like to marry into children—but I couldn't withstand that. Mom says Ally and I are all she needs. As long as we have each other, we'll be okay.

"I hope we're not in trouble for missing the first week of school," Ally says.

I kiss her head. "Nah. It'll be fine. Grade one is premium. They'll love you there. Can't you feel it? It'll be great."

She nods to convince herself. "It'll be the best year ever."

TWO

Mom drives us to school in a car that smells like a chemical spill. It's glorious not to walk. It's only a mile and I don't have much to carry, but I like pretending we're still rich. Ally sits behind me with a red backpack on her knees, crammed with emergency undies, gym shoes, jump rope, lunch box, whiteboard and twenty fat markers I secretly covet.

We drop her off first. Her schoolyard is a fenced field of concrete and sand writhing with a thousand children in grades one to four. Girls squeal around the play structures. Boys chase each other down the pavement. Loners hang by the fence and wait for the bell. Ally surveys them hopefully, searching for her friend, then walks away alone.

"Melissa must be sick," Mom says.

"No." I point to the entrance doors. They won't open for another eight minutes, but hundreds of uniformed children wait there with ID badges in hand. "Isn't that Melissa near the door? With the yellow pack?"

Mom nods. "Her whole class is lined up. I wonder if Ally missed something important last week."

"Oh yeah. Xavier said she missed a math assessment and a vaccination."

"How would Xavier know what goes on in grade one?"

"He knows everything."

"Was it a flu vaccine?"

"I don't know. Ask him."

She rolls her eyes like I ought to be on top of my little sister's immunization record.

The high school is a five-minute drive down the road. It's larger and more stylish than the elementary and middle schools, with six black glass-and-concrete units—ambitious architecture for this part of town and so spacious it's unsettling. There's only one academic high school in each of New Middletown's quadrants. Three-quarters of the city's children go to trade schools. Academics cost more and they require a B average right from grade one. It's always competitive, but kindergarten is dog-eat-dog. Once you're recommended for trade school, there's no coming back.

I'm in Secondary Two, which means tenth grade. We're not allowed in the buildings reserved for grades eleven and twelve. The higher the grade, the fewer the students still maintaining a B standing, the more space and attention each student receives. And they need it because once they graduate they'll have to compete with foreign students and private-studies graduates. There's no point paying hundreds of thousands of dollars for twelve years of academic school if you fall behind when you finally get out. You might as well educate yourself online for free.

Tuition is bleeding us dry, but Mom never mentions it. She pulls up to the school gates and smiles like there's nowhere else she'd rather see me. "First day of grade ten," she says proudly.

"And I'm already a week behind," I add.

My principal, Mr. Graham, rushes outside to greet us. He must have seen the car and assumed we were premium people. Confusion spreads across his face when I step out from the passenger seat. Sweat rolls down his temples into his shirt collar. He's another fat bald white man who can't take the heat. The army should enlist them all, stick them in their own division somewhere temperate. They wouldn't need uniforms because they already look identical. An armed battalion of fat bald white men would scare the crap out of any enemy. Just one of them gives me the shivers.

I lean on the hood with my hands clasped, while my mother tells my principal what a good boy I am. "Max knows how fortunate he is to be in academic school. He assured me he won't skip class or get into any fights."

"I'll try not to," I say. "But if someone starts a fight, I'm going to protect myself."

They stare at me like I'm a recall.

"My grades are premium," I remind them.

Mom sighs. "He'll do his best to stay out of trouble."

"Don't worry, Mrs. Connors," Mr. Graham says. "Everything will be fine once our support system gets up and running. What I'm more concerned about is that we didn't see you on the parent board last Friday. Did you watch from home?"

She shakes her head. "I completely forgot about it."

"I hope you'll come out for the fundraiser at the end of the month," he says.

She shrugs. Mom never quite lies. She just avoids answering.

Mr. Graham frowns. "I'm sure you're doing your best under the circumstances." He looks down his nose at me and the car, memorizes the license plate so he'll never again mistake us for someone he cares about.

"Told you he was a beast," I say after he leaves. "He pretends to be nice so he can use you, then he feeds you to the sharks."

"There are no sharks anymore," Mom says.

"He has his own private shark pond. He dangles me over it when I skip detention."

She smiles and tells me she loves me. "Have a good day."

I search for Dallas among five hundred uniformed ninth and tenth graders milling the grounds. They clump near the fence, gab in groups, take photos, message madly. Once we're inside, all RIG use is prohibited except for Blackboard, the school network, so everyone stays out until the final bell. I see my football team huddled around the picnic tables, reviewing plays I missed in last week's game. Brennan Emery, the coach's son, shouts, "Nice to see you back, Max! Sorry about your aunt."

"Hey!" I reply. I can never think of anything fit to say to Brennan. He outclasses me in every way. He's tall, unselfish, a winning quarterback, an elected president of the Students of Color Association. He has what people call natural leadership ability—but since he's an ultimate, it's not entirely natural.

Dallas jumps up from the picnic bench and slams my shoulder. His jacket strains at the armpits and his pants hover above his shoes. We ordered our uniforms in August and he's already outgrown his. Life is not fair. "Did you hear about that poor Chinese kid who was beaten to death with a fencepost?" he asks. "Disgusting."

"Yeah, I saw that. What a bunch of freaks."

"What would you rather be beaten with? Fencepost or barbed wire?"

"Fencepost," I say.

"Me too."

Xavier stands alone across the grounds, waving. The sun shines off his hair like a halo, rippling as he makes his way over to us. He's three sentences into his speech before he's within earshot.

Tyler Wilkins rushes in and trips Xavier, who crumples into the pavement. The crowd parts to ensure him a painful landing. Tyler laughs and shouts, "Walk much, unit?"

Tyler is a funhouse mirror image of Xavier. He's six foot and blond, but skeletal and homely. He reeks of deli meats and cigarettes. One day he'll slash Xavier's face out of jealousy. We all know it, every one of us, but we'll be sure to act surprised.

Tyler's goons leap over Xavier's legs, giggling. Tyler puts a foot on his back to stop him from getting up.

It's like watching the planets align.

I strut over to Tyler and throw a right hook that staggers him. The crowd steps back to form an arena. Xavier commando-crawls to the edge of it.

Tyler swears at me and rubs his jaw. "You're dead, Connors."

Somewhere in my brain I wonder if I should be nervous. Nah. I spent two hundred and twenty hours of summer preparing for this moment. I'm zesty.

I let Tyler take a shot. I block it easily with my left forearm and wallop him in the gut with my right fist. I knock the wind out of him and follow with an elbow to the cheek. A hoot of excitement escapes my lips. The crowd starts buzzing.

I bounce on my toes and laugh. Tyler is bleeding and shocked. He knows I'm going to win this fight. But he's a scrapper, nerve-deadened and self-important. Backing down is not an option for a kid like him. He wipes his cheek on his sleeve and comes at me, spitting.

I pummel him in the face—hook, jab, elbow strike. *Pow, pow, pow.* When he returns the blow, I grab his arm and twist it behind his back. I force him to his knees and kick him into the ground, much harder than I intend to. I hear groans from the watching girls and giggles from the gay boys.

Tyler drags himself up and tries to hit me, but he's angry and embarrassed, and I can read his moves before he makes them. I dodge his blows, hopping away so he has to come at me; then I rush in and trip him. He slams into the pavement, just like Xavier did five minutes ago. The crowd gasps, laughs, narrates their recordings.

I'm ready to beat Tyler Wilkins to a pulp of sodden flesh, but Mr. Graham steps between us with his arms outstretched. Tyler shoves him aside to get at me. I laugh—shoving the principal won't go over well—and take him down hard with a wrist lock.

Two security guards pull us apart. Bystanders start yelling. "Tyler started it!" "Max started it!"

The principal is shaking, he's so mad. It turns his stomach to be in a crowd of teenagers. "You are both suspended for the week," he says through gritted teeth. "Wait outside the front doors until your parents collect you." He walks away, probably to wash his hands.

So I'm stuck at the front of the school with two security guards and the kid I hate most in the world, waiting to tell my grieving mother about my latest wreckage. My heart thumps. My hands throb. Yet I feel absolutely premium.

They say violence is wrong and such and such, but I have never felt as happy in my life as I do now. I've shaken off a future of swallowing Tyler Wilkins's waste. I have cleared my road with my fists and feet. I can walk wherever I want to now.

True, Tyler and his friends might take out my eyeballs with a spoon tomorrow, but right now he's bleeding and I can't get the smile off my face. It widens every time he glances at me, his nose swollen and his eyes miserable.

"When did *you* learn to fight?" he asks.

I snort and bare my teeth.

He shakes his head and wipes his bloody lip. "I must be out of practice."

I hope he'll practice up on me. I could squeeze a beating into my Monday schedule: pack lunch, walk Ally to school, beat the crap out of Tyler Wilkins, get suspended.

My happiness plateaus when my mother trudges up the school driveway. "I just signed in the car when I got the call from your principal," she says.

I hang my head and hope it looks repentant.

"Is someone coming for you?" she asks Tyler. He shrugs.

The tallest guard steps up to Mom and says, "He has to leave with his own guardian."

She nods. She knows the guards will regret that rule after they pass the entire school day sitting on the front steps waiting for Tyler's parents to show. "Okay, Max, let's go. Goodbye, Tyler."

"Bye." It surprises me when he adds, "Bye, Max." Like we're friends, like we got into trouble for skipping class together.

"I'll see you," I say. I don't mean it to be menacing, but after I say it, I like the way it sounds.

Mom doesn't speak on the walk home.

"I can get my assignments off Blackboard," I say. She doesn't glance at me. "I was defending Xavier," I add. She just sighs.

When we get to our building, I want to race up the flights of stairs, but I slow myself down for Mom's sake. She yawns and says, "I haven't slept since Saturday night."

"Technically, it was Sunday morning."

She stares at me like I'm the biggest ass in the world. And maybe I am. But as I review the fight in my mind—I add an announcer in the background, cameras on the side—the crowd goes wild.

I thought I'd spend my suspension exercising and watching *Freakshow*, but Mom puts an end to that dream when she wakes up in the afternoon. Instead of making me a sandwich, she makes me a list of chores: *dishes, dusting, laundry, clean Ally's room, supervise Ally's homework.* When I add *wipe Ally's ass* to the list, she is not amused.

"Okay. I'll do chores," I say. Then I continue watching *Freakshow* until she stares me down.

I work my way to the bottom of the list by six o'clock. I help Ally with her homework while Mom makes supper. I am not a premium teacher. It frustrates me when Ally doesn't understand her work. It makes me think she's a recall, and I hate that thought because I love her so much.

Her spelling words are strange but simple: *duty, job, joy, love, power, help, hurt, good, bad, boy, girl.* That's a damaged mix of words, but they're phonetic—except *love*, which is irregular in every way.

"No!" I say for the fourth time. "It's h-u-r-t, not h-e-r-t!"

"I'll take over, Max. You set the table," Mom says. She smiles at Ally. "Remember that *U* can get hurt. Not *E*."

Ally laughs. "An *E* can't get hurt, can it?"

I arrange knives and forks and feel like a creep.

"There's something wrong with the kids at my school," Ally says when she dissolves her screen. "I think they're sick."

Terror fills Mom's eyes. Four million kids died in the Venezuelan flu epidemic. "Are they coughing?"

Ally shakes her head. "Not sick like that. Sick like their heads are cloudy."

"Are they slurring their words? Losing their balance?"

"No. They're just not right. They're all slowed down."

Mom looks at me as though I might be able to elucidate.

I shrug and say, "I'll look around when I take her to school tomorrow."

* ·

I'm ready for Tyler when I leave the apartment in the morning. I have a steak knife in my jacket pocket but no idea how to wield it. Fortunately, he's sleeping in, as all suspended children should be.

Ally chatters about rodents the whole way to school, a stream of useless facts like, "Mice have poor eyesight," and "Chipmunks nest underground." She shuts up as we approach her school, pushes me away when I hug her goodbye.

I linger by the fence and chat with the eight-year-olds who rush up to me, make faces, tattle on their friends, ask who I am.

"Hello, Max," Xavier pants. He towers at my side, half-naked, as if he teleported from a gymnasium. He smells like raspberry crumble. "I ran five miles cross-country and now I'm sprinting to school. Will you run with me?"

"I'm not allowed at school this week," I remind him. He looks confused. I raise my swollen hands. "Remember how Tyler tried to waste you and I beat him down yesterday?"

"Yes."

"I got suspended for that."

Four high school girls fall silent as they approach. They gawk at Xavier, who's wearing a pair of shorts that reach his knees, a pair of sneakers that reach his ankles, and nothing else except a sheen of sweat.

I give the girls a wink. They giggle and walk on, whispering and glancing back.

"You should get to class," I tell Xavier. I smile like it's premium fun being suspended, then turn back to Ally's schoolyard.

The first graders line up early again. Their ranks have swollen with a few dozen grade twos. Melissa stands near the front, staring at the closed doors. A supervisor walks the line, watching me where I lurk outside the fence. I wave and say, "Hey!" She doesn't wave back.

The older kids play on the jungle gyms, run across the concrete, throw balls at the fence and try to scare me. When the bell rings, the sour-faced supervisor calls in the stragglers. "I can't wait till next week!" she shouts to another supervisor across the concrete. Ally looks my way but doesn't return my wave. The supervisors yell at her to get in line.

Where the youngest children wait near the doors, the lines are royally neat. No jostling, no hopping, not even pairs of girls holding hands. The line snakes out as it lengthens. The fourth graders at the back are toxic, switching places, yapping, pushing each other down. The supervisors yank on their arms to no effect.

Eventually everyone slithers inside, and I'm left standing with my fingers threaded through the fence, staring at silent concrete. Xavier jogs on the spot beside me. "What are you still doing here?" I ask him. "You're going to be late for class."

"Will you run with me?" he repeats.

I laugh. "I have to go home, Xavier. I'm suspended for saving your life."

Xavier can deconstruct my personal mythology faster than I can fabricate it. "I don't like you to fight," he says. "I like you when you're nice."

Sometimes Xavier reminds me of Ally because he's kind and innocent. But once in a while when he's not speed-talking—because he looks so old and white and serious—he reminds me of my father. It saddens me and I don't know why.

"Go to school before you're late," I tell him. "I can't run with you today."

"Okay. Bye, Max." He sprints away, supremely fast and strong, out of sight in thirty seconds. If he could manage relationships and violence, I'd recruit him into football.

Stray children rush past me, trying to get to school on time. Older teens and adults ride to work on bikes. I watch them for a while. Then I have to admit that I have nowhere to go but home.

"You forgot to put the garbage out," Mom says when she wakes at two o'clock.

I look up from my RIG. "Sorry."

"We'll have too much next week, Max. They raised the fine to forty dollars."

I shrug. "I could dump it in the park."

"That's wrong."

"It keeps people employed."

She digs up a half smile. "Did you do anything at all today?"

"Nah. The only kids online are throwaways and Tyler Wilkins."

"I meant anything useful."

"Oh." I look around the kitchen. My cereal bowl sticks to the counter, the flakes bloated and gummy in the bottom. My pasta bowl sits beside it, crusty with dried tomato. Mom opens the microwave and gasps like someone's bunny exploded in there, when really it's just a bit of spaghetti splatter. "I guess I could clean up," I say.

She heats a cup of water in the dirty microwave and scoops in a spoon of coffee. She taps her foot as she stirs. "You only have a few minutes before you have to get Ally, so you might want to start cleaning now." *Tap, tap, tap.* She cracks the whip, this mother of mine.

⋅⋅⋆⋅

Mom is gone when I bring Ally home from school. The kitchen screen reads, *Called in to work early. Be good.*

"Want to go to the park?" I ask.

Ally runs to the cupboard and grabs a handful of sunflower seeds for Peanut, her squirrel friend. Mom used to feed peanuts to the squirrels when she was young and lived in the country. She has a lot of animal stories. Ally's favorite is how one fall a bear and two cubs came into our grandparents' orchard and ate apples off the ground. They swallowed three bushels in ten minutes, then had a snooze beneath a tree, the little ones flopped across the mama's big belly.

Eventually, when they awoke to eat more apples, my grandfather scared them away with a shotgun. The mama bear nudged her cubs, and they all loped off back to wherever they came from.

Ally loves that story. Mom never tells the ending, where the mama bear gets shot the next place they steal apples and her cubs are put in cages for the rest of their lives. Mom pretends the happy bear family went to a national forest and stayed there, safe and shining, for the rest of their days, telling stories in bear language about the afternoon they ate apples and dodged bullets.

I'd like to think that were true. I tell Ally it's true. But it's not true. Those bears are dead.

Ally would like to see a bear, but she makes do with whatever wildlife is at hand. She saves a worm from drowning in a puddle on the way to the park, picks it up and settles it on the grass, saying, "There you go," like she helped an old lady across the street.

The park is just down the street from our apartment complex. It has a large playing field flanked by oaks and maples, two swing sets and a jungle gym fit for chin-ups. Two eight-year-olds, Zachary and Melbourne, use it as their gladiator arena. They throw sand, smash heads into monkey bars, knock down baby bystanders, kick and scream. Today Zach pushes Melbourne face-first off the jungle gym. Melbourne's mother jumps from the bench with a hand raised like she's going to swat Zachary. Zach's mother jumps up like she's going to swat Melbourne's mother. Melbourne latches onto Zachary's ankles and yanks him off the platform. The mothers sit down like all is well.

"Hey, there's Melissa," I tell Ally.

Melissa stands on the sidewalk, long skinny legs and arms jutting out of flowery shorts and a frilly blouse. She holds her father's hand and stares at her feet. He leads her to the edge of the play structure and nudges her into the sand. She walks to the slide, climbs up and spirals down without a peep. Her father turns her toward the swings. "Stretch and bend!" he shouts. "Get some momentum going!"

She swings until Melbourne and Zachary shout, "Get off! We want a turn!"

"All right," her father says. "Let's go."

I point Ally in their direction. "Go say hi."

She shakes her head.

"Hey, Melissa!" I shout. "Want to play with Ally?"

Melissa looks at Ally like she never met her before. Her father checks his watch. "I don't know," he says.

"That's okay!" Ally shouts. "We don't have time to play either." She turns her back on her friend as they leave the park.

"Why did you say that?" I ask. "That's not like you, Ally. You hurt her feelings."

She shakes her head. "She has no feelings anymore."

I laugh, thinking it's a joke, but when she looks up at me, she's almost crying. "Hey, hey, what's wrong?" I ask. "Trouble making friends this year?"

"There's something wrong with them. They're fuzzy and slow. They just go along." She looks around to make sure no one's listening. "At first it was just my class, but now all the grade ones and twos are strange."

I kiss her little head and twirl her braids. "Don't you have any friends at all?"

She sighs and looks away. "I want to find Peanut."

She sits before the tallest oak tree and clicks from the back of her throat, *"Kch, kch, kch."* A black squirrel peeks out of its nest, twitches its tail, runs down the tree. "Peanut," Ally whispers. She throws a few seeds on the ground.

The squirrel pauses, twitches, descends, backtracks, finally hops to the earth and inches closer. It cracks the seeds with orange teeth, chews them speedily, glancing up at me with nervous black eyes.

Ally holds the rest of the seeds in her palm. She giggles when the squirrel's mouth nuzzles her skin. She pets its head and calls it beautiful. Peanut stays with her even after the seeds are gone, answering her questions with grunts and trills, until a scream from the swings sends it up the tree.

"Let's go," I say.

Ally rises and waves goodbye to the squirrel. Her eyes blaze with love, and it saddens me that she has to grow up and make friends with humans. I hear the future coming for her. *Stomp, stomp, stomp.*

THREE

I spend the final morning of my suspension punching a padded tree, sketching, and reading the *Freakshow* contestant bios. My money is on Zipperhead, a twenty-two-year-old with a head like a boulder, covered in scars from surgery that separated him from a conjoined twin.

Two of this season's contestants are from New Mexico. That's a rarity. Usually everyone is from Freaktown. I can't remember the real name of the place—it's been called Freaktown all my life. It was christened twenty-five years ago when two transport tankers spilled untested agricultural chemicals on the banks of the Saint Lawrence River. No one cared much until the birth defects showed up: conjoined twins, spinal abnormalities, missing limbs, extra limbs, enlarged brains, external intestines, missing genitals, extra organs. When the same defects appeared in the babies of agricultural workers all over the country, the poisons were taken off the market and the shoreline was cleaned up.

It came too late. Even today, one in three babies born in Freaktown has deformities. Nobody visits the city anymore. Strangely enough, nobody ever leaves the place either.

Deformed babies are sad, but deformed adults are supremely fascinating. Four years ago, a savvy media company started a weekly documentary about Freaktown's twentysomethings. They called it *Freakshow*. It started off as an educational program, but it soon evolved into a contest, with voting and prizes and betting pools. It's called a charity program now. Xavier says it's controlled by organized crime.

I came fourth in the New Middletown *Freakshow* betting pool two years ago, but I couldn't claim my prize because I was underage and Mom wouldn't step up for me. She says the show is reprehensible. I know the time is coming when she won't refuse any money, no matter where it comes from, so I lay a bet on Zipperhead.

After lunch I do my homework, tidy up and jog to Ally's school for the three o'clock bell. I don't hear much of what she says on the walk home, because I'm on my RIG fighting communism in the Chinese Civil War. I don't play often, not like throwaways, but New Middletown just added the game *Underdog* to our network. Your ISP marks your alliance, so every American logged on right now playing the 1946 China map is a Kuomintang. Every Brazilian is a Communist. It makes gaming an act of patriotism.

A soldier spawns into my projection and stands there doing nothing for so long I suspect he's a Commie spy. I'm about to knife him when he says, "Stop wasting your youth, Max.

Log off and apply for the manual arts exhibit. I'm coming over after football." Somehow Dallas always finds me idling online. I knife him before he exits.

I skim the manual arts application at home and submit my portfolio with an essay on why I should be a representative artist. I lie like a rug, apologize for my three graffiti convictions, flaunt my grades in art and architecture, and claim to be a productive citizen.

Ally tugs on my earpiece. "There's someone at the door."

A redheaded man with a handlebar mustache stands in the hallway holding a bowl of apples. His smile is lopsided and his teeth are blackened, but there's no mistaking his vocals. "They said these apples are organic, but I found pesticide residue on them so I'm sending my samples to a laboratory for testing because they've stretched the certification definitions beyond reason."

I smile. "Come on in, Xavier, and we'll slice them up."

When Mom gets home from a double shift at six o'clock, Xavier and Dallas are lazing on the couch watching an ancient movie about machines that take over the world. Dallas is wearing the red wig and mustache. Xavier is chatting through the action scenes.

"Why aren't you in there with your friends?" Mom asks me.

I point to the kitchen screen, where I've projected Ally's homework. "We're working."

Mom skims Ally's ethics assignment: an evil bunny paints graffiti on the wall of a grocery store, all the nearby plants are poisoned, distracted drivers crash into bikes, the store gets robbed, and all hell breaks loose until two tattler bunnies save the day by ratting out the evil bunny, who repents when interrogated. The follow-up asks, *What makes a good community member? What should you do if you see someone harming property?* "Wow," Mom says. "That's advanced for grade one." She frowns with worry, then sits next to Ally and asks me to heat supper.

I wear my earpiece to drown out Ally's struggle with every sentence. I don't know why Mom won't let her use the speech editor—half the country can't read or write, and they're not missing anything except the odd evacuation notice. They're on question four of ten when I ladle out the soup. "Dallas! Xavier! Want to eat?"

Xavier streams the movie through his RIG and brings it to dinner. Mom hates electronics at the table, but she'd never hurt Xavier's feelings.

"Elaine was asking about you today," she tells me. Elaine is a patient at the geriatric center. I adopted her as my community grandparent for a sadistic school assignment in grade seven. "Why don't you come for a visit tomorrow?" Mom asks.

I cringe. I would rather eat vomit than go back to that place. Elaine is sweet and funny but that just makes it worse, her being stuck there with thousands of people pissing themselves and rotting slowly. "I'm getting my hair cut tomorrow."

"No!" Ally says. "I like your hair long."

"Me too," Xavier adds. His own hair dangles in his tomato soup.

Dallas laughs. The mustache falls off his face into his bowl. He pinches it between his fingers, holds it up dripping like a severed tail. "Max has high-maintenance hair," he says. "We should cut it for him."

"My sister does hair," Xavier says.

"Oh, I wish she'd do me," Dallas says. I smile. Mom rolls her eyes. Ally and Xavier don't get it, but that's just as well.

·—x·

I go to the cheapest hair salon in the quadrant: Kim's Trims. It's the size of my bedroom, with a wall of mirrored tiles to plump it up. It reeks of hairspray and Kim's musky perfume. She's a middle-aged beautician who lives in a carpark by the highway outside of town. She and three other stylists take shifts at the salon. She probably bathes in the sink where she washes my hair.

Mom says carparks used to be places where people parked their cars before they took a bus to work in the morning. They'd return on the bus at the end of the day and get back in their cars and drive home. The cars would still have gasoline, and the tires would be on, and even the music systems would be in place, just as the owners had left them. That's the kind of safety full employment used to bring.

Now, of course, carparks are places where people live in cars that don't work. They're the hallmark of modern efficiency. When you have a host of vehicles no one can afford to drive and a horde of people who can't afford a home, a carpark makes royal sense. Especially if you live alone, like Kim. Then there's lots of room.

Kim talks so much it takes an hour and a half to trim my hair, and it's only two inches long to start with. Mostly she holds up her scissors and stares in the mirror, waiting for me to answer whatever her last question was.

"Huh?" I say.

"When I was your age, the student council met with the governing board every week to keep the dialogue going," she says. This explains why I zoned out. "But my nephew tells me his student council just chooses the color of the year-book. It doesn't influence school policy."

I shrug. "I'm not on the student council."

"You should join it."

I laugh. "They wouldn't let me. I missed the past two weeks of school."

"If you let other people make the decisions, you can't complain about what they decide," she says. "That's what I tell my son. He's always got his head in an engine. He doesn't take any interest in what's going on in the world. Then he raises his head and wonders how things got so bad."

I should tell Xavier that the field of hairdressing is wide open to him. It's a legal way to trap people in a chair and force them to listen to you for hours.

"Like the new education program they started this fall," Kim says. "There's not one student council that had any input into that decision."

I wish I'd let Dallas cut my hair.

❖

"My mom cuts my hair," Dallas whispers into his RIG. "That's how the rich stay rich." He would never give anyone else that information. It's like confessing that your parents grow their own meat or knit their own mittens. You might as well sign up at the psychiatric recall center.

He runs a hand through his silky bangs. "Who did you vote for on *Freakshow*?"

"Zipperhead. You?"

"Juice and Tiger."

I don't comment. Tiger is a teenager tattooed with stripes to complement his pointy ears and golden eyes that are probably plastic. Juice is almost twenty-five and so defective that he leaks from all orifices. There's no way he'll win—either he'll be exposed as a fake or he'll die of blood loss.

"Who do you think would win in a fight?" Dallas asks. "A tiger or two cougars?"

"There aren't any tigers left."

"I think there's a few in zoos."

"Then a tiger would win for sure."

"I think so too."

Austin shoves his face into the screen. He has a cracked lip, swollen purple ears and white goo on his chin. "Ice cream! Ice cream!" he shouts like an idiot child. "Dad bought me ice cream after my fight. None for you units. Hah!"

Dallas ignores him. "If you could only have one dessert for the rest of your life," he asks me, "what would it be: chocolate cake or ice cream?"

"Xavier told me that chocolate cake doesn't contain chocolate."

"So? Ice cream doesn't contain cream. They still taste good."

"Maybe chocolate cake."

"Me too," Dallas says.

Austin whacks him on the cheek. "Ice cream is better, unit."

Dallas swats Austin's hand away and accidentally hits the ice cream cone to the floor. There's a moment of silence before Austin jumps on Dallas's head. The screen dissolves. It seems that in every two-child family, only one child is normal.

My first day of classes falls two weeks into term. Everyone is angry at me for missing so much school. Fortunately, my favorite teacher, Mr. Reese, is taking his weekly hypochondriac day, so I get a midmorning break from the nagging. A substitute stands at the front of history class, wringing her hands as we take our seats. She's young, homely, scared. I can't resist.

I answer the roll call for Pepper Cassidy before Pepper can get her hand up. The sub squints at me like she thought Pepper was a girl's name but you never know these days. "Maxwell Connors?" she calls out next.

I wait. There's a risk to jokes like this. I might lead the classroom fun or I might be laid to waste. Fortunately, word has spread on how I thrashed Tyler last week. Brennan Emery raises his hand and says, "Here." I'm stamped with approval, checked off the list.

When Brennan's name is called, three hands shoot up, all wanting to be him. Montgomery from cheerleading stands to attention. He lowers his voice and squares his shoulders. "I'm Brennan," he says, trying to look straight.

Dallas answers for Montgomery. He snaps his fingers and sings, "Have no fear! I am here!" Dallas is a supreme actor. He played a drag-queen elf in the grade nine Christmas production, and the entire football team avoided him for weeks afterward. He jumps at the chance to revive the role. Mincing opportunities are rare for a fifteen-year-old giant whose entire family is named after parts of Texas.

Pepper answers for Kayla Farmer, the ultimate cheerleader. Pepper wiggles her fingers, jiggles her boobs, cheers, "That's me! I'm Kayla. K-A-Y-L-A. That spells Kayla!"

Soon everybody has a new name and personality except the honest kids whose names start with A and B and Tyler Wilkins, whom nobody answers for.

I play a premium Pepper, but Dallas steals my limelight. No one can take their eyes off him as he mimics Montgomery, who's flamboyant even for a gay boy. Dallas doesn't hold back. He opens a pack of mints and waltzes up the aisle— literally, spinning and stepping, *one, two, three*—past all the girls and average guys, right up to Brennan, who's playing me. "Hi, Max," Dallas says. He leans across Brennan's desk, stretching to pull his shirt up over his muscled belly. He bats his lashes and whispers, "Want a mint?"

Brennan tries not to laugh.

Washington Anderson swears from the desk in front of them. He's Tyler's ugliest goon, a rabid homophobe and racist who's stuck playing his own damaged personality this morning. "You reeking hemorrhage, Richmond," Washington mutters. "Get back to your desk."

Dallas sticks a mint between his teeth and pulls back his lips. He leans close to Washington, daring him to take it.

Washington leaps to his feet and raises a fist.

The substitute teacher screams.

Dallas lifts himself off Brennan's desk and stands up to his height of six feet two inches, transforming instantly from a happy fag into a serious fighter. He crushes the mint between his teeth.

Tyler hurdles a desk to hover beside Washington. I hop beside Dallas, smiling at the opportunity to kick Tyler's ass again. Brennan stands up next to me with Bay, the biggest, blackest boy on the football team. "You don't want to do anything rash," Brennan tells Washington. The room is silent and tense.

The sub looks from us to the surveillance camera to the door, too scared to say a word.

Dallas smiles at Washington. "Do you have a problem with my mints? Not your favorite flavor?"

Washington snorts and swears, clenching his fists. His eyes gleam with fury. But his grades are borderline and a suspension might get him sent to throwaway school, so he backs off with a muttered, "Outside." The sub resumes her lecture on climate change in the twenty-first century. She stutters so quietly I can barely understand her.

"I'm wasting face time on this?" Kayla asks.

"It's worse than a virtual tutor," Montgomery agrees.

The tension slowly fades, and we pick up our alternate personalities where we dropped them. Brennan sketches, I dance, Montgomery calls a huddle, Dallas and Pepper cheer.

In the hallway, everyone pats my back in thanks for livening up the lecture. I feel supreme—I need successes like this to raise my standing, especially given my height.

"See you at practice," Brennan shouts as he walks down the hall with Kayla—quarterback and cheerleader, the love story that never grows old, just more expensive.

Sage Turner, Pepper's best friend, leers after them. "Do you think Brennan's the best-looking guy in school?" she asks.

Pepper glances at Dallas for a moment too long before she says, "I don't know."

Dallas doesn't rub my nose in it. He says, "No way. You know who the best-looking guy in school is?"

Pepper smiles at me and we all shout at once, "Xavier!"

Dallas, Pepper and I sneak to the skate park up the road for lunch. It's empty except for a few kids our age, probably throwaways skipping class. Four boys skate around a bowl while two girls watch them, leaning against a railing, sipping on sodas.

Pepper keeps one eye on the boys while she calls her father. "Did Mom find a place for those people we spoke of?" Her parents help relocate New Yorkers whose homes are sinking into the sea. They're an unusually close family. My mother never talks to me about her patients. Dallas's father can't talk to anyone without shouting.

Dallas falls back on his standard topic. "Who do you think would win in a fight? The guy in the black shirt or the Asian kid?"

The Asian throwaway skates up the bowl and somersaults into the air. He lands in a crouch and zooms back down. The white kid dressed in black tries to copy him but chickens out on the somersault.

"Is the fight on skates or shoes?" I ask.

"Skates."

"Maybe the Asian, if the other three don't gang up on him."

Dallas swats my arm and points across the park. "Look!"

Tyler Wilkins is leaning over the railing near the girls, watching the throwaways skate. Washington Anderson steps up beside him, fury still gleaming in his eyes.

The Asian kid and the white kid zoom down opposite sides of the bowl toward each other. They link arms in the center, jerk hard and spin madly before they let go and zoom away laughing. The Asian boy flies up the concrete and flips in the air, lands on his wheels at the top. The girls clap as he takes a bow.

Washington nudges Tyler. He's found an outlet for his rage.

There's a reeking backlash against China these days. The news says it's a result of drought and famine and inflating food values, but that's crap. Guys like Tyler and Washington always brim with hatred, and right now they're taking it out on Asians because blacks and Latinos have had enough.

Tyler shouts something at the Asian kid—I can't make out the words, but the meaning is clear. The boy's smile disappears. He looks around the park to assess his situation.

"Shit," Dallas mutters.

"I have to go," Pepper says into her RIG. The three of us rise to our feet.

"What do we do?" Dallas asks.

I shrug. "He has three friends."

"I'm not so sure," Pepper says.

The Asian boy skates to the bottom of the bowl where the others stare up at Tyler and Washington. Then the three white kids step away, leaving the Asian kid to stand alone.

"What do we do?" Dallas repeats.

"There's a time to fight and there's a time to walk away," Pepper says.

"Yeah, but which time is this?" Dallas asks. "What do you want to do, Max?"

Last year we would have slunk away, posting the news and photos. But once you stand up to someone, you're expected to keep standing.

I roll my eyes and sigh. I do not want to do what I'm about to do.

I toss my pizza crust into the compost and walk to the edge of the concrete bowl. Dallas moves to my side. It's a shining gesture but it only makes me look short in comparison.

"What do you faggots want?" Washington shouts.

Everyone looks our way. The girls step back from the railing and whisper. The skaters block the sun with their hands and look up at us. I feel like I should be wearing a cape.

The Asian boy picks up his bag while everyone's distracted. He speeds up and over the edge of the bowl, past us, down the sidewalk, out of the park.

Dallas laughs. "I guess this is the time for flight." He turns to Washington and shouts, "We want to learn to skate like that kid!"

Washington looks around the park, shakes his head and swears, checks his watch.

Tyler rubs his hand up and down the railing and says something rude to the girls. Then he mutters to Washington and they walk away.

The skaters keep their eyes on me and Dallas. The girls wait for something to happen.

"We should get to school," Pepper says.

Dallas puts his arm around her. "What would happen if you got caught off grounds?"

I pull her out of Dallas's embrace. "Imagine the shame," I say.

Pepper walks away from both of us. "I don't like trouble."

Dallas and I hustle to catch up with her. I don't remember when this competition began. Our other contests are clear— who's fastest, who's tallest, who played better in the last game. But with Pepper, we're both convinced we're winning.

A guard awaits us at the school gates, no doubt tipped off by Tyler. Pepper slips behind a shrub and glides into school unseen while Dallas and I crawl to the principal's office. Coach Emery is there with Mr. Graham. "I need these boys at practice," he says. Instead of detention, we're assigned hall duty during the afternoon break.

It's humiliating. We wear striped yellow vests and peer around corners for loiterers and contraband. All the kids who clapped my back after history class now laugh in my face.

High school is a fickle arena.

⋆

"Dad's upset with you for missing two weeks of practice," Brennan warns me in the football trailer.

"And our first game," Bay adds. "Which we lost."

"I know," I say. "He called me a pig-dog and a lamebrain."

Coach Emery sticks his head inside and shrieks, "Get your midget ass out here, Connors!" He makes me fill the water bottles and carry out the benches. Traditionally that's the job of ninth graders. I was looking forward to lording it over them this year. Instead, they survey me with ridicule.

Brennan grabs one end of the bench I'm dragging, but his dad shouts, "No helping! He didn't help you at the last game, did he? Let him do this by himself."

The coach pretends he's tough, but I know he loves me. His exact words to my mother at the end of last season were, "Don't worry. He'll turn out fine."

Unfortunately, he doesn't show me the love at practice. First he makes me sprint, drop and do push-ups up and down the field. Then he lines us up for chute drills and pairs me with Bay. After beating on trees all summer, I was looking forward to slamming into humans today. But with Bay, there's not much difference. I'm in a sweet sort of agony by the time we split into practice teams.

Mr. Reid, the assistant coach, leads my team. We used to have two assistant coaches, but Bay's father found a job and no one else volunteered. I've seen Xavier's old movies about small-town high school football with stadium seating and floodlights and uniforms that match, where half the town comes out to watch the games, girls drop their panties for all the players, and coaches review plays in screening rooms after hours. That is not New Middletown football.

Maybe that still goes on in public schools in open cities, or maybe it only happens in movies, but it doesn't happen here. We don't have the money anymore, and if we did, we'd upgrade the chemistry lab. We are the academic elite of a crumbling empire. There may be fifteen-year-olds beyond the walls who risk their ligaments for sport, but we will never meet them—although Dallas will invent the vehicles that carry the lucky few to their games, and I'll design the factories and prisons to house the rest of them. We're not sloughing off brain cells for a long shot we don't require.

As a consequence, the New Middletown Northeast Secondary junior football team really bleeds. We're called the Scorpions but we have no sting. No one comes out to watch our games, the only panty offering we've had was from Montgomery, and assistant coaching is a straw too short to pick your teeth with. We have thirty-six players this year, but half of them don't know the rules of football. They're here because two physical activities are mandatory, and cross-country running fills up fast. The only real players are Brennan, the quarterback, and Dallas, a receiver. They both have football-crazed fathers who suited them up at age seven. Since we only play other academic schools, we usually win. Brennan throws to Dallas for the touchdown over and over until the opposition catches on, at which point Brennan hands the ball to me and I run it to the end zone with Bay blocking. We call Sarah Havelock off the bench when we need a kicker. That's our entire playbook.

Running is the reason I'm on this team—that and my fondness for inflicting and suffering pain and violence. Coach Emery says I run like the devil's chasing me. I told him that when I look at a field, I don't see the players so much as the space between them, like negative space in a work of art. He told me to shut my mouth and run.

Today I run faster and shiftier than ever. Mr. Reid asks if I'm on speed meds.

"Fighting strengthened your game," Brennan says as we clear the field.

Dallas agrees. "You're not a coward anymore."

Coach Emery jogs up and asks, "How do you go so fast on midget legs?"

I explain the mathematics of leg length and pendulum swing, but he doesn't appreciate it.

"You're assigned to the middle school team on Saturdays," he tells me. "They requested an assistant coach and I'm giving them you."

"Are you serious? Grade sevens and eights? They're five feet tall."

"Then you'll fit right in." Coach Emery walks away, leaving everyone laughing except me.

⁕

"Why are you watching a movie when your homework is unfinished?" Mom asks when she gets home with groceries. She's always in a bad mood after spending money.

"Did you never relax after school when you were a kid?" I ask.

"I did my homework first, unless I forgot it."

I can't imagine carrying books and papers back and forth to school. I'd forget them every time. Then Mom would have something concrete to flay me with instead of intangible things like "going that extra mile," which is a damaged metaphor now that fuel is so expensive. Going an extra mile is unjustifiable.

"I'll get to it after dinner," I say.

"Show me what you have." *Crack* goes the whip.

I scroll through the day's homework. "The human organism—an anatomical diagram with system descriptions.

A law review—three pages, I did it in class. Two chapters of North American history—Xavier says it's all a lie. A translation of some psycho religious text—I did that in math class. Trigonometry—piece of cake. And I should plan my art exhibit in case I'm selected."

Mom whistles. "School is so demanding these days."

"Only academic school. Throwaways just read and count."

"Don't call them that. They're children just like you and Ally."

She opens the day's announcements on Blackboard and reads: *Students in grade four will receive Hepatitis vaccinations next week. Nurses are needed to administer needles. An honorarium will be paid to volunteers.* She messages back with her cv, seizing the chance to make a dollar in exchange for a few hours of sleep.

"You can't come to my school," I say.

"It's not your school. It's Ally's school."

"But whenever they get to my school, you can't do shots there."

"Why not?"

I shudder. "School nurses are not good, Mom. They're dregs who work for minimum wage. You can't associate me with that."

When she speaks, her voice is icy. "Are you calling me a dreg?"

"No. But you'd look like a dreg if you came to my school." She stares at me, eyes black as coal, but I persist. "It doesn't matter what kind of people we are, Mom. It matters what kind of people we appear to be. You can't do shots at my school. It would kill me."

Thankfully, Dallas calls at that moment and asks me over to work on science. I run to the door and Mom shoves me out. Finally we agree on something.

I jog to my old neighborhood and greet Dr. Richmond with a shining smile. He grunts and opens the door just wide enough for my shoulders to pass.

Austin jumps off the couch and towers over me with his fist raised. His father snickers in my ear. As the fist heads toward my jaw, I duck, so Austin punches his father in the throat. Dr. Richmond explodes in coughing and profanity.

I flee to Dallas's room, smiling all the way.

"Hi, Max. Did you do your drawings?" Dallas sits behind a massive metal desk, diagrams lit up before him, preparing for a future of leadership and advancement. He shows me his progress on the respiratory system, and I open what I have on circulation.

Austin is kicked out of the living room, so he loiters outside Dallas's door, calling us faggots. I can't concentrate through his idiocy.

"You should augment your memory," Dallas says.

"No way. It wastes the adolescent brain. Kids in the trials are recalls now. Even the meds are dangerous. Remember when you tried them?"

He laughs. "Remember my dad?" He duplicates his father's scowl and wags his finger. "'There's always an adjustment period. This behavior is perfectly normal.'"

"I thought you were going to die," I say. "You were demented. You wouldn't shut up about your hallucinations."

He shakes his head at the memory. "Thank god Mom let me stop."

"You don't need meds, Dallas. Your brain is supreme."

"Yours too, Max."

"Parents always make you do more than you have to. I pull nineties with moderate effort, but that's not good enough for Mom. I should exhaust myself for hundreds."

"No kidding. Dad would do anything to make me more employable. He won't stop pushing until I break."

"It bleeds," I say. "It's not natural. We shouldn't have to try harder."

Austin pounds on the bedroom door. "Help, guys!" he shouts. "I'm stuck!"

Dallas opens his door to his giant brother, who's bending over with his pants down, laughing maniacally.

"Then again," I say, "maybe some of us are not trying hard enough."

⚮

It's raining as Ally and I walk to school. She hangs her head and looks for drowning worms. She's happy, but it saddens me. She's at the mercy of a merciless world. If she had to cross a river and a crocodile said, "Step on me. I'm a log," she'd say, "Really? You look like a crocodile." "No, no," he'd say, "I'm a log. Step on me and you'll see." And off she'd go, never to be seen again.

I keep her company outside the school, holding her umbrella while she saves one last worm.

I don't carry an umbrella for myself. I'll take my hood down when I get near school because hoods are not fit, but I wear it on the road to protect my hair.

Unfortunately, it blocks my peripheral vision so I don't see Tyler Wilkins and his goons sneak up behind me. They grab me tight, Washington on one arm and some grade nine beast on the other. I drop Ally's umbrella. I'm so startled I barely have time to exhale before Tyler hits me in the gut.

I come up fast and furious. Instead of struggling away, like they expect, I lean into Washington to get some leeway for my arm, then I elbow him in the throat. He lets go fast, freeing my hand to grab the head of the grade nine goon and jerk it forward into the spot where Tyler's next punch is aimed. *Kapow.* I'm like a movie star. Then Ally's umbrella trips me up so I take another shot from Tyler.

That makes me mad. I kick Tyler's kneecap as hard as I can, twice. He squeals and falls forward. I ram my knee into his jaw. His head cracks back with a sound that cuts through my frenzy.

Ally screams.

I grab Tyler's throat, partly to be tough but mostly to make sure his head doesn't fall off in front of my little sister. I look him in the eye and say, "There's not going to be a next time. If you need more than two guys to take me down, it's time to give up." From the regurgitated crap of Xavier's damaged movies come the words, "There's no honor in this for you."

Tyler's goons stand back. Washington holds his throat, and the other boy staunches a nosebleed.

I shake the rain from my face and pull Tyler to his feet. "I don't want to fight you again," I say. "You're nothing to me now."

He eyes me intently for a few seconds. I can't tell if he's going to knife me or confess that he's in love with me.

He nods and spits on the ground—but nowhere near me or Ally because I'd take his head off if he did that. He wipes his face and glances at the school to see how many first graders have witnessed his humiliation. "Jesus Christ," he whispers.

I look over too. Washington and the other goon look over. Ally looks over. We all stand there speechless, staring at the schoolyard.

There are no faces glued to the fence watching our fight. Nobody watches from the play structures. Nobody pauses in a puddle, points an umbrella or strains for a better view. Nobody.

The schoolyard is a silent field of concrete. Twelve hundred children stand before the closed doors, holding umbrellas over their heads and identity cards below their chins, waiting for admittance. They're thirty feet away from us, but not one head turns in our direction. They stand in long straight lines in the pouring rain, eyes forward, mouths closed, feet exactly the same distance apart, like gravestones.

One supervisor stands beneath the eaves and stares at us like she wishes we were dead. She digs up a fake smile and shouts, "Alexandra Connors! Come join your schoolmates!"

Ally walks through the gate with her face in the rain, dragging her busted umbrella. She doesn't even say goodbye.

FOUR

"Let's do surveillance on the middle school."

Dallas throws me a scornful look. He chases a fourth slice of pizza with a second carton of milk and grows another half inch taller. "Why?"

"I want to see if it's like Ally's school."

He shakes his head, mystified, but he follows me.

Everything about the middle school is short and squat, like the kids who go here. "I always hated this place," I mutter.

A thousand students in grades five through eight are crammed into three flat-roofed concrete units only three stories high. A single-story addition serves as a music conservatory. Music floating across the barren grounds would be glorious, but the conservatory is soundproof. They wouldn't want to accidentally inspire a mind.

"You got in so much trouble here," Dallas says, smiling.

I was nearly expelled in eighth grade after my third graffiti conviction. The principal didn't understand what bare white walls could do to a kid like me. The third time I was suspended, my mother cried and my father raced to the school to see my piece before they pressure-washed it.

"It's too hot," Dallas complains, sniffing his armpits. "Everything looks smaller than I remember. This driveway was miles longer. Who was the kid who always hid in the ditch?"

"Wheaton Smithwick," I say.

"Wheaton. Yeah. I haven't seen him since the first week of school."

"Maybe he was downgraded."

Dallas points to the conservatory. "We climbed that roof to fetch him down once, remember? It looked a lot higher then. And that soccer field was farther away."

We walk toward the conservatory behind two eighth graders. One of them is taller than me, skinny, with cropped hair and too much makeup. She pushes her short friend into the ditch.

"Some things never change," I say.

Dallas smiles and shoves me over, inches from the drop. We block the path of three fifth graders who wear their ties tight at the collar. "I was never that little," Dallas says.

"Excuse me," I tell the tiny white kids. "We're taking a survey."

They walk right by me.

I grab the last one's arm, flimsy as a toilet-paper roll beneath his gray uniform. I give him a pat and a smile. "Can I ask some questions?"

He shakes his blond head. "I don't talk to strangers."

Dallas rests a hand on the boy's shoulder. "Just a few questions, kid."

The boy makes eye contact with Dallas's ribcage. He looks back and forth between us and shrieks, "Help! You don't belong here!"

We shrink away from him.

The boy's friends turn on us and yell, "Help! You don't belong here!" A little black girl up the driveway shouts, "Help! You don't belong here!"

The eighth graders snicker. "You're in for it now!"

The blond boy stares up at Dallas with eyes glazed over like a doll's. "Help! You don't belong here!" he yells again. This time a dozen fifth graders join in. Their shrill voices ring off the concrete and burrow into the ditch.

"Let's get out of here," Dallas says.

We sprint up the driveway and keep running till we're at our school.

"That was damaged," Dallas says. "I should have recorded it."

"They must be teaching kids differently this year."

"Yeah. Maybe it's part of the drama program."

"That reminds me," I say. "You owe me ten bucks for the *Freakshow* elimination. Juice is history."

⸱⸱⸱⸴⸱

The football team gets off at lunch on Friday to prepare for the afternoon game. We rub our classmates' noses in the announcement. They boo us as we leave. This is New Middletown school spirit.

The primary colors are blazing outside—clear blue sky, severe yellow sun, blood red leaves on the distant maples. It's dry and dusty and difficult to breathe. The field is hard as concrete and prickly with dead grass.

Coach Emery works us easy but talks us to death. *Do this. Do that. Grind those Devils into dust!* The Blue Mountain Devils are the visiting team. They're from the southeast quadrant—rich kids. They wrecked us in the playoffs last year because Brennan had pneumonia and no one else can throw a ball.

The Devils descend from their bus in brand-new blue and beige uniforms. Some Devil's daddy must be a generous football fan. We grumble in our faded black and white jerseys.

Thirty students straggle out to watch our game. Pepper sits in the bleachers wearing a Scorpions hat and waving a clacker. Every time I look at her, she's watching me. She's almost never watching Dallas.

The Devils left their cheerleaders at home, so ours relax in the absence of competition. Kayla leads three dull songs, then sits on the dirt with her friends while Montgomery shimmies and shouts, "Let's go, team!"

It's a tough game from the kick-off. Two new Devils are as big as Bay and as aggressive as throwaways. We can't get two yards with the ball before we're taken down. They pile into Dallas wherever he goes, slam into Brennan each time he raises his arm. We give it right back to them, but they live up to their name and take one to the end zone.

It's 7–0 at halftime, and it stays 7–0 till there's only five minutes left of the last quarter. We call a time-out and kick the crumbs of our mental stamina into a huddle. Kayla revs up her cheerleaders. *Go, team, go.*

Coach Emery doesn't waste time yelling. "We lose the play when the ball's in the air," he says. "Get the ball to Connors and help him clear a path. Do not throw it to him. He cannot catch. Just hand it to him and let him run, son."

Dallas and I wince at the word *son*—me because I have no father to call me that anymore, and Dallas because his father reserves the word for Austin.

As if on cue, Dr. Richmond thumps down from the stands and breaks into our sacred team pep talk. He looks uniformed—black pants and vest, white shirt stained a wet yellow at the collar and armpits. He reeks of alcohol. It's shocking—it's barely four o'clock and school policy is zero tolerance. He drapes an arm over Coach Emery's shoulder. "What these boys need is to pull off their goddamned pantyhose and start playing football!" he shouts. "I've never seen such pussies in my life, and, believe me, I've seen a lot of pussies." He breaks into drunken laughter, wheezing and coughing, honking deep in his throat.

Dallas stares at his father with his eyes and mouth gaping.

"You!" Dr. Richmond grunts. "You're the worst one out there. You're losing the ball to kids half your size! You want Austin to sneak into uniform and help you out?"

Scarlet blotches bloom behind Dallas's mask.

"Or how about that pretty cheerleader?" his father adds, leering at Kayla. "I bet she could get you boys going." He smiles around the huddle with his brows raised.

"Get out of here," Dallas says, but the words grate across his throat in a whisper.

Coach Emery pulls Dr. Richmond aside with a fake smile. Dr. Richmond stumbles and laughs, waves at the cheerleaders.

"Oh my god, look how drunk that guy is!" someone shouts from the bench.

Dallas shudders beneath his padding.

Austin jogs down from the stands and walks his father back to his seat. "Keep it up, ladies!" he shouts.

Coach Emery turns straight to Dallas. "You block for Connors. I want you to take all the anger you're feeling right now and plow it into that big white Devil, number seventy-three. I want him out of this game. You got that?"

Dallas nods until I have to nudge him and say, "Stop nodding."

Dallas is an unstoppable force when the game resumes, one hundred and eighty pounds of unloved shame and fury. Number seventy-three limps off the field after eight seconds of play. When I hit Dallas's shoulder in thanks, he shoves me away. His face is blank.

I've seen him like this before. When we were eleven, we built a fort in his backyard out of scrap wood we'd found in an abandoned lumberyard. We spent two weeks at it, every day all day, hammering and cutting and measuring wrong and cutting again. It was a feeble fort with a crooked window, but we spent our summer in it, playing virtual games and drinking stolen soda and showing every kid in town what we'd made. Then school began, and Austin had to build a model cottage to scale for applied mathematics. We came home to find Dr. Richmond in the backyard tearing down our fort. "Your brother needs this wood," he said. Dallas came to school the next day but he wasn't there, wouldn't look at anyone, wouldn't speak. He hit a teacher with a garbage bin and broke his teeth, snapped out of it when he saw the man's blood on his shoes. He was a nice teacher. Mr. Navarro. Dallas can't believe he ever hurt the guy. It's strange how easily you can do things you swear you could never do.

He's like that again now—no expression in his eyes, not even hate—but it's scarier because he's huge. He could snap bones and shatter skulls. We watch him and tremble.

"Pay attention to the play," Brennan reminds me.

The moment I get the ball, I know I'm going to score. I feel like that every time I get the ball, but this time I'm sure I'm right. The Devils' defense spreads too far, and Dallas knocks them over one by one. I scramble my way to some clear field and tear through thirty-two yards, skirting bodies until they're all behind me. My eyes blur, my heart ignites, my head throbs like a ticking bomb, and I blast into the end zone yards ahead of my pursuers.

I cartwheel and flip and roar. I wave to Pepper and dance one of her moves. She's on her feet, screaming, shaking her clacker like she loves this game.

Dallas doesn't rush over to celebrate. He paces back and forth through his own field of negative space.

Sarah kicks us an extra point, and we buzz with the hope of winning.

When the Devils get their turn, we're on them like psychotic lovers desperate to get our sweet ball back. They can't take a step before we put them on the ground. Their plays last three seconds: *oomph, crash, crack.* The quarterback passes long, and it looks like they might get somewhere, but Dallas heads for the receiver like a bull. Even I want to run away when I see him coming. The Devil fumbles, and Dallas leaps through the air, coming down hard on top of the kid with the ball in his hands. He's not smiling when he gets up.

Coach Emery is worried that either the Devils will score again or Dallas will kill somebody. We make it to twenty seconds, tie game, third down, when Dallas says, "I want the ball." Those are his first words since his father appeared. He doesn't repeat himself and no one argues. He straightens up and takes his position on the line, eighteen yards from goal.

"Don't let him go home like this," Brennan whispers as we head to our places.

When the game resumes, Brennan throws long to Dallas, who smashes through the Devils that surround him. He shoves helmets, wrenches hands, nearly takes a kid's arm off. He rushes the ball to the end zone and scores—wins— with one second on the clock.

He doesn't smile or slap shoulders, doesn't prance for Pepper, doesn't even play out the game and shake hands with the losers. He walks straight off the field into the showers.

He's still there when the rest of us arrive. He stands naked under a showerhead, hands against the wall, hair hanging black over his eyes, water streaming down his face.

Kids who were on the bench when Dr. Richmond appeared squint and whisper in Dallas's direction, but they taper off when no one joins in. We wash in silence while Dallas stands there, unmoving. He takes occasional shuddering breaths, but I can't tell if he's crying or fuming. I exchange "What the hell do we do?" looks with my teammates, but they have no answers.

I dress and sit on a bench by my locker until they all leave. Dallas is still in his own private waterfall, blazing white and way too naked. He's bleaching pale as a corpse, and the whole place reeks of chlorine.

I walk up beside him, tap his arm. "Hey hey, we have to go. Brennan said I should take you home."

He clenches his jaw but doesn't open his eyes. Hot water bounces off his shoulder into my face. He sucks in a slow breath.

I can't leave him here, but I don't want to touch him again. I don't know how to manage this, so I fall back on a joke. "Brennan stared at your fat white ass for twenty minutes and then he said, 'Max, if I was you, I would take that big boy home.'"

Dallas breaks a tiny smile, snorts quietly. He peeks at me from under his hair and lisps, "I was wondering when you'd notice."

I laugh. His blue eyes are bloodshot pools, but he's better than I feared. I swat his arm. "Come on. Let's go paint graffiti on the old Home Reno or something." I cringe as I realize that's the lumberyard we pilfered from years ago to make our backyard fort. "I don't know why I said that. I just meant let's go do something constructive. We could do anything you want."

He sighs and raises his head, wipes the water off his face. "I know why you said that." He turns off the tap and grabs his towel.

Outside, the grounds are empty. Even Pepper is gone. Coach Emery waits by the trailer, holds the door open while we store our pads. "Good game," he says.

Dallas tries to smile. Then he sees his father and brother in the parking lot. Brennan and Kayla wait beside the bike rack. We have to pass them all to get to the road.

We avoid eye contact, pretend we're strolling on our own. "Come to my place," I say.

"Sure. Maybe we can order chili."

Dr. Richmond staggers over and shouts, "You know Maxwell and his mother can't afford a restaurant. It takes all their money just to send him to school."

Brennan and Kayla stare at me like I'm an armless dwarf who's been beaten up by kindergartners. The only way I could be more pitiful is if I had an asshole for a father.

Dr. Richmond tries to drape an arm around Dallas, but Dallas steps away, knocking into me, shaking with fury.

"Why don't you all come to our place?" Dr. Richmond shouts. He looks at Kayla and winks. "Come have some fun."

Brennan shakes his head in disgust. "We have things to do." Because he's kind and generous, he adds, "Sorry, Dallas."

"You played well today," Kayla says before she climbs on her bike.

Dr. Richmond leans forward to ogle her ass.

"These children are fifteen years old," Coach Emery says as he leaves. "Remember that."

Dr. Richmond's glance passes over the coach like he's a servant without a tray, and lands on me like I'm shit on his shoes. "I guess it's just *you* left."

Dallas looms in front of his father. "We're not going anywhere with you. Don't make social plans for me. I am not your little boy."

Dr. Richmond steps back, cocks his head, tries to focus his sight. *Blink, blink.* "Come home with your brother and we'll order pizza."

Dallas moves into his father's face again, looks down into his watery eyes. "Don't ever walk onto that field while I'm playing."

Dr. Richmond looks from Dallas to me and back. "What were you two doing in the school for so long?"

Dallas bristles. "Don't talk to my friends. Don't talk to my team. Don't talk to me. Don't even come to my games. I don't want you here."

"I'm helping you out!" Dr. Richmond shouts. "If I ever saw a kid who needed help, it's you. I can't wait till you get the goddamned support treatment because you need it bad."

"I don't need any help from you," Dallas says. "I hate you. I hate everything about you. You're a reeking drunk." He walks away, toward the road.

"I'll give you and your buddy a ride!" Dr. Richmond shouts.

"Just fuck off!" Dallas shouts back.

It's amazing the kind of lip a kid can get away with when his father doesn't have the sperm to make another one.

⚜

Xavier is camped in my living room, watching an ancient movie on the big screen while his sister helps Ally with homework at the kitchen table. Celeste's blond hair cascades over a flowery pink shirt that hugs her breasts.

Dallas poses in the archway flexing his biceps, like she might otherwise overlook someone his height.

"Mom's not home yet?" I ask.

"She got an extra shift," Celeste says. "There's some kind of outbreak killing the old people, something to do with mice. She should be home by eight."

I kiss Ally's head. "We won our game. Did you eat?"

She nods and whispers, "The burger made me sick."

"You want to go lie down?"

She smiles and flees from the table, leaving her homework unfinished on the kitchen screen. I dissolve it before I open the fridge.

"Stop! I'll order in," Dallas shouts, whipping out his RIG. "Will you stay for chili and chips, Celeste?"

"That's sweet of you, Dennis, but I ate with Ally."

I laugh. "Dallas. His name is Dallas."

She shrugs like it's irrelevant to her life. "Come on, Xavier. Time to go."

Xavier doesn't move.

"What are you watching?" I ask him.

"*Body Snatchers*."

"Looks demented."

Celeste streams the movie through her RIG and lures Xavier to the door with it.

His face is split by a fake scar that rips from his left eyebrow across his nose and cheek down to his jawbone. "It's about space creatures that make themselves into clones of every human on the planet," he says. "They kill all the people and take their place in society."

"Why not just set up their own society?" Dallas asks. "Why bother cloning us?"

Xavier rubs his scar off absentmindedly as he processes the question.

Celeste takes his hand. "It's a metaphor," she says.

Xavier smiles. "Yes. Exactly. It's a metaphor."

"For what?" Dallas asks.

"For what makes us human."

"Of course," Dallas says. He turns to me and shrugs.

When Celeste is gone, and we don't have to pretend to a level of maturity we'll never attain in our lives, Dallas and I settle comfortably into chili and *Freakshow*. "Gusher," he moans when Tiger hits the bottom three. He hugs the couch pillow for comfort.

"Hey, what's that?" I pick up a slim black RIG that had been hiding under the pillow. "Xavier's. And it's connected."

Dallas hoots and clicks his heels together.

Over the next two hours, we break up couples, match up singles, fire all the teachers in our school, tell a dozen old ladies they won the lottery, and book three days of hairdressing appointments with my chatty stylist.

We're almost peeing our pants laughing when Mom walks in. She can tell we're up to no good, but our joy is contagious. "You guys are crazy," she says.

We send one last message to Mr. Graham to let him know he's New Middletown's Principal of the Decade.

"That's enough!" Mom shouts from the kitchen. "Where's your sister?"

"In bed."

"Is this chili?"

"Dallas ordered it."

"Help yourself," Dallas says. "I have to head home."

"Do you want to take it with you?" Mom asks.

He smiles, lowers his eyes, shakes his head. He knows our money is tight but he can't imagine money being tight enough to worry over a tub of leftovers.

Five seconds after he leaves, he's back at the door.

"You can't have it. I already ate it," I lie.

He smiles. "Thanks for waiting for me, Max. At school, I mean. I didn't want to go home."

"I wouldn't want to go to your home either," I tell him.

⸻

None of our teachers show up for class on Monday morning, but there's a big sign at the front office congratulating Mr. Graham on his supreme accomplishment as Principal of the Decade. People believe anything they're told.

FIVE

I raise my hand during Communications.

"Yes, Maxwell?" Mr. Ames draws out my name like I've been annoying him all afternoon.

"Is there a new principal at the elementary school?"

He lifts his glasses and rubs the bridge of his nose. He shakes his head, rolls his eyes at me, replaces his glasses.

I raise my hand again.

He sighs so hard his lip flops in the breeze. "What is it now, Maxwell?"

"The kids at the elementary school are different than they used to be."

"That's because new children enter the school system every year."

"Ha ha, good one. That's not what I meant. They act different. They don't play. They're neat and quiet."

"Ah." A smile crawls over his face. "Nesting. It's a new direction in class management. They use motivational leadership."

I picture group chanting, sweat lodges, shunning—there has to be more than a sticker chart keeping those brats in line.

In the front row Montgomery raises his hand.

"Yes, Monty?" Mr. Ames chirps.

Montgomery swings his legs into the aisle and takes in the whole room with his gaze. "It even works at home," he tells us. "There's a third grader in my neighborhood who used to bother me and my friends. She's toxic with jealousy. I think she's a freebie. But now she stays in her room all day and does her work."

"You don't think that's damaged?" I ask.

He slaps me a hard look. "I wish everyone was like her."

Mr. Ames nods like that's what he wants to hear.

"But *you're* not like her," I tell Montgomery. "You can't walk down the hall without skipping."

Montgomery holds up his hands like he's staging a stinging comeback, but I continue. "And that's fit. That's who you are. You play music and make up cheers. You don't sit in your room doing schoolwork all day. Nobody does that. Why is it good for that girl?"

He laughs. "Because she was annoying!"

"Half the school finds you annoying," I remind him.

Across the room, Washington snickers. Tyler stares at me so hard I think his eyeballs might bleed.

"I don't find you annoying," Dallas tells Montgomery with a smile.

Saturday morning, I withstand on the middle school soccer field watching seventh graders in oversized pads do laps. They have no muscle, no hormones, no anger. The field is equally ill-equipped—no benches, no goalposts, not even a trailer to store the ball. The yardage is marked with pylons. It's like a game of midget dress-up.

The sun has barely risen, but Mr. Hendricks, the gym teacher, sweats through his third cup of coffee. "Everybody in!" he shouts.

As the midgets trot toward me, I realize I should call them something else because the expensive ones are taller than me.

Hendricks hurries them through the rules of football. He teaches them basics by shouting insults. Then he splits them into practice teams and lets the big kids demolish the infants. "What is wrong with these children?" he asks me.

"They're twelve."

There's only one player who shines—Saffron, an eighth grade girl who throws harder and runs faster than any of the boys. No one can catch her. She reminds me of me at that age.

Frankie and Chicago, two hulking seventh grade ultimates, refuse to let Saffron have the ball. They ignore the plays and leave her open, slap hands when she's tackled. They can't bear their inferiority to a black girl.

Hendricks mutters, "I can't wait till Nesting next week."

"Nesting?" I ask.

"Yeah. Next week. You can't run a school these days any other way. We're losing to the competition. We need motivational leadership."

I look toward the conservatory where two snappy white girls, older teens, bounce a ball against the wall. "I know what you need," I say.

I swagger over to the girls. "Would you ladies watch the football practice for a while? It's a new team and they need motivation."

The blond snorts at me. I think I've seen her on the high school grounds but I can't be sure. She looks like a million others: long hair, short clothes, pink makeup, plump flesh. "Do we look like cheerleaders?" she asks.

"Yeah."

She rolls her eyes. "We walked my baby brother here. We didn't come to cheer him on."

"You don't have to cheer. Just watch for a few minutes."

She puts me under a microscope, examines my shoes and haircut, decides what I'm worth.

"Like we're judging them?" her friend asks. She's small and slippery, with spiky black hair, green eyes and clothes like lingerie. My hands could meet around her waist.

"Sure," I say. "Judge them."

They stare from me to the soccer field. They shrug, smile, follow me over.

Immediately, the football players try to fill out their uniforms. Even Saffron toughens up under the new surveillance.

The girls flaunt their power by shouting praise and insults. "Hit him harder!" the blond likes to say. The elfish one hops and claps.

I'm starting to enjoy myself when Xavier appears at my side, shirtless and sweaty. "Hi, Max. Your mom said you were here.

Do you want to run cross-country when your practice is over?"

"Sure. Why not?"

Once the girls catch sight of Xavier, they couldn't care less about midget football. They flank him, brushing up close, not even faking nonchalance. Their voices slide from their mouths, their giggles flutter like lashes. They whisper questions and lick their lips.

"Bye, Max!" Xavier shouts thirty seconds later. "I have to cancel our run. I'm going for ice cream!" The girls laugh as they pull him away.

Mr. Hendricks checks his watch. "Oh, boy. I have to pick up a vehicle at ten. Just run them through fumble drills before you send them home, all right? Put the balls and pylons in the storage room. Make sure it locks, would you? Thanks, kid."

This is my Saturday morning.

I end the practice ten minutes later. "Premium work," I tell Saffron. To Chicago and Frankie, the hulks who hogged the ball, I say, "Not so premium for you guys. Stick to the plays next time and let everyone do their jobs."

"Yeah, whatever, midget," Chicago says. Frankie laughs.

"Here, Coach." A tiny blond boy holds out the pylons he collected from the field. He's the most timid player on the team, a seventh grader drowning in his aquamarine jersey. He's feeble, but I like the way he called me Coach. "Do you know where my sister went?" he asks.

"Sorry, kid. I think she left."

He looks around, nodding. "Okay. Thanks."

There's no trailer and the gymnasium's locked, so the kids walk home in their uniforms and cleats, helmets dangling from their fingers.

I tuck the pylons and balls in the storage room. It's crammed with maintenance tools, gym gear and school supplies: hula hoops, soccer balls, ladders, light bulbs, garbage bags, gardening tools, cleaning solutions, rolls of tape, bottles of glue and ink, buckets of storage chips, stacks of paper and cardboard, and a stunning spectrum of paint that leaves me breathless.

Ever since I flipped open my first box of sixty-four crayons at the age of three, art supplies have made my heart race. Paint, ink, my mother's nail polish, even the juxtaposition of wet and dry concrete makes me tremble. My mind reels around tonal variation, the sheer number of blues you can lay side by side.

The paints in the storeroom are impossibly numerous, a rainbow sliced and dehydrated into tempera cakes stacked in knee-high columns on the floor. And on a shelf above them, dozens of aerosol cans in banner red, regal blue, ivory, glossy black, aluminum.

It's too much. I can't help myself.

I toss a basketball from hand to hand, trying to look casual. I throw it higher each time. I let it get away from me twice before I hurl it against the wall and—oops—smash the surveillance camera above the door. *Bang, crash, thunk.* I stuff two garbage bags with paint cakes and cans, so excited my tongue hangs out. I don't take it all, but I take a lot.

I spend the next three hours spraying the back wall of the middle school conservatory. I fill the background quickly, choking on vapor, then take my time with my subject. I make a premium end-to-end piece: two baby white boys who look like Frankie and Chicago pick their noses in shitty blue diapers and jerseys while eleven supreme black females jog past them in spotless red uniforms, helmets tucked under their rippling arms. The lead player has Saffron's face: powerful, focused, deadly serious. She looks like she's off to war.

I keep it simple—blue sky, green field, brown and beige bodies. I restrict the red to uniforms and a wee dab on Chicago's snot. I swipe with a paper bag and dig in with my sleeves and fingertips before it dries. It takes me into the afternoon, leaves my hands and face stained, my clothes a mess, my mind shining free.

When I get home with the burgled paint cakes thunking at my side, Mom is napping and Xavier is in my living room watching a movie with Ally.

"Did those little kids paint you?" he asks.

"No. Did those big girls paint you?"

"They were very physical."

"I'll bet. What are you watching?"

"*Stepford Wives.*"

"Looks damaged."

"It's about a town of men who build robots that look exactly like their wives and then they kill the real wives and replace them with the robots."

"Why don't they just keep the robots and get divorced?"

"It's a metaphor." He doesn't hesitate this time.

I have to laugh.

I pause on the sidewalk outside the elementary school and reach out to Ally for a hug. Her arms hang limp at her sides. "Give me a hug!" I tell her.

She extends her arms obediently.

I kneel down and hold her to me.

"I have to act like the other kids," she whispers.

I glance over her shoulder and through the fence. A thousand zombies line up at the entrance to her school. "They're pretty scary, aren't they?"

She nods slowly.

One supervisor hangs out by the monkey bars, gabbing into her RIG. She sees me watching her and takes a photo of me and my sister.

"You do whatever you have to," I tell Ally. "Stay on their good side."

She joins the line of zombies facing front. I can't tell her apart from the rest of them.

"Hey, Connors!" Tyler Wilkins struts up the street, smoking a cigarette. He waves at me with a stained hand. "I saw you at the middle school this weekend."

I nod self-importantly. "I coach their football team."

He snickers. "That's not all you do. I passed by at lunchtime and saw you making some art. I never knew you could paint like that. You should go to a special school."

"Funny, I always said the same about you."

He butts his cigarette and holds his RIG up to my face. I try not to breathe him in as I watch a movie of myself defacing the middle school conservatory. All I can think is, *Am I really that short?*

"You're bright enough to pick the wall with no surveillance," he says. "But not bright enough to look over your shoulder once in a while. I must have been there twenty minutes."

I sigh. "What do you want, Tyler?"

"What do you mean?"

"What are you going to do with the recording? Are you posting it?"

"I don't know. I just took it."

"If you're going to get me suspended for graffiti, I might as well beat the crap out of you first."

He spits on the concrete, leaves a brownish yellow splatter by my feet. "Why do you have to say that? You think I'd run to the principal with your picture?"

"Then why are you showing me? Are you trying to blackmail me?"

"What have you got that's worth taking, asshole?" He scowls and shakes his head. "You don't know anything about me. I don't want to talk to you, unit." He walks away flexing his fists.

He hunches and sways, sad and slow, like a crooked little man, and I suddenly realize that he was trying to compliment me. Someone like Tyler never gets to be anybody else. I want to shout, "Sorry!" but I don't have the balls, and he's too far away. The word sits inside me like a stone.

I convince Xavier to hack the school surveillance system and take one wall of tenth grade lockers offline. He does it happily—he likes breaking rules he doesn't believe in. At lunchtime I zoom in on my RIG and watch Montgomery punch in his locker code. Two minutes later, I watch Washington punch in his.

While everyone's in the cafeteria, Dallas and I open the lockers and transfer their contents. Washington's beloved photo of a naked woman with a python snaked around her hips now hangs on Montgomery's door. Montgomery's construction workers and chorus line cover the inside of Washington's locker.

We hover nearby when the boys get back from lunch. Dallas records Montgomery shaking and flapping his hands like he's been assaulted. "Where's my jacket?" he shrieks. "What's all this?" He looks at the locker numbers around him, then back at his own. He removes a blue sweatshirt and holds it between two fingers like it's covered in waste. He sniffs it, cringes, drops it on the tile floor. Then he marches off to find an authority figure.

Washington trips in with Tyler and Jersey, bragging about fourteen-year-old throwaways they've molested. The boasting stops when Washington opens his locker. Jersey laughs and says, "That's some damaged action you're into."

A few bystanders peek over their shoulders. Washington burns crimson as their laughter snowballs and more students gather round the handsome carpenter and chorus line. "That's not mine!" he shouts.

"You have the same jacket as Montgomery?" Jersey cries.

I have to hide around the corner, I'm laughing so hard. Dallas maintains his composure and keeps recording.

Washington throws everything from his locker onto the floor, shaking and shouting, "This is not mine!"

Dallas zooms in on a vein throbbing in his forehead.

The principal marches over with Montgomery, who gasps and falls to his knees beside his belongings. He seizes a photo of a chorus girl like it's his dead mother.

"Pick those clothes up," Mr. Graham tells Washington.

"What were they doing in my locker?" Washington shouts.

Montgomery huffs to his own locker and throws the rest of Washington's belongings on the floor. He stomps on the snake girl.

"Hey! There's my stuff!" Washington yells. His eyes light up like he's made a fantastic discovery. It takes him another five minutes to comprehend that he and Montgomery are victims of a prank.

Tyler crosses his arms and stares across the hall at me and Dallas, smirking.

Mr. Graham shouts, "Whoever did this, I know you're watching! Let me warn you that your antics have been recorded." He points to the disabled camera above his head. "This is the last time you'll be enjoying yourself at someone else's expense."

Expense. What a feeb. Like twenty minutes of confusion is such a cost.

✦

"I know it was you," Pepper whispers in geography class. "The locker switch? Don't ever pull that joke on me."

"So I should take my football gear out of your dance locker?"

She laughs, throws her head back and stretches her neck like an invitation. "I'm picturing you catching a ball in my dance clothes."

"I dream of it."

She nudges her shoulder into mine. "There might not be many days left for pranks."

"You think retinal scans are coming this year?"

"I don't know what's coming." She looks me in the eye and whispers, "My parents are talking about moving away."

"No way! Where?"

She shrugs.

Ms. Reynolds calls us to attention and describes the adolescent initiation practices of extinct indigenous cultures. It could provide good fodder for jokes, but now I'm too depressed to bother.

"Did Pepper tell you she's moving?" Dallas asks in science class.

"She told you too?" I whine.

"No talking, Maxwell!" Mr. Thompson shouts. He continues his illustration of the digestive system, step-by-step illumination of a burger turning to shit.

In Communications, we read fairy tales in five languages. Frogs into princes, rags into riches, sweet tongues into sharp teeth. Everything in school today is about transformation, but I'm jammed into place, same day every day, with no way out.

Xavier takes over from Mr. Ames and expounds on the psychological necessity of heroic tales.

Tyler interrupts him. "Why aren't you in college, Lavigne? You look like an adult. You think like an adult. Why are you here?"

Xavier looks around in confusion. "I need my diploma. Education is the key to freedom."

"Xavier is fifteen like you, Tyler," Mr. Ames says. "But he spends his free time studying instead of fighting."

"That's not fair," I say. "Tyler studies and fights in equal amounts."

Everyone snickers. Tyler gives me the finger.

"I'm serious," I say. "There are no slackers in this school."

Mr. Ames snorts so hard his glasses fall off.

"It's true!" I shout. "We know that if we fall below seventy we'll be sent to the school for throwaways."

"Trade school," Mr. Ames corrects.

"Trade. Royal. The trade of dismantling old technology and recycling its parts."

"What's your point, Maxwell?" Mr. Ames sighs.

"My point is that none of us is stupid and no one lets school slide. You might think we mess around, some of us, but not one student here works less than two hours a night."

"Two out of how many?" Mr. Ames asks. "Seven? Eight? Is that really so much homework?"

"Are you serious?" I ask.

He smiles. "Let's take another look at the Big Bad Wolf."

"There aren't any wolves anymore," I mutter.

Dallas leans over and whispers, "Who do you think would win in a fight? Red Riding Hood or Grandma?"

※

In history we compare the recent Venezuelan flu to the Black Plague in the 1300s.

"Both were times of increasing social control," Mr. Reese says.

Xavier gushes at the magic words *social control*. He leans into the aisle and leads us all astray with a comparison of our national government and the medieval papacy, neither of which had anything to do with health care. Mr. Reese is kind and neurotic—he gives Xavier a long leash.

Brennan reaches the end of his own rope. "I understand what you're saying, Xavier, but in the modern world, social control is necessary. It's too easy for insane people to unleash disaster on the rest of us."

"Don't tell me the Venezuelan flu was spread by terrorists," Montgomery says with a sigh. "I am so tired of that theory."

Brennan lowers his eyes. "We know the California nuclear disaster was a terrorist move. What if something like that happened in a city? We have millions of environmental refugees from drought and rising sea levels. We can't add to that burden with industrial sabotage and terrorism."

"We should have closed our borders years ago," Washington says.

"No. It's immigration that keeps our economy strong," Xavier says. "Our openness is what made us great."

"The point is," Brennan says, "our technology has become too lethal to allow the same freedoms we used to have. Look at what happened to Freaktown, and that was just an accident."

"That was the Canadians," Washington says.

"It was our own industry," Xavier argues.

"It was an accident that our enemies want repeated," Brennan says. "We have to limit civil liberties for our own safety."

"We have to limit *corporate* liberties for our safety," Xavier argues.

"What liberties are you talking about, Brennan?" Dallas asks. "We're under surveillance on every street of this city and every room of this school."

"We need that in the rest of the country," Brennan says.

"At least they're getting universal IDs," Montgomery says. "That's step one."

"They'll never implement that," I say. "The southwest signed on to get their water supply back, but they'll never enforce it. Texas barely has zoning laws."

Dallas laughs and says, "That's where I'm moving."

"Should there be places with no surveillance?" Mr. Reese asks.

Xavier shouts, "Yes!" and Brennan shouts, "No!"

"Ask Connors," Tyler says. "He knows all the places with no surveillance."

I smile. "I like knowing that someone is keeping an eye on other people, but when they start monitoring my every move, it could be a problem."

"Who are *they*?" Mr. Reese asks.

"Chemrose," Tyler says. "And the government, the cops, the school, you."

Mr. Reese gasps. "Me?"

Tyler leans back in his chair, bites his yellow fingernails, bitterly surveys the class. He points at Brennan. "So are you. Quarterback. Ultimate. President of This and That. Of course you want more control." He points at Dallas. "Your daddy runs the school board, doesn't he?" He turns to me. "You'd like to be one of them, wouldn't you, Connors? But you just don't fit in."

"We're all *them*," Pepper says. "You too, Tyler. Compared to the rest of the world. Even compared to the rest of the country. Look at us. We have everything."

"Just because we're privileged doesn't mean we control anyone," I say. "Or want to control them."

"*You're* not all that privileged, Max," Dallas says with a smile. "And you can't be one of *them* if you're sneaking around behind their backs, can you?"

"I'm not the one who sabotages the surveillance and hacks out of the communications network," I say with a glance at Xavier. "But even if I was, I wouldn't be dangerous. I wouldn't need to be controlled."

Brennan raises his brow and shrugs.

"People always find ways around social controls," Xavier says. "Good people or bad people. That's the problem— there's no end to it. Governments and corporations will set up more and more controls for as long as we let them, until we're all living in a prison."

"Prison might be better than a carpark," I say.

"It's not funny," Xavier says. "One by one, our rights are being stripped. Freedom of movement, freedom of speech, freedom of organization. You don't care because you're where you want to be. But one day they'll control us in a way that matters to you, Max. Then you'll have to choose if you're going to go along with them or fight back."

Tyler laughs almost hysterically, shaking his head in disbelief. "What are you, insane? They are never going to give us a choice, unit."

Dallas comes over Friday for the *Freakshow* elimination. "No!" he groans when Tiger lands in the bottom again.

Tiger talks about the recent death of his daughters. The host grimaces—she doesn't consider it a significant loss since they were conjoined twins.

"He's too young to have kids," Dallas says. "He's three years older than us."

I shrug. "Not much else to do in Freaktown."

Zipperhead, who was a conjoined twin himself, hauls his massive head toward the mike and says, "I'm really sorry for you losing your baby girls, Tiger. People don't know how much pain and suffering these malformations cause us. The toxins are still poisoning our city and—"

The host whips the mike away and turns her back on Zipperhead.

Dallas laughs. "I bet he was supposed to say, 'We've all lost loved ones, but it's their memory that keeps us going.'" That's the line every contestant uses when asked about the dead.

Mom gets home with Ally just before they announce the loser. "We had a parent-teacher meeting, and I lost my front tooth!" Ally shouts. She giggles through the gap in her smile. "I'm going to take my picture."

"Did you get some supper, Dallas?" Mom asks. "We have chicken, lab-grown, fully humane." Her voice is heavy and slow. Her head hangs with fatigue.

"No, thank you," Dallas says. "I'll just stay for the end of the show." He leans forward to hear every word.

"One of you will move on to next week's show," the host announces. "The other will go back to Freaktown and spend the rest of his life as a social outcast, scraping a living by begging or thieving."

The camera closes in on the two faces, now full of shame and dread on top of their freakishness. Tiger's eyes look plastic to me. But Squid's eyes almost pop out of their sockets. He has three arms that end at the elbows, a curved spine, a huge forehead, and he can barely string three words together. He deserves another week.

"After eighty million votes," the host says, "the contestant who will be staying with us next week is…Squid!"

Squid's inky black smile is so disgusting that even the host winces. Tiger hangs his head. His ears twitch.

"Shit," Dallas says. "Sorry, Mrs. Connors. But, shit. I love that guy. Now he has to be a beggar."

"Thief," I say.

"You think so? What's worth stealing in Freaktown?"

The four contestants staying another week line up onstage.

"Please turn it off now," Mom says. "It's so sad."

"It gives them a chance to win money," I say.

"We've had this talk before, Max. Turn it off."

"I should go," Dallas says. "Austin has college entry coming up and I said I'd test him tonight."

"This early in the year?" Mom asks.

Dallas nods. "If they don't make it, they need time to apply to the state schools. Bye, Mrs. Connors. Bye, Ally!"

Ally's voice sings from the bathroom, "Goodbye, goodbye, good Dallas, goodbye!"

He smiles. "See you later, Max."

The moment the door closes, Mom launches into a lecture about the messy house, forgotten chores, unfinished homework.

"I'm saving it for Sunday after cross-country. That's when the teenage brain is at optimal performance level."

She doesn't even smile.

I follow her into the kitchen. "Are you okay? I can do the dishes."

She shakes her head, sighs, pulls a paper document from her handbag. "Ally has to go to another school."

The hair on my neck stands up and squirms. "What?"

"She's been transferred."

"To the school for throwaways?"

"Don't call them that."

"But is that the school you mean?"

"That's the only other school there is."

I sink into the counter. "I should have helped her more with homework."

Mom runs her hand over my hair. "It wouldn't have mattered, Max. She can't keep up. A hundred grade ones are

93

together with one teacher now, and the new curriculum is just too hard."

"Where *is* the school for throwaways? How will she even get there?"

She moves her hand under my chin and forces me to meet her eyes. "You have to stop calling them that. It's a trade school. They're children." She keeps her hand there until I nod. "It's near the core, less than a mile from here, where the interactive carnival used to be. She'll walk with some other children in the building. I have a list of names. Your old friend Lucas is on it."

I groan with guilt. I passed time with Lucas when we first moved to the complex, but he's feeble and in a different social tier, so I dropped him. Hard.

"I'll call his parents tonight to make sure she can walk with him," Mom says. "Their school starts at eight and runs till four."

I bang my head on the counter, grinding my forehead into a mess of toast crumbs. I picture Ally training eight hours a day from the age of six to recycle copper wire and disentangle plastic from food waste. "Does she know?"

Mom nods. "They told us at the meeting. They made it sound like fun. Maybe it's fun."

"But—"

"Don't."

I bite my tongue.

SIX

Ally wakes me early on Saturday morning, so I take her to the park before coaching. Summer vanished in the night, chased by a cruel cold front. We shiver in sweaters while the wind blows all the color off the trees.

"Fall was Daddy's favorite season," she says. I don't know how she remembers that.

Zachary and Melbourne are at the park with their mothers. They swing and slide carefully, speak pleasantly to each other, smile for their proud parents. Zach's mom says, "Time to go, sweetheart," and her little brat walks right over and takes her hand.

"I don't like it here today," Ally says.

"Do you want to go home?"

She shrugs.

"Do you want to decide with a rhyme?" I ask. "If it lands on me, we stay. If it lands on you, we go."

She points back and forth, whispering, "One, two, three, the bumblebee. Stung my nose and away he goes." She's pointing at herself.

I smile. "Let's go."

She hangs her head.

I bend down and kiss her cheek. It's wet. "Ally, are you crying?"

She pulls a handful of sunflower seeds from her pocket.

"Hey hey, we don't have to go. Do you want to feed Peanut?"

She sniffles and wipes her eyes. "Yes, please." She takes my hand and leads me past zombie Melbourne to the oak tree.

"You only had to say so," I tell her.

She shakes her head. "It's not good to speak out."

At the middle school, half the kids I'm coaching are not right. All the seventh graders seem altered, though I can't pinpoint the change. It feels like they're falling behind the grade eights, but they run just as fast, hit as hard, follow plays as closely. It's as if there's a cushion around their thoughts. Their arrogance is gone, and it's hard to see what's left.

There's a muddy dip near the end zone where the water ran when they washed my painting off the conservatory wall. The eighth graders sidestep the puddle. Frankie and Chicago squelch through. When a small kid fumbles the ball, Frankie shouts, "Try again!" When a big kid limps off the field, Chicago apologizes for his rough tackle.

"What's going on with the younger kids?" I ask Mr. Hendricks.

He smiles. "Nesting. New Education Support Treatment. It's the future, kid. The foundation of motivational leadership. It'll take our community where it needs to go. Take the whole country where it needs to go."

Saffron cartwheels after a touchdown. Eighth graders pound her shoulder in joy. Seventh graders clap like they're at an assembly.

"Did you see that drawing on the conservatory wall last week?" Mr. Hendricks asks. "There'll be no more of that. We don't have resources to waste cleaning up after troublemakers."

"I didn't do it," I say.

"I know *you* didn't do it. But whoever did won't be doing it again. We've gone too far treating children like they're precious when actually there are billions of them in the world and most of them are good for nothing. We need to educate them to work harder at whatever work is available."

"Hey, Max, why don't you do some coaching today?" Dallas shouts. He's across the field, setting up lawn chairs with Austin. They wear leather coats and cowboy boots that make them look even taller. "Xavier told me he met some girls here. I'm hoping they come back."

"Pick it up, defense!" Austin shouts.

The older kids give him the finger. The younger ones don't give him a glance.

Mr. Hendricks squints. "Is that Arlington Richmond's oldest?" He heads over to shake Austin's hand.

"What about the practice?" I yell.

Dallas helps me divide the team in two for a practice game. "Who would you rather fight?" he asks. "The big guard or that girl?"

I watch Chicago clap for Saffron's touchdown. He keeps a beat with all the other youngsters, *Clap-clap-clap, pause, clap-clap-clap.* "Neither," I say. "I wouldn't go near any of them."

⚜

On Monday morning, Mom leaves a note for Ally on the kitchen screen: *Have fun at your new school. We love you.* There's a picture of us waving, with Peanut pasted in.

Ally spills her cereal and juice in her excitement. "I have to get out all my giggles," she says. "They're not allowed in school." I tickle her to get them out, but they just keep coming, slipping through the gap of her missing tooth.

Lucas arrives at the door with another white boy my age. They wear gray polyester uniforms, paler and less stylish than mine—shapeless pants that bag at the knee, jackets with round metal buttons fastened to the neck. I feel like they should lead me on a tour of some museum.

"Hello, Maxwell," Lucas says. "We're here to take Alexandra to school." His voice is young and sincere, with no trace of a grudge.

"Thanks, Lucas. Get your bag, Ally."

Ally squares her shoulders. "I hope I like it there."

"You will if you take an interest," Lucas says.

She smiles. "I'm interested in animals."

"Good," Lucas says. "The school trains for trades in pest control."

"She *likes* animals," I say. "She couldn't stomach pest control."

He blinks repeatedly, disapproving. "There are detentions for being late. You should meet us in the lobby from now on."

I kiss Ally's cheek. She wraps her arms around my neck and says, "I'm going to like my new school."

"Yes, you will," Lucas says, butting into our goodbye. "Children who have trouble at academic school belong in trade school. You'll graduate earlier, ready to work in your field."

"I'm going to miss you so much," I whisper.

"Shh," Ally whispers back.

She steps lightly out the door and walks toward the stairwell. She looks tiny in the greasy hallway, with her red rubber boots and backpack, her hair a mess of short braids all around her head. She's six years old and already a throwaway. I just want to cry.

Lucas reaches out to shake my hand. I pull back instinctively. "We are not throwaways," he says as if he read my mind. "Our school has a higher job placement rate than yours. We're lucky to be there."

"Hear that, Ally?" I shout. "You're lucky to go to your new school."

"Alexandra!" Lucas yells. "Answer your brother!"

"Don't tell her what to do," I snarl. I step into the hallway, into his vacant face.

He looks over his shoulder at the surveillance camera, then back to me. The kid behind him does the same. I expect them to shout, "Help! You don't belong here!"

Ally turns around. She doesn't smile or frown. She looks as blank as Lucas. "I know I'm lucky, Max. Every child who goes to school is lucky."

"Exactly," Lucas says. "Goodbye, Maxwell."

Then he and his zombie friend walk away with my sister.

***

I used to complain about walking to school with Ally, stopping every ten paces to transplant worms or collect feathers, arriving at the high school just ahead of the bell, no time to socialize before class. Now I'm jostled by crowds of elbows and laughter and nodding heads, and I hate it.

"Hello, Max," Xavier says. "I never knew you came to school on time."

I message Mom seventeen times. *What if Ally gets put in a trade she hates? What if Lucas ditched Ally in the middle of nowhere? What if Ally walks too slow and gets detention?*

Mom replies once. *I have to work, Max. The virus is hitting hard. Elaine sends her love.* Like that's going to cheer me up, a deathbed love note from the granny I'm neglecting.

***

I'm heading to football practice when Pepper takes my arm. "Walk me home?" she asks.

Dallas jogs toward the gym without noticing us. "Sure," I say.

She barely speaks on the walk but she lets me hold her hand. I'm almost pissing myself with nerves.

She lives in a four-story row house. It's a bracket up from my apartment complex but nowhere near as nice as my old place. She has an end unit with a flower bed in front. We stand inches apart outside the door, saying goodbye under a security camera.

I reach my hand behind her head and lean in to kiss her. She smells like cherry candy. The back of her neck is the softest thing I've ever touched. She kisses me warmly but much too briefly before she pulls away. Her hands rest on my chest, small and delicate. I can't tell if she's feeling my heartbeat or holding me off.

"Thanks for walking me home, Max."

I stroke her hands, along her arms, up to her bare brown neck. I lean in to kiss her again, but she lowers her head so I end up smelling her hair.

"I just wanted you to know where I lived," she says. She uses the past tense.

My shoulders slump as history and gravity pull me down. I stumble back and scratch my head, slap an arm in the air. "I'll see you, Pepper." I walk away before I have to watch her shut the door on me.

I can't go home. Mom's there with Ally, and I don't want to hear how great trade school is.

I check the time. Late. I don't care. I run back to school.

The team's still doing drills when I arrive. I rush into the trailer for my gear.

"Why do you bother?" Coach Emery yells when I step onto the field. "You missed half the practice!"

I play hard, wiping Pepper and Ally and all my wasted hopes from my mind. The coach eases up on me eventually.

In the last play of practice, Dallas throws me the ball. I tuck it tight and clear a path down the field, dodging and dashing so fast I make it look easy. Bay plows through everyone who comes close, but soon he's far behind me. I've got a clear view of the end zone and I run like the devil's chasing me.

I see Brennan coming at me from the side, broken through his block. He's fast, maybe faster than me. He's huge, too, and if he tackles me from that angle at this speed I will certainly suffer.

I pump out an extra burst of speed as Brennan bends for the tackle. I spring into the air and leap over him, my hand shoving down his helmet, my legs scrambling above his arms. I clear his reach and land steady, running down the field. I throb with adrenaline through forty yards of open space.

I slam the ball into the end zone. I scream and stomp and walk on my hands, kicking my heels and raining down dirt, until my team arrives and knocks me over. Dallas almost takes my shoulder off. He laughs so hard he drools on his mask.

Coach Emery and Brennan jog up together. When I see them like that, shoulder to shoulder, I wish my dad were alive.

Brennan slams my shoulder and hugs me, lifts me off the ground, drops me, slams into me again. "Royal escape, Max. Premium. Award-winning. Do that at our next game."

I do some kingly prancing. I pat Brennan's back and say, "Good try." We all break into laughter.

I'm the first to walk off the field. Coach Emery catches up to me by the trailer. "I'm glad you made it today, Connors. I'll remember that jump for years."

I figure this is a good time to tell him I'll miss Thursday's practice.

His smile disappears. "For what reason?"

"The middle school has its first game."

He frowns. "It's good that you take your coaching seriously, but you can't let it interfere with your own practice."

"I need to be there, Coach. I'm asking my mom to come. You should come too."

My teammates pass us on their way to the trailer. "Way to go, Max," they say.

The coach lays a hand on my shoulder to hold me at the bottom of the steps. "Why on earth would I go? I have a practice to lead."

"To see the kids. There's something wrong with them. They're like—"

"I've heard about the good children at that school," he interrupts. "I'm glad you find them a pleasure to coach." He glances up at the security camera while he pats my shoulder. Then he steps backward and collides with Bay. It's strange—even with weak peripheral vision, you can't miss somebody as big as Bay.

Coach Emery straightens up and says, "Let's get out of the way." He leads me to the back of the trailer where there's no surveillance. "What are you organizing at this game?" he whispers.

I'm used to him shouting, so I'm unnerved. "I'm just asking people to see the kids."

"Who are you asking?"

"My family. Dallas."

He gasps. "Richmond's family?"

"No. Just Dallas."

"Don't invite Arlington Richmond. And don't invite any other teachers."

"Why not? They should see these kids. *You* should see them. They're not right."

"Keep these opinions to yourself, Connors." He holds me by the back of the neck and stares into my eyes. "I mean it. Do not go around talking this way."

I don't know if that's a caution or a threat.

⊱⊰

"I don't have time for a football game," Mom says. "*Your* games, yes, I love those. But the little kids? No. I'm tired at the end of the day. My shifts start at five AM this month."

"You have to come, Mom."

"I know you've been working hard coaching them—"

"I told you, it's not like that!"

"My teacher says you shouldn't raise your voice to an adult," Ally says. She sits across the table from me, eating her sandwich crusts. "The kids in my new school barely speak at all."

"That's too bad, Ally," Mom says. "But Max and I are having a private conversation right now."

"My teacher says private conversations are not good," Ally says. "We work quietly all day long."

Mom stares at her sadly.

"It's not so bad," Ally says. "There's coloring and building."

I interrupt before I have to hear the lonely details. "I need you there, Mom. I need to know if I'm imagining things."

She sighs. "How long is the game?"

"An hour and a half. You could catch the end."

She considers the minutes of lost money and sleep.

"Please," I beg. "When have I ever asked you for anything?"

She thinks about that. "Never," she says in surprise.

⁕

The middle school erected bleachers for the Warriors' first game, and they're full of students, uniformed and neatly spaced in rows.

A dozen parents stand on the sidelines, gabbing about the impending rain. Fathers scowl and pace with their hands on their hips, bellies sagging over polyester trousers. Mothers push the limits of their stretch pants and stare at the field with constipated squints.

The Chiefs bus over from the southwest quadrant. They're no bigger than the Warriors but they look premium in red and orange uniforms that shimmer when the sun breaks through a cloud.

Mr. Hendricks shakes his head. "They're a bit behind in Nesting. We're never going to beat them." Motivational leadership in action.

I shout at the Warriors as they pass by on laps. "Slow down, Frankie, save some for the game! That's right, Chicago, get those feet off the ground!"

Mr. Hendricks rolls his eyes at me.

"Where's Saffron?" I ask.

He points to the bleachers. Saffron sits at the end of the top row, watching her team jog around the field.

"Did she break a bone?"

"She quit," he tells me. "It's just as well. Boys slamming into her like they did? There was something about it that didn't feel right."

My mouth hangs open. I flap my hands around as if they're going to come up with a response on their own. I give up on Hendricks and run up the bleachers.

Saffron looks at me politely. "Hello. How are you?"

"Why did you quit the team?" I yell.

"Girls need their own teams to express themselves adequately. I'm tired of competing with boys."

"But you kick their asses. Is there a girls' football team at this school?"

She shakes her head.

"Get in uniform."

She looks at the field, looks up at me, shakes her head. "There's no place for girls on this team."

"Did the coach tell you that?"

She frowns. "I don't remember who told me that."

"You're the best player on the team, Saffron. They need you."

"I don't like this conversation anymore." She turns to her friend, a tiny black girl with purple hair clips and a white zip-up sweater.

"No girl has to converse with a boy if it makes her uncomfortable," the friend says.

Every student in the back row nods and waits for me to leave. They have the same eyes, same words, same minds. I shudder and nearly stumble off the bleachers.

The coach calls in the team and the game begins.

Mr. Hendricks was right. The Warriors have no hope of winning. The Chiefs are no bigger or faster but they have the advantage of not yet being zombies. They jump and scream on the sidelines, "Go, Matty, go! Come on, come on, come on!" They dive for tackles they have no chance of making. They run the ball like they're fleeing spear-wielding cannibals. When they score, they shout and leap and slam into each other joyously.

The Warriors stand on the sideline and shout stock phrases for no particular reason. "Good try! We're the best!" They only dive for tackles they can take. They run the ball like they're jogging to school. And when they score—which they only do once—they clap politely. *Clap, clap, clap, pause, clap, clap, clap.*

Mom arrives late and stands apart from the other parents, nervous and out of place. Ally stands beside her like a mechanical doll waiting for someone to wind her up.

"Do you see what I mean?" I ask.

"Your team's not very good," Mom says.

"Not good? Look at them, Mom. They're not right. None of them. Even the eighth graders are defective now."

Chicago runs for the ball, but he fumbles and a Chief throws himself on top of it. Chicago smiles and brushes off his hands.

"See that?" I ask. "He lost control and he doesn't care. He's not angry. He's not embarrassed. You should have seen that kid two weeks ago. He was a mouthy little punk with an ego bigger than this field. Now he's a robot. They all are. Look at them."

"They're like the kids at my school," Ally says. She holds her teddy tight to her chest. "They're all slowed down."

Mom frowns. "They run almost as fast as the other team."

"Inside," Ally whispers. "They're all slowed down inside."

"They are a bit quiet," Mom says.

"Hello, Karenna!" a huge white woman shouts. She walks over, smiling and wheezing. "I thought that was you."

"Linda MacMillan," Mom says. "I haven't seen you for ages. Look, Max. It's Linda. She worked at Manor Heights with me and your dad."

I don't recall ever meeting Linda, and she's not someone you could easily forget. She weighs about five hundred pounds and she doesn't wear them well.

"Isn't this the best week of your life?" she shouts. "All these good children! I'm so thankful for Nesting."

"Nesting?" Mom repeats.

"The New Education Support Treatment." Linda looks at Ally and says, "She must have been done the first week of school. She's in grade one, isn't she?"

Mom opens her mouth to say something, but then she closes it tight and puts a hand on Ally's shoulder.

"You notice it most with the little ones," Linda says. "It's harder to tell in the older grades until you get their marks—then you'll see the difference." She looks me up and down and snorts. "You're a hefty boy for eighth grade. You should be out there on the field." She wags her finger and says to Mom, "I recall you saying this one was a bit of a trouble-maker. I'm sure you're glad that's over. What's he like now?"

"Max is as good as gold," Mom says softly.

"These clouds are getting darker by the minute," Linda says. "I hope we're not rained out, though god knows the grass could use it. Did you see that mess of paint at the end of the field? It's not right, letting the paint wash into the grounds like that. I don't know why they didn't just paint over it. How much does a can of paint cost these days?" She shakes her head at the conservatory and mutters, "You won't see any more graffiti once they do the high schools this month. Thank god. These kids are out of hand."

A fat black woman struts up to us. She holds out her hand to Mom. "I'm Denise Atkins. I work at the school. Thanks for coming out." She nods toward me and Ally. "It must be so stressful with two of them. How did you manage before?"

Mom shrugs. "They're not much trouble."

"I'm sure they're not now," Denise says. "You wouldn't believe the calls I've had this term. A lot of families are happy at last. No more constant battles. No mouthing off. No fighting over homework. No lies."

"No need to worry about their future," Linda adds. "That's the main thing for me. With the new class sizes, every minute counts. I don't want my child's grades falling because some troublemaker is wasting time."

"My Saffron is a gifted student," Denise says. "Her talents were wasted in the old system."

"You're Saffron's mother?" I exclaim.

Denise and Linda turn on me like I called them fat cows.

"She's an excellent football player," I add.

"Have you noticed any side effects?" Linda asks, surveying me closely. "Some kids on other meds get confused and have outbursts like that. Just like in Manor Heights."

"Side effects of what?" Mom asks.

Linda and Denise exchange glances. "Aren't you on the parent-teacher board?" Linda asks.

Mom shakes her head. "Not this year. I haven't even read the minutes."

"You don't know about motivational leadership?" Denise gasps.

Mom shakes her head.

"Honey, you have to get on that," Linda exclaims. "Parent participation is essential to program success. We can't be giving the kids mixed messages."

"You should have read the guidelines weeks ago," Denise sneers. "These outbursts can't be ignored."

Linda pats her friend's shoulder. "He just got done this week, Denise. It's a lot for a boy to take in." She turns to Mom. "Chicago had a bit of an adjustment last week when they did the grade sevens, but he's fine now. Better than fine." She points to Chicago, who stands like a zombie in a line of zombies. "He's the best player on the team."

I snort with laughter. It's stupid, I know. I regret it immediately. But it's impossible for me to leave that statement in the air without snorting at it.

Suspicion and hatred fly from the fat women's faces.

I scratch my nose and cough and snort some more like I'm having a respiratory attack until at last they stop staring at me.

"Nesting saved Chicago's academic career," Linda says. "He never got anywhere on time. He always left his homework to the last minute and messed around in class. But now that's all changed."

Denise gives me a thorough inspection, scrutinizing my face, my arms, even peeking round my backside, like I'm a slave she might purchase for field work. "You don't play football?" she asks me. "I saw you talking to the coach earlier. Why aren't you on the field? Or sitting in the stands with your classmates?"

Mom puts a hand on my shoulder, just like she did with Ally. "I like having my children near me."

Linda smiles. "We have a lot in common, Karenna. I'm a softy, too, where my boy is concerned." She stares across the field and nods. "I was there for his treatment and I'm glad for that. It makes a difference to know it's done right. Plus it's extra money. I was let go from the hospital this summer. We're mostly living on the one income." She slaps a hand in the air and adds, "I'm sorry, honey. That was thoughtless. You've been on one income for a while now, haven't you?"

Mom nods.

"You should come do vaccinations with me!" Linda grins and jiggles like she's planning a garden party. "I've been telling them I need help, and they just said yes."

"I work until three," Mom says.

Linda shrugs. "You never know. I might be doing some after school. I'll check at work tomorrow."

"Thank you," Mom says. She stands stiff and awkward, gripping me and Ally tight. When thunder rumbles way up in heaven, she squeezes us so hard it hurts.

⁕

"We lost the game," I tell Dallas on my RIG. "They were useless."

"You shouldn't have bothered."

"You should have been there." I describe the fat ladies and what they said to Mom and how it fits with the zombie children who yelled "You don't belong here!" at us.

He laughs. "They thought you were in grade eight?"

"That's not the point."

"What *is* the point? You think the hepatitis vaccinations are turning kids into zombies? That's what it sounds like you're saying."

"That's what I'm saying."

He shakes his head. "You're crazy, Max. Why would they do that? We're their children. We are the future of this country."

"Maybe the future of this country requires a lot of slaves."

Dallas laughs and the screen dissolves.

SEVEN

We receive two announcements Monday morning. First, we can wear costumes to the Halloween dance next Friday. Second, we'll be vaccinated over the lunch hour, grade nine students today, grade ten tomorrow. "As you know," Mr. Graham says on every screen, "you are not allowed to leave the school grounds at lunch. Not any day."

"But tomorrow they really mean it," Dallas whispers.

"I don't plan on being here tomorrow," I say.

"Afraid they'll zombify you?" he scoffs. He hangs out his tongue and extends his arms, rolls his eyes at me when I don't find it funny.

We sneak out for lunch—through the chemistry lab, across the parking lot and over the football field, hiding our faces from the cameras. We eat in the skate park, slurping limp noodles from thermoses, while two grade twelve ultimates perform skateboard stunts for their gorgeous girlfriends.

"I haven't been on a skateboard since I was thirteen," Dallas says, like it was decades ago.

One guy rides up the bowl, spins and crashes, spills backward onto the pavement. He removes his shoe and wiggles his ankle with both hands.

"I can ride better than that guy," Dallas says.

The other guy walks up to the railing and kisses his girl for a long time, one hand at the back of her neck and the other hand spinning a wheel on his board.

"Maybe not better than him," Dallas adds.

I'm dying to say that I kissed Pepper, but I'm afraid he'll tell me they've been sleeping together all term.

He elbows me. "Remember that time you tried Austin's board?" He wails like an ambulance and laughs.

"I'm not good with wheels," I admit.

The feeble skateboarder clatters to the pavement again. He rubs his ass and laughs hysterically, then lies back on the concrete and lights a cigarette, blowing smoke rings at the cold blue sky.

"How would you rather die?" Dallas asks. "Burning in a fire or drowning in icy cold water?"

"Fire. No contest."

"Fire? You're crazy. No one picks fire."

I shrug. "I don't like being cold."

"So burning in a fire or drowning in a hot tub?"

"Hot tub."

"Good man. Want to head back?"

"Not yet." I take a picture of the skater and his girl, his hand in her gray pocket, her red hair blowing in the wind, brown leaves dying all around them.

Dallas grabs my RIG and scrolls through my photo albums. He pauses on my conservatory mural and snorts. "I can't believe you did that."

"The piece was supreme."

"Not the piece. The *stealing*. From a *school*." He holds up his hands and asks the air, "What do the children do in art class this year? Nothing. Because Max stole their paint." He shakes his head at me. "I would have bought you paint if you'd asked. What are you going to do with it all anyway?"

"Use it in my art exhibit."

"You took fifty cakes, Max. How much do you need for one project?"

"I'll have a big canvas. Mom found an old army tent at the surplus store. There's a guy at the carpark who'll cut it and stretch it for me."

"You're painting a whole tent?" He snorts and looks around for backup mockers.

A vision of a silent gray tent leaps before my eyes: square canvas walls, flat roof, closed flaps hiding the interior. "I was going to cut it into canvases, but maybe I shouldn't." I see the tent walls blossom in graffiti—messy tags, shocking stencils, some masterpiece I can't yet picture. I rise to my feet and pace, wagging my finger at Dallas. "A tent to represent the school. I have enough paint to do all four walls."

He shakes his head. "You know what you should do with that paint."

"No way. I might get caught giving it back. I'd be expelled for something like that."

"You *should* be expelled for something like that."

I'd argue with him but I'm too excited by my vision.

"Let's get going," he mutters. He won't look me in the eye but at least he stops shaking his head.

⚜

We arrive at school sullen and late. The principal catches us outside the front gate when the bell rings. "Detention!" he shouts. "Connors! Richmond! Three thirty today in detention hall!" That's all he says. His main qualification for the job is an uncanny ability to remember names.

Mr. Reese is on his weekly stress leave from history class. In his place is my least favorite substitute, Mr. Warton. We call him Werewolf because of his excessive body hair. Back of his neck, back of his hands, everywhere from cheekbones to toenails, he's a blanket of fur. "Oh joy, oh bliss," he says when Dallas and I enter the room. We gave him a razor for Christmas last year and he hasn't forgotten our thoughtfulness.

I sit behind Pepper's empty desk.

"Pepper hurt her ankle in dance practice," Xavier tells me. "Her father picked her up and took her to the hospital."

"Are you serious?"

He nods. "I saw him. He's bald."

"White or black?"

"In between."

"Shaved head or naturally bald?"

"Detention!" Werewolf howls at me. "You too!" he tells Xavier. "Three thirty in the blue room for talking out of turn."

"But I never get detention," Xavier says.

"You do today," Werewolf snarls.

I make a big deal of it, pleading and whining, saying I'll be kicked off the football team if I don't make practice, my girlfriend will quit me if I leave the team, and my adolescence will be ruined. Eventually Werewolf gives in just to shut me up. "All right," he says. "But keep quiet for the rest of class."

"You mean it?" I jump out of my seat and shout, "Oh, thank you, thank you, Mr. Warton." Then I sit back down and say, "Nah, wait. Actually I already have detention for being late. But thanks anyway, man."

The class bursts into laughter. Werewolf turns purple. "It was a good effort," I tell him.

Dallas cracks up, cackling like a witch.

Werewolf turns on him. "Detention!"

"But—"

"Not one word!"

"But I already have detention," Dallas squeaks.

The class laughs along with him.

"You'll be singing a different tune soon enough," Werewolf snarls.

Dallas and I start to hum quietly.

<hr />

The detention room buzzes with *Freakshow* gossip. Kids spin in their chairs, stick their legs in the aisles, hug their seat backs and chat to neighbors. There's no supervisor yet. The teachers are probably in the lounge, drawing straws.

Xavier docks his RIG at the desk in front of me and hacks through Blackboard to change his science grade. "I deserve an A," he says in explanation.

The kid kills me.

I groan when the teacher finally shows up. It's Werewolf again. When he calls the roll and I answer, "Here," he tells me to shut up. He files the attendance list and paces the aisles. He rests a butt cheek on my desk and smirks at me and Dallas, who sits next to me in the back row. "You'll be getting a little present in a minute. Something your parents will thank us for."

"What kind of present?" Xavier asks. "Is the present for everyone or just for Max?"

Werewolf snickers. He walks to the front of the room and announces, "Your classes are having their vaccinations tomorrow, but you people are getting yours early. We know that some of you detention types like to skip out on lunch, and we certainly don't want to miss you."

"Shit," I mutter. I look at Dallas, but he rolls his eyes at my distress. "I don't want any vaccinations, sir," I say.

Werewolf raises his bushy brows. "Too bad for you."

I start to sweat. I consider running for it, but the doorway is suddenly blocked by Mr. Graham in all his bald white enormity.

The principal shakes a paw with Werewolf and takes the floor. "You all know how it's done. You'll get two shots, one in each arm. They won't interfere with your ability to do your homework while you're here. Please be polite to our nurses."

He peeks into the hallway and beckons Linda, the fat white woman from the middle school football game. She walks in wearing a pink polyester shirt the size and shape of a barbecue cover. A stainless-steel serving cart rolls in behind her. The top shelf is cluttered with tiny brown bottles, syringes, a heap of sterile needles, stacks of gauze, huge square bandages. One of the cart wheels sticks so it drags across the floor tiles, *shhhh, shhh, shh.*

I shudder as I look up at the black woman pushing the cart. It's my mother. She stares at the floor like there's no one here she knows.

"Hey, Max—," Xavier says.

"No talking!" Mr. Graham snaps. "Let's get this done quickly and quietly. If anyone speaks out of turn, Mr. Warton is instructed to put them on tomorrow's detention list." He smiles at Linda. "I'll leave you to it. Make sure you submit the attendance records at the office. We wouldn't want to shoot them twice." He chuckles. Werewolf snorts. Linda smiles like a clown. Mom looks down at the tray, humble as a slave.

Werewolf walks the principal to the door, then closes it and leans against it like a security guard.

At the click of the latch, Mom lifts her head and stares at me. Hard. I have no idea what she's trying to communicate. Run? Stay? Goodbye? I don't know. Her mouth is tight with worry, her skin tugs on her cheekbones.

"All right, children," Linda says. "Take off your jackets and roll up your sleeves, please. These will go in the upper arms, one on each side." She smiles at Mom. "Can you do the right arms?"

Mom chooses a brown bottle and a syringe. She fits on a needle, rips off the security plastic, fills the syringe with god knows what. She holds it in the air the way my stylist holds scissors and looks down on the boy in the first seat—Michael or Martin something; he's on the cross-country team with me and Xavier. He offers his arm, flexes his muscle, winks at my mom.

"You're eager," Linda says with a big smile. "What have you got there, Karenna? The inhibitor? I'll do the Hep then."

Mom nods without the slightest bit of feeling in her face. I wonder if she dosed herself in the hallway.

She sticks a thermometer in the kid's ear and nods after she reads it.

"This won't hurt much," Linda yaps. "Needles are so thin these days. You should have seen them back in my mother's time. Almost as thick as a pencil! Do you kids use pencils anymore?" She pinches the kid's skin and rams in the needle. She does not have a delicate touch. No wonder she was fired from the old folks' home. They're so skinny there, she must have hit bone every time.

Mom places two gloved fingers on the boy's gangly right arm and aims her needle between them. She leans into him a little and whispers something just before she sticks him.

I watch the syringe push the fluid into his muscle, and I know that he's being zombified. I wonder who he was and who he'll never be again.

Mom pulls the needle out and presses a tiny gauze square over the entry point. "Hold this in place, please." She reaches for a large square bandage, removes the packaging, peels the backing, checks the gauze for blood and delicately positions the bandage on the kid's arm.

"These patches we're putting on have to stay in place for a week," Linda announces. "They're not Band-Aids. They're part of your treatment, and if you pick at them, you'll make yourself sick. Don't worry, you can shower in them. Your parents will be sent more instructions over the next few days."

I sit like a stone and watch my mother move down the row of students, *shhhh, shhh, shh*, closer and closer to me.

"Of course, being in detention doesn't mean you're bad," Linda babbles. "It just means you've done something wrong and you're not going to get away with it."

When they're two desks away, I can hear what Mom is whispering in every child's ear. *I'm sorry.*

I start to shake. I want to get up and leave, but I can't move with all these kids here, and the camera and Werewolf and my mother.

Xavier is ahead of me, staring at his RIG. Mom gasps when she sees him. He looks up and smiles. "Hello, Mrs. Connors."

She breathes slow and deep. "Hello, Xavier. How are you feeling today?"

"Fine."

"Oh my goodness, you're a good-looking boy!" Linda says. "How old are you? Eighteen? Twenty-five? You belong on a poster in a college dormitory, that's where you belong." She laughs and looks at Mom. "I know they're mostly all good-looking these days, but this boy is something special, wouldn't you say?"

Mom rests her hand on Xavier's shoulder. "He's a very beautiful boy."

Xavier smiles shyly at my mother, speechless for once.

When the thermometer beeps, she shakes her head. "He has a bit of a temperature. We should wait until he's well."

Linda scowls. She reaches across Xavier's desk and snatches the thermometer from Mom's hand. She wobbles her head around and mutters, "Well, hmm, I don't know. It's just on the edge. We should do him anyway." She jabs her needle into Xavier's left arm.

Mom stares at the needle in her own hand. She swallows and tries to smile. "I don't think so. I know he takes other medications and there may be contraindications, especially with a temperature."

"It's critical that we get the detentioners done quick," Linda says. "Don't make me regret offering you this job."

Mom groans and sucks in her lower lip, stares down on Xavier's angelic face. "What other medications are you on, dear?"

Linda huffs and snorts. She tries to squeeze behind Xavier's chair, but there's not enough room. She stomps around the back of my desk and comes up on the other side, her fat shoes squealing along the floor. She seizes the syringe from Mom's hand and plunges it into Xavier's right arm.

"Ow!" he shouts.

"No," Mom moans.

Linda yanks out the needle, scowling. "That's the sort of consequence hesitation brings." She hands a patch to my mother. "We are here to do these children, and we are doing these children. Now let's get a move on."

Mom presses the patch on Xavier's arm, stroking it gently to fix it to his skin.

"Thank you, Mrs. Connors," he says.

She turns to me with the saddest face I've seen since Dad's funeral. "Hi, Max." Her voice is soft like a little girl's.

"Oh my goodness!" Linda shouts. "This is *your* son! He's at *this* school!"

All the kids turn around and strain to get a look at my mother while she fills a syringe just for me.

Linda laughs and slaps the air. "No wonder he was so odd at that football game! Oh my goodness. You'll see such a difference after this. Oh, you'll love it."

Mom sticks a thermometer in my ear. It feels obscene, and I cringe away from her. She leans into my desk, smelling of latex and toxins. "I'm glad you explained it to me," she tells Linda. "I'm glad I could be here for this."

"Don't you mention it," Linda says as she readies her needle. "It makes all the difference to be there for them."

Mom reads my temperature and nods.

"Mom—," I start to beg.

She pinches my arm, tight and twisted, digging in her nail. "Be quiet, Max!"

I feel like I'm six years old.

She lays her gloved fingers on my right arm. "It will make all the difference for me to be here."

I open my mouth to speak, but nothing comes out, not even air.

She leans toward me and whispers, "Don't say anything."

"Mom, don't—"

"Shh."

Linda jabs my left arm.

"That doesn't hurt, does it?" Mom asks softly. I look up at her. She smiles. "Does it hurt, Max? I tried to do it gently."

There's no needle in my right arm. There's something cold and wet against my skin, but no penetration. I peer down, but Mom's hand covers the syringe and I can't see what she's doing. A bitter chemical stench rises into my face.

"Almost done," she says.

She presses gauze to my skin, reaches for my hand, lays my finger over the tiny white square. "Hold this in place, please." She flicks the needle into the garbage, lays the syringe on the white tablecloth. It's empty. She takes a patch from her pocket, removes the wrapping, sticks it on my arm. "There," she says. "That didn't hurt at all, did it?"

I can't respond.

Mom turns to Dallas at the desk beside me. "You're next."

"I'll come round the other side," Linda says. "You might as well stay there and work your way up on the left. I don't mind walking around." She wheezes and squeaks as she walks behind me. "That's one row down and four to go. We'll be out of here before four thirty, but don't worry, we get paid for the full hour no matter what."

Mom slips on a fresh needle and stabs it into a bottle. I watch the syringe suck up a pale dose of zombie. She sets the bottle down and holds the needle high.

"Mom, you can't—"

"That's enough, Max," she hisses.

Students stare at me like I'm a freak.

"Voices down," Werewolf reminds us.

"Is he afraid of needles?" Linda asks.

"Yes, but he needn't be." Mom turns to Dallas. "Ready?"

Dallas smiles like she's offering ice cream.

I lay my head down on my desk to get a better view of his arm. Mom cups her left hand over the needle so it's hard to see. Her right thumb pushes slowly on the syringe. It looks like she's really giving him the shot. My heart thumps as if my blood is too thick to push through the valves.

"Ow," Dallas says. He looks up at Linda, who just stuck him in the other arm.

"A big boy like you afraid of a little needle?" Linda shouts. "I'm surprised anything can get through those muscles of yours. They're hard as a rock."

"Almost done," Mom says softly.

Dallas looks at her, smiles, tries to see what she's doing to his arm.

"There," she says, pressing gauze to his skin.

He opens his mouth to speak, but she says, "Don't talk. Just rest. Hold this in place."

She flicks the needle into the garbage and grabs another patch from her pocket. I stretch back in my chair and get a brief but clear view of Dallas's arm. There's no mark, no piercing, just a moist gloss.

Mom presses on the patch and pats his shoulder. "All done."

She works her way up the aisle of desks, whispering, "I'm sorry" to everyone. Everyone but me and Dallas.

She stops and sighs when she gets to Tyler Wilkins. "Hello, Tyler," she says sadly. She looks across the desk at Linda, but she doesn't bother speaking.

"My goodness, child, you smell like cigarettes," Linda chatters. "Do you know how many toxins one cigarette contains?" She looks at Mom and her smiles fades. "Oh for God's sake, what is it now? Does he have a temperature?"

"No, but—"

"Then get to it, Karenna. We have to do them all."

Mom looks at Tyler's homely face. "I'm sorry, Tyler."

He laughs and runs a hand down his tattooed arm. "It's all right. I'm not afraid of needles."

I watch the drug go deep into his skin.

I'm not sorry to see Tyler Wilkins zombified. But I suppose there are people who'd say the same about me.

There's a dear little home in Good-Children street—
My heart turneth fondly to-day
Where tinkle of tongues and patter of feet
Make sweetest of music at play;
Where the sunshine of love illumines each face
And warms every heart in that old-fashioned place.

For dear little children go romping about
With dollies and tin tops and drums,
And, my! how they frolic and scamper and shout
Till bedtime too speedily comes!
Oh, days they are golden and days they are fleet
With little folk living in Good-Children street.

From Eugene Field's
"Good-Children Street"
in *Love Songs of Childhood* (1894)

PART TWO

ADJUSTMENT

EIGHT

My mother sits on her bed, folded small like a child, hugging her knees. She's in pajamas at dinnertime. Ally's eating a sandwich in the living room, watching cartoons.

"How did you know?" I ask.

Mom sniffles and shrugs. "Parents are always notified of detention."

"I mean how did you know about the drug?"

"Oh. Linda told me when she called. I recognized the name."

"As what?"

"It's a derivative of one we use at the home."

"On who?"

She shrugs or shudders, I can't tell which. "Everyone."

"Everyone," I repeat. I lean against Ally's dresser, rattling her plastic dolls. They fall on their sides, backs bent, legs splayed, smiles painted pink.

"It's not how you think," Mom says. "Our patients are in pain. They're lonely and bored. Antisocial. That's how this drug started out—for mood disorders."

"Elaine wasn't antisocial." I recall stepping into the geriatric center with my class three years ago. From the sad ranks of old folks slumped in rows of collapsible chairs, Elaine jumped up and shouted, "Hallelujah! There are children alive in the world!"

"She wasn't disordered," I tell Mom. "She was a firecracker."

My mother stares at me, biting her lip.

"I guess she's no firecracker anymore," I say.

She huffs and scowls. "These drugs help my patients cope, Max."

"All of them? How could you drug all your patients? Most of them aren't even sick. They're just old."

"I can't give them happy lives, Max. I can't make their children visit. I can't find them jobs or make them feel important. I feed them and bathe them and give them their shots."

"Did they ask for those shots?"

"There are seventy-two patients under my care every ten-hour shift! That's eight minutes each. That's what I give them. The other nine hours and fifty-two minutes, they are ignored. They used to lie there and cry. Remember when you visited? It's not like that anymore. They eat well, they take part in social activities, they exercise, they have hobbies."

"I bet they line up neatly too."

"They are happy to be alive now, Max."

"They're not happy, Mom. They're just not crying anymore."

"You don't understand."

"No. I don't understand. Why not just give me the shot if you don't think it's wrong?"

She gapes at me, outraged. "It's not for children. It's for people with nothing else in their lives. It's wrong to give it to children."

"*You* gave it to children!" I remind her. "Why didn't you call the police? Why didn't you stop it?"

She squints at me, confused. "It's not illegal. The school has the authority to treat students for behavioral problems."

"We don't all have behavioral problems."

"Sure you do, Max. Everybody does. Everybody can be improved—you've told me that yourself. They've just never done it on this scale before."

"Why didn't you take us out of there?"

"Take who out? I'm not allowed to take your friends out of school. I doubt if I'm allowed to take *you* out."

"You still should have done it."

"And put you where? It would be the end of education for you and Ally. Linda says they've already treated the trade schools. There is nowhere else to go."

"Take us to another town."

"And live on what? How will you find work if you never finish school? Do you know what the rest of the world is like, Max? We're lucky I have a job here."

"A job where you drug people against their will."

"Stop it! I did what I could today." She looks away and lays her head on her knees.

"How did you fake it?" I ask.

She grabs a dirty napkin off the cluttered nightstand and peels back the layers to reveal a small stained sponge. "I was scared to try it with Xavier. I didn't know how much it could hold. I only brought two patches anyway, for you and Dallas." She sighs and shakes the memory from her head.

"What's in my patch?"

"Estrogen."

"Estrogen? No way. Am I going to grow boobs?"

"I don't think so."

"You don't *think* so?"

"It's just a month's worth. But you have to keep it on for three."

"Three months? Linda said the patch was for a week."

"She lied."

"Why? People will take them off early. Is that safe?"

"Their parents will tell them to keep them on. Don't worry. The patch is part of the treatment. It balances the side effects of the shot."

"Will kids get sick if they take them off?"

She sighs. "They won't take them off, Max. By tomorrow or the day after, they'll do whatever they're told."

I scratch my head and stare at the ceiling, trying to think of something to say. I hear Ally singing in the living room, "A—my name is Ally, my husband's name is Arnold, we live in Arkansas, and we sell apples!"

"You'll get a new patch in three months," Mom tells me. "Make sure you take it off and put the empty estrogen patch back on."

I nod at the ceiling.

"Then in six months, you'll get another shot," she tells me.

I look at her in surprise. "How many drugs are they giving us?"

"It's the same drug, just another dose."

"It wears off? So there's a chance for Xavier?"

She shrugs. "I think so. My patients get a slow-release shot that lasts two years, but Linda said they reduced the dosage for children."

"So Linda's coming back to drug my class again in six months?"

Mom nods. "I'll try to be there for it."

I pick up two of Ally's dolls and hurl them at her. She's so surprised, she screams. Ally's song ends abruptly. "How about you don't?" I shout. "How about I find another school? How about you find another job?"

Mom picks up a doll and straightens out its clothes and hair. "I'm not taking you and Ally out of New Middletown if I can help it. This is the safest city on earth."

I walk over to the bed and lean into her face. "You came into my school and stuck people with something that makes them do whatever they're told. I don't feel very safe."

She lowers her head and pinches her bottom lip. "I'm sorry, Max. I want you to finish academic school. Your life will be so much easier if you do that. I can be there for your shots. No one will ever know."

"What about everyone else?"

"They'll be fine eventually. They'll become much more focused on their studies." She lays the doll down and sits up tall. "Everyone says it's for their own good. Maybe this new variant—"

"Don't even try it," I interrupt. "I've seen the results at the other schools. I don't want to be like that."

"Okay. I know. I don't want you to be like that either." She reaches out for my hand, but I back away from her. "You'll have to pretend you've been treated," she tells me. "It's not just that you have to work harder. You have to take school more seriously. You have to act like the others."

I remember Ally saying that outside her school weeks ago.

"I've already spoken to Ally," Mom says, as if she read my mind. "She's so well-behaved that no one noticed. But you, Max." She looks me in the eye and shrugs. "You *have* to be good."

"I have to be *good*?" I repeat. "*Good*?"

"You know what I mean. You have to be obedient. Your teachers will be watching you."

"So the teachers know what's going on?"

She looks at me like I'm a lost little boy. "Everyone knows, Max. This is school policy. They've been planning this for months. They'll increase the dosage for anyone who doesn't respond."

"Is that what you do at the old folks' home?"

She ignores me. "Tell Dallas not to fight with his brother. Arlington will be watching and Austin won't be treated for another week or two."

"They're doing the grade twelves?"

"They're doing all the grades, Max. Everyone."

"Everyone," I repeat, hating her.

Celeste comes over after supper with a box of face paints. She wears white woolen stockings and a tight blue sweater that hangs to her knees. She pulls back her hair and ties on a beige apron. "You're so much darker than the kids," she says as she smears Mom's cheek with makeup. "This is way too light for you. Your skin is gorgeous for your age."

"Thank you, dear. How's your brother?"

"Xavier? He's fine. He's actually sleeping. He fell asleep at the table, he's so tired. It's all that cross-country running."

Mom frowns and hunches. She's quiet while Celeste applies two darker tints. Her face takes on subtle stripes, like faded war paint. "I hope he's all right," she mutters.

"Xavier?" Celeste asks. "Sure, he's just tired." She cleans Mom's face with white cream. "Can I try tomorrow with other colors?"

"Yes, dear."

"Thanks." Celeste sways down the hall under the eye of the camera.

I stay up late watching a movie from Xavier's favorite site: *1984*. It's about a poverty-stricken world where the government watches all the workers as they pretend to enjoy their reeking lives. They're all ugly, white and underfed. It's probably a metaphor.

Mom knocks on my bedroom door.

"Shouldn't you be asleep?" I ask. "Don't you have to get up at three?"

She sits on the edge of my bed, wiping her eyes. I pause the movie. "Xavier could never fake being a zombie," I say. "He talks too much. They'd dose him again right away."

She sniffles and pats my hand. She's tired, her eyes baggy black, her lips stretched thin. Her hair is frizzy, and it's been too long since she had it cut. "Your hands are so young," she says. "They look brand-new."

I can't smile at her, but I squeeze her fingers. "Thanks, Mom."

"For what, honey?"

"For saving me and Dallas."

"Oh, baby." She leans her head and shoulder into me. "I should have taken you home."

I shudder at the memory of her wheeling the tray into class. "When you walked into detention, I thought it was some kind of punishment. For the way I am."

"I thought you'd know why I was there. I couldn't lose you, Max."

"You wouldn't lose me. I'd just be a zombie."

She smiles. "That's a funny thing to call them. Zombies are corpses that crawl out of their graves and eat people's brains."

"No way."

She laughs. "Yes. They eat people alive. They're not calm at all."

"That's crazy."

"You should call them something else."

"What do you call your patients?"

She stiffens and pulls her hand away.

I don't take it back. I don't want to make it easy for her. "We could call them robots," I say. "Or mindless slaves."

"It's not like that, Max."

"Yes it is." I unpause the movie and watch skinny people in shapeless uniforms hide from giant cameras. "What if they do everyone? The whole country?"

"Don't be silly," Mom says.

"Remember that airport guard who frisked me? I bet she was a zombie. I bet they'll do the nurses eventually. One day you'll come home from work and you'll be one of them."

"Who would even notice?"

I want to smack her face for asking that. "I would."

She leans into me again. Her hair is dry and stale as dust.

"I love you, Mom," I whisper.

"I love you too, Max."

Tyler Wilkins stops on the sidewalk where I linger outside Ally's old school watching the zombies. "Hello, Maxwell. Aren't you going to class?" He looks at the schoolyard and frowns. "There's something strange about that. We spoke of it before." He winces and holds a hand to his chest. "I'm getting a cold." He smiles at me without malice.

"You don't seem yourself," I say.

"I don't feel right," he admits. He checks his watch. "We should be going." There's something in his eyes, some rule-following gleam, that makes me keep up.

I don't talk much the rest of the way. He asks strange questions like, "How's your family?" and "Did you have a healthy breakfast?" He rubs his forehead and chest every few minutes, stumbles more than once, doesn't smoke or swear. He ditches me on the school grounds and heads inside.

Dallas pulls me to the fence and whispers, "My dad interrogated me last night! Mom said he'd been waiting since he heard I had detention. He checked my blood pressure and reflexes." He stops talking when Bay walks near, doesn't make eye contact, doesn't wave. After Bay moves on, he continues in a whisper. "He gave me a list of rules to memorize. I made a joke and he recorded it. Then he said, 'You're going to do so well from now on, *son*.'" He shakes his head, leans in close. "Like he's proud of me now that I'm a zombie."

I nod. "They all know about it."

"Why? Why would they turn us into zombies?"

"I don't know. But Mom says zombies are actually undead creatures like werewolves who hunger for people's brains, so we should call them something else."

"Werewolves aren't undead," Dallas says. "They're just cursed."

"Well, zombies are undead. They crawl out of their graves half-rotted and go looking for brains to eat."

"No way. I thought they were hypnotized people who did some evil guy's bidding."

"Zombies don't do anybody's bidding. They drag around after brains."

Dallas snorts. "So what are we supposed to call them?"

I shrug.

"Let's still call them zombies," he says. "It's a good word."

I agree.

"What would you rather be killed by?" he asks. "A zombie or a werewolf?"

"Werewolf."

"Me too."

I take out my RIG. "Let's record people before they're all brain-eaters. Have you seen Pepper?"

"No. But get the Scorpions."

We tell our teammates we're composing a message for the Devils. They growl and roar, gesture rudely at my RIG, shout, "We're coming for you, ladies!" The bell rings too soon. Montgomery is yards away, teaching a dance routine to the cheerleaders. I raise my RIG high, hoping to record a few moves, but I'm too late. He picks up his coat, hangs it over his back with one hooked finger and heads inside.

His casual happiness lays me low. I'm limp and heavy suddenly, while all these lives bustle by me. Their voices and expressions are so distinct. They strike me down with their joy and bewilderment and lust and fury. I need to collect them in my RIG, but there's no time.

"Get a grip on yourself!" Dallas hisses as he yanks me toward the doors. "What do you think Graham will do to us if you walk in crying?"

"Sorry. It must be the estrogen."

He shoots me a look that shuts me up.

※

Mr. Ames keeps the class in for shots at lunch. He walks the aisles and highlights the absences: Pepper, Brennan and Xavier are all home sick. "You're not on the list, Maxwell."

He points his finger at me. "You must have had detention yesterday."

"Yes sir."

"Were you in detention with Maxwell yesterday?" he asks Dallas.

"Yes sir. I was in detention yesterday."

"Everyone will remain in their seats as we wait for the nurse," Mr. Ames announces. "Except Maxwell, Dallas and Tyler, who had their shots yesterday and are free to go."

The class groans. "It isn't fair that we lose part of our lunch hour when the recalls who got detention don't lose anything," Montgomery whines.

I can't let that lie, even if he is about to be zombified. "Who are you calling—?"

"You have to do what Mr. Ames says, Montgomery!" Dallas interrupts. He shoots me a warning glance.

Mr. Ames looks back and forth between us. It's my first morning as a zombie and I'm already arousing suspicion.

Tyler stumbles on his way out and puts a hand to his heart. "I don't feel well."

"That's to be expected," Mr. Ames says. "We'll see how you're feeling after lunch."

"Stop smiling at the cameras," Dallas whispers once we're in the hallway. "Where are you going?"

"Skate park?"

He shakes his head. "We're not allowed off school grounds till the final bell."

"Yeah, but we're not seriously going to stick around, are we?"

"We have to go to the cafeteria, Max." There's no expression on his face, but his voice squeaks in exasperation. "We have to follow all the rules."

The cafeteria is half full. Ninth grade zombies eat their soup in silence. Tyler Wilkins eats a sandwich at a table by himself, rubbing his temples. "This is damaged," I mutter.

Mr. Graham stands behind us in the lineup, chatting to the cook. "What a nice Halloween dance we're going to have next week. Have you seen the decorations?"

Beads of sweat cling to the lunch lady's whiskers. She doesn't acknowledge the principal's small talk. She's like a tall version of my airport molester. She slaps my lasagna onto a white plate. Red lumps of meat slide out from under the noodles and onto my garlic bread. I groan.

Dallas stiffens beside me while Mr. Graham watches closely.

I'd hate to fail so early in my acting career, so I find a reason for the groan. "This lunch doesn't meet the daily food guide requirements," I tell the lunch lady.

"Pardon me?"

"It's every student's right to have a meal that meets the national guidelines for good health," I say.

Dallas turns to me with a sparkle behind the eyes in his blank face. "You're right. This dish does not contain one-and-a-half cups of fruits or vegetables."

"It's mostly pasta, which is a grain," I explain.

"We should get a free salad," Dallas says. "I want potato salad."

"I want fruit salad," I say.

Dallas turns to me with his eyebrows raised. "Did you know that one cup of fruit salad contains two fruit servings?"

"I did *not* know that! That's excellent nutritional value."

"Indeed."

We don't smile, but inside we're laughing. Our shoulders relax and our breath comes easy. We've found a way to hide ourselves in what they want us to be.

"I guess we'd better pull up our socks," Mr. Graham says.

The lunch lady wipes her lip.

I pause outside Xavier's door on my way in from school. His mother answers. She wears bright blue pants with a khaki sweater. I can't tell if Celeste has made her up to look old or if that's just her face. "Yes?" she asks. "Oh. Max. Hello."

"Hello, Mrs. Lavigne. I noticed that Xavier wasn't in school today and I wanted to make sure he's all right."

She looks over her shoulder into the living room. "He's fine. He has a migraine, so we kept him home."

"Will he be coming to school tomorrow?"

She squints like she doesn't trust me. "It depends on his health," she says and shuts the door.

The hallway smells like carpet cleaner. I imagine people sitting behind the walls surveying me, waiting for me to slip up.

I collapse onto our sofa and call Pepper.

"Hello, Max. How are you?" she says. Ponytail, monotone. No lip gloss, no smile. She's not right.

"I noticed you weren't in school today," I say.

She doesn't respond.

"I'm calling to make sure you're fine," I add. I pop my eyeballs at the screen, trying to convey a secret.

"Yes. I'm fine." She doesn't even blink.

"Why weren't you at school?"

"I sprained my ankle, and the doctor said the walk to school might be damaging."

"That bleeds."

She stares at me like I'm a stranger. "Is there anything else?"

"You missed the vaccinations."

"They had vaccinations at the clinic."

My heart thumps. I breathe through my mouth and wait for a sign that doesn't come. "I have to go," I say at last.

Ally tiptoes into the room with a packet of licorice to share. "What's wrong?" she asks.

"Leave Max alone for a while," Mom calls from the kitchen.

Ally threads a licorice string through my fingers and sings, "All my friends were here, but all my friends have gone. All my friends were here, but they left me all alone." She kisses my cheek. *Pat, pat, pat.* "It's okay, Max. *I* still love you."

I hold her to my chest and drench her in hormones.

NINE

Pepper's back at school on Friday with a bandage around her ankle and a patch beneath her sleeve. When I ask if she wants to eat with us, she says, "I prefer eating with my girlfriends," and limps away.

"I bet they taste good," Dallas whispers. That phrase is our new password. He's such a premium actor, I needed a code to prove that he's not a zombie. Whenever we meet or message, one of us says, "Zombies eat brains," and the other says, "I bet they taste good." If we answer properly, we can let our guard down. If we don't—I don't want to think about that.

"Spending time with her fellow dancers may improve Pepper's skills," Dallas says.

I nod. "Perhaps we should spend time with our fellow footballers."

"I believe there is a practice after school today."

"That will present a fine opportunity."

We turn to each other and nod. We take our humor dry these days.

Zombie football is no fun. It's hard to describe what's different about the team, but it's easy to feel. There's no energy or emotion. It kills me to feign disinterest as a thousand pounds of zombie pile on top of me over and over again.

"We might have to quit the team," Dallas whispers at the edge of the field.

"I can't. I love football."

"That's why we should quit."

I conduct a zombie survey in search of inside information to improve my faking. I tell my teammates I'm exploring the role of sports in adolescent bonding. I call it "adolescent bondage" but the irony gets depressing when no one cracks a smile. I record their answers to questions like, "How do you experience tackling as a social interaction?" and "How does it feel to score?"

"I'm proud to carry out the play," everyone says. Everyone except Brennan, who mutters, "You know how it feels, Max."

I pocket my RIG and ask, "Does it feel like it always felt?"

"Only for some of us."

"You weren't at school Tuesday," I whisper. "You missed the vaccinations."

He shakes his head. "Nobody missed those vaccinations. I'm allergic to eggs so I took the shot at the hospital."

"The hospital where your mother works?"

He nods. "They have medical staff in case of emergencies."

"Good decision," I say.

Coach Emery walks over and pats Brennan's shoulder. "Time to go, son."

The whole school comes out for Monday's football game—more fans than I've ever seen. It's drizzling and windy, but students crowd the bleachers. They sit in uniform side by side, gray and greasy like zombie sardines. Parents claim their own section. My mother sits behind Dr. Richmond, bundled up and biting her lip, waiting for the worst.

Kayla climbs to the top of a zombie pyramid and shouts, "Go, Scorpions!" with a big vacant smile on her shiny face. Brennan turns away—Kayla split up with him this weekend. She says fifteen is too young for romance. He pretends not to care.

The Blue Mountain Devils descend from their bus in silence, heads high, helmets cradled in their arms like rifles. "Looks like the other quadrants have been vaccinated," I whisper.

Dallas nods. "My father says it's happening everywhere."

The Devils are devils no longer. They don't look our way while they warm up, don't say a word on the cold muddy field. It's like we have no history.

The game is freakishly quiet. There's still the thud of feet, clash of armor, scream of whistles, but there's no shouting, no laughing, no swearing or grunting. We make the plays with a vague dedication, like we want to do what's right but we've all forgotten why. We're big and strong, we run fast and hit hard, but nobody cares. We're just taking a ball and putting it somewhere else.

Whether we lose our ground or gain ten yards, each whistle is followed by a feeble clap from the spectators. The bleachers gleam with wet bared teeth that pass for smiles.

Dallas fakes it well. I don't. Not at all. I just don't want to. I want to run.

I intercept a pass by leaping four feet in the air and landing in a sprint. Zombie Devils are easy to dodge and shove. I guard my ball like a stray dog and run it for twenty slippery yards. The wind roars in my ears. My heart pounds in my head. I feel like I might rise from the ground. I tear into the end zone and slam the ball to the earth. I jump up, kick my cleats, and turn to the friends who are supposed to be running over to congratulate me.

They stand scattered across the field, yards away, smeared in mud. They're identical but for the numbers on their jerseys. Dallas leans on his left leg, clapping out a rhythm with the rest of them. I don't know why the sight hits me so hard. It's like my team is part of the background—they blend with the dead grass and cold skies, the naked trees beyond the bleachers, the rows of staring, vacant eyes. I'm yards away from them and the space between us forms a void instead of a path.

A scream flies up and out of me from some hollow place I didn't know I carried—a long drawn-out fury that rises in pitch and intensity until it pierces the clapping from the field and the stands, then tails off in a guttural growl as my breath runs out.

I can't bear the thick silence that follows. I drop to my knees and rest my butt on my cleats, rocking and moaning in the end zone like my baby just died. Mud soaks into my skin and I want to melt with it, lay myself out on the field like compost.

Dallas jogs to my side and shields me from the rain. He shakes my shoulder and says, "What are you doing, Max? Get up."

I sway in his shadow.

Coach Emery squats beside him. "You can't be here, Richmond. Go back with the team."

Dallas shakes his head.

The coach wraps his fingers around Dallas's mask and stares him scared. "Your father is in the stands watching you right now." He rises with a fake smile. "Go back with the team before you're both caught."

Dallas nods and walks away, leaving me exposed.

Coach Emery performs a first-aid check: airways, circulation, scrapes and abrasions. "Stretch out your legs," he says.

I can't move. I'm too depressed. I'd rather be a zombie than feel like this.

My mother is suddenly all over me, looking for wounds. I shift onto my ass and let her take me apart.

"He has a very bad sprain," the coach tells her. "Could be broken, judging by the pain."

"I'm a nurse," she says.

The principal walks up, hands on his hips, bald head glistening. "This is a strange situation."

"A very bad sprain," Coach Emery repeats.

Meanwhile I'm sitting like a stone while Mom prods my extremities. Mr. Graham stares down at us, unhappy. Mom pinches my Achilles tendon.

"Ow!" I pull my leg away.

"Yes, it's badly sprained," she says. "But the bone's not broken."

"Are you telling me he screamed like that because of a sprained ankle?" Mr. Graham asks.

Coach Emery chuckles. "These tough kids. They tackle each other all day without complaint, but pull a muscle too far and they cry like little girls."

"Should that happen?" Mr. Graham asks. "I didn't think that was supposed to happen."

"With purely physical pain, yes, it can still happen," Mom says like she's being interviewed. "But, as you can see, it's very short-lived." She points to me, quietly slumped in the mud.

"Brennan! Richmond!" the coach calls. "Help Mrs. Connors take her son off the field!" Mr. Graham surveys me as Coach Emery helps me stand. "Right now!" the coach shouts. He turns to Mom. "He'll have to take a break from football until this heals. No Halloween dance either. Have him study from home this week and keep him off his feet."

Brennan and Dallas close in on either side of me. They sling my arms over their shoulders and wrap their hands around my waist. I fall short between them, childish and broken.

"Don't put any weight on your right ankle," Mom says. She stares at my feet, firmly planted on the ground. I lift my right heel and lean into Dallas.

"You'll be all right, Max," Mom says.

"Of course he will be," the coach says. "Just give him time to heal."

Dallas squeezes my ribs and I hop along between them. Brennan doesn't say a word, doesn't even glance at me. For all I know, he's a zombie. It's getting hard to tell us apart.

"I can borrow a car from work tomorrow," Mom tells me. "We could take your canvas for cutting."

I look up from my RIG. "I'm going to keep it as a tent."

She frowns. "Campsites are so unsafe, Max, and it's an ancient tent. We'd need a stove and a cooler—"

"I mean for my art exhibit. I'm going to paint the whole tent."

"That will take weeks."

"Nah. It's mostly tags and bombs. They don't take long."

She hovers in the doorway of my bedroom, shifting from leg to leg. "You mean graffiti?"

"Yeah. Layers of it in different styles."

"Do you think that's wise?"

"It'll be glorious, Mom. It's all coming together." I return to my homework—five hundred years of dates to memorize and half the animal kingdom to classify.

Mom leaves the room, biting her lip.

　　　　　　　　　　　　·

"I thought you hurt your ankle," Ally says as I walk her to the park.

"I'm a fast healer."

"So you're going to school tomorrow?"

"No. Next week."

"Did you get suspended again?"

"No way. I've been good. I'm just supposed to stay off my feet for a few days."

She stares at my shoes, so I tap out a dance. She giggles and hops. I twirl her on the pavement like a princess. "Stop," she whispers.

A woman watches us from her living-room window—a vague pale shape in an unlit room. She could be anyone. We continue in silence.

The reformed gladiators, Zachary and Melbourne, are at the park again. Their mothers stand behind the swings, chatting, pushing their children through the air.

Ally walks to the oak tree. I shield her from view. Peanut darts down and devours the seeds while Ally whispers soothing words, "You're such a pretty girl, such a good little mama." She chats and giggles and blows kisses and gives this squirrel all the love she would have spent on friends if they hadn't been turned into zombies.

"What on earth are you doing?" a woman shouts behind us. Peanut scurries up the tree. Ally drops the seeds on the ground and covers them with her skirt.

I turn to meet the angry eyes of Melbourne's mother. She's young and plain, with shapeless clothes and brown hair pulled back. She stands with her hands on her hips, waiting for an explanation. "We're not doing anything wrong," I say.

"You can't tame these animals! There's a disease going around spread by these creatures."

"It's spread by mice," I say.

"What's the difference? They're all the same species!"

"No, they're not." I stare at her zombie-style. "They're not even the same family. Mice and squirrels have been evolving separately for forty million years. They're in different suborders of Rodentia."

She huffs. "Just stay away from them! Don't be training them to come near my child."

I glance at her little zombie on the swing. He wouldn't care if a hundred squirrels took a dump on his head. "Like that would be so awful," I mutter.

"What did you say?" she yells, her face ugly and twisted.

"I said that would be awful."

She looks me up and down, scowling, before she leaves.

Ally brushes off her bottom. "Let's go now."

"Sure. Peanut will find these seeds later. She'll know they're from you."

Ally nods, takes my hand, walks home without twirling once.

***

Dallas comes over on Saturday for Halloween fun at the Spartan. "I can stay till eleven! I told Dad we're working on science." He smiles with all his heart and dances with his arms above his head.

"How was the dance last night?" I ask.

"The dance? Oh my god, the dance. How was the dance?" He laughs, sighs, collapses on the couch.

"Yeah. How was it? Did you dance with anyone?"

"Think about it, Max. It was a dance full of zombies dressed in costumes. What do you think it was like?"

I shrug. "I don't know. That's why I'm asking."

He leans forward and clasps his hands together. "How can I describe it? It was like wading through a river of shit, Max. No, actually, it was like standing in a gymnasium of shit for three hours while people flicked elastics at my head and stuck thermometers up my ass and I asked for more. That's exactly what it was like. That's what you missed." He leans back, smiles. "It was glorious. I can't wait till the Christmas ball."

"Whoa. Are you okay?"

He laughs. "Am I okay? Am I okay?"

"Seriously, Dallas. Take it easy."

He spreads his legs and slouches into the couch cushions, lays his head back and stares at the ceiling. He mutters a string of senseless curses, laughs hysterically, then closes his eyes in a state of bliss. "Man, it's so good to be here. You don't know what it's like." He turns his head toward me, cracks an eye open. "For you it's a job. You go to school, put in your time, come home and relax. For me..." He closes his eyes, shakes his head, breathes deeply. "It never ends, man. It's every fucking second."

Ally hops into the room. She's been dressed like a rabbit since ten in the morning. Celeste painted her face and gave her whiskers. "Hi, Dallas! You said a bad word. Where's your costume?"

He sits up and smiles, tweaks her bunny ears. "We're going to make our costumes." He turns to me excitedly. "Unless Celeste would do us. I'm not above begging."

"I already asked. She's at a party with some guy."

"What are you going to make a costume with?" Ally asks.

Dallas smiles. "With my imagination!"

Ally takes a step back. "My teacher says imaginations get us into trouble."

Dallas laughs so long that I just leave him there and make some lunch.

Twenty minutes later we're eating fries at the kitchen table, swallowing the fact that we have no imaginations. "What should we make?" I ask for the tenth time.

He shrugs. I shrug. I look around the kitchen. He looks around the kitchen. I hum. He whistles. I pick up the salt and pepper shakers—boring silver and glass cylinders—and shake them to my tune. He snaps his fingers and says, "Excellent. But I'll have to borrow something gray."

We wear gray T-shirts, gray pants and gray ski caps with holes cut out of the crowns. "This is a waste of two good caps," Dallas says. "No one is going to see the tops of our heads."

"Speak for yourself. Half the building is taller than me."

He paints a big *S* on his shirt and wears it with his white skin. I paint a big *P* on mine and wear it with my black skin. We show Mom. "Ta da!"

"That's it?" she asks. "S and P? Is that a product?"

"We're Salt and Pepper!" I whine. "God, Mom. We're shakers."

She laughs. "Salt and Pepper. That's what your dad used to call us when we were first dating. He was *so* white." She stares us up and down and shakes her head. "We were *real* salt and pepper. You two are more like cinnamon and garlic powder. Have you looked in a mirror?"

Dallas and I pose in the bathroom, trying to look cylindrical and spicy. "We look like recalls," he says at last.

"It's the hats."

"We look way too old for trick-or-treating."

"If we had masks, we could at least act like ourselves."

"So we're not just defective salt and pepper shakers, we're defective *zombie* salt and pepper shakers."

We slump out of the bathroom, ready to call off the whole adventure.

Ally hops away from the window and shouts, "Hey! Salt and Pepper! What a great costume!"

And we're back on the scene, giant candy bags in hand.

We head down the hallway, knocking on doors. "Is Xavier trick-or-treating tonight?" I ask Mrs. Lavigne.

"No, he's still not feeling well."

"Still?" I let slip a note of concern. Dallas jabs me. "That's a shame," I say. "It's important to feel well every day. If we don't feel well we should see a medical practitioner."

She closes the door in my face.

On the second floor, we run into Lucas. He's alone, dressed like a box of cereal. Dallas eyes his costume and mutters, "We could have done that."

"Hello, Maxwell. Hello, Alexandra," Lucas says. "I like your costumes." He stares from me to Dallas like he's trying to figure it out.

"Thank you," Ally says. "I like yours too. I'm going to trick-or-treat at your house."

"It's that one." Lucas points to the apartment directly under ours. There's a wreath on the door made of dried vines and pine cones. "I'm going upstairs. Good night." He doesn't ask to join us. He's perfectly happy to walk the halls in a cardboard box without a friend in the world.

After we tap every door in the Spartan, Ally looks in her candy bag and says, "I have enough. It's heavy."

We drop her at home, where she dumps a feeble collection of chocolate and candies on the kitchen table.

"Let's visit the rich houses," I say.

"Better goodies," Dallas agrees.

We head outside into the most disturbing Halloween of my life. All the young kids walk in orderly fashion, alone or with parents. They wait their turn to knock on doors. They say, "Thank you," after every treat. And they never—not once—look inside their bags to see what they got. They are clear and present zombies.

The older teens yell and laugh and push each other around. Six boys dressed as mutilated bodies shout, "Boo!" as they pass us. "What the hell are you two supposed to be?" one asks. "P and S? What's that?"

"Salt and Pepper," Dallas mutters.

"What, unit?"

"Salt and Pepper," Dallas repeats.

"Salt and Pepper?" the kid says. "What have salt and pepper got to do with Halloween?"

They mock us and walk on. They yell "Boo!" at a ten-year-old girl dressed as a giraffe. She pouts and says, "With every year, we should grow more responsible toward ourselves and those around us."

They roar with laughter and call her names. *Feeb. Defect. Recall.* I want to join in.

Dallas sadly surveys their costumes. "We could have done that," he mutters.

Two teenagers spray-paint a billboard on the corner, covering a pharmacy ad with sloppy tags. I ache to join them, but Dallas holds me back. "They'd spray-paint your face, Pepper."

The name stabs my heart. I don't want to be reminded of Pepper. Yet here I am dressed in a pepper costume. The subconscious is cruel.

"I saw Pepper dancing this week," Dallas says. "She didn't seem like a zombie."

I turn on him. "Was she at the dance last night?"

"No. I saw her at lunchtime with her group."

"Why would you go looking for Pepper?"

"I wasn't looking for her. I just saw her."

"And?"

"And she didn't dance like a zombie."

"I thought her ankle was busted."

He shrugs and says, "Could be, but I wasn't watching her ankle."

"She doesn't even like tall guys, you know."

He smiles his dazzling ultimate smile. "She thinks I'm the best-looking guy in school, remember?"

I snort. I have nothing to say to this friend who's trying to get his tall white mitts on my brown zombie girl.

"Oh my god," he whispers. "Max, look! It's Tyler. What is he wearing?"

Tyler Wilkins is twenty feet away from us and closing fast. He's alone and dressed like a caterpillar. He wears stretchy polyester pants striped black and green, with a skin-tight green T-shirt that shows off his nipples, and a black ski cap that sprouts long spiral antennae. His hair is tucked under his hat so his bony face is blindingly bare. The tip of his nose is painted black like a pup's.

I crack up. I can't help it. I double over and pretend to be coughing. I can barely breathe, I'm laughing so hard.

Dallas steps in front of me to block Tyler's view.

"Hello, Dallas. How are you?" Tyler asks. His antennae wobble when he speaks.

Dallas starts to lose it. "I'm well, Tyler. How are you?"

"My doctor says I should be fine, thank you. Is that Maxwell behind you?"

"Yes, it is," Dallas squeaks.

I straighten up a little and wave.

"Salt and Pepper," Tyler says. "Very clever." He nods twice. His antennae sway back and forth. "Happy Halloween."

Dallas and I flee down the street and break into laughter that feels like it's never going to end.

TEN

Dallas invents history and communications projects that require extensive teamwork. He comes over almost every night, giddier each time. The stress of living as a zombie under constant surveillance is wearing him down.

On Friday he helps me set up my art tent in the living room. It's like a small canvas building, ten by ten and six feet high. It has no floor—it's last-century war surplus—so we put it over the couch. It's stiffer and heavier and more complicated than I'd expected. We're swearing our asses off by the time we straighten it out.

"This is a huge tent," he says. "You haven't got much living room left. Are you sure your mom won't mind?"

"Nah. She never sits in here. I'll lay down sheets before I paint."

We tie back the flaps and sit inside. It smells like a moldy basement. The stained plastic windows barely let in any light.

"Ally will love it once it airs out," Dallas says, bouncing on the couch. "It's every kid's dream."

Freakshow is down to the final three contestants. Zipperhead was in the lead, but they did a Saturday special on Squid and his dead parents, which earned him a boost in support.

"Dorsal's got to go," I say. Dorsal is crippled by a bulbous curved spine and a lumpy skull, but her brain is normal. She takes virtual college courses in library sciences. They did a show on her a few weeks back, stressing how hard she worked to go that extra mile like Mom always talks about. Not that Dorsal could even sit in a car, let alone drive an extra mile.

"Zipperhead always looks sad," Dallas says. "It makes the show depressing."

Celeste knocks at the door. She's blue, literally and metaphorically, wearing alien makeup and a frown. She's not withstanding so well these days.

"Hey, come on in," I say. "Want to sit in our tent?"

"No, thank you." She smiles like everybody has a military staff tent in their apartment. "I have a favor to ask you, Max."

"Anything."

"Will you walk to school with Xavier tomorrow? It's his first day back since he got sick, and he's still having dizzy spells."

Dallas peers through the tent window and shouts, "Come camping with us, Celeste! Wow, this window makes you look completely blue!"

"I guess Dennis isn't doing so well either," she whispers. "Poor thing."

Xavier barely speaks when I arrive at his door the next morning. He doesn't smell right. His fruitiness has fermented. He hunches inside his gray suit and his hair hangs stringy. He has a Christ-on-the-cross sort of beauty that dazzles me. I want to offer him a cup of water, sling him over my shoulder, carry him somewhere safe.

"Take care of him," Mrs. Lavigne says, her face tight, resigned to whatever's coming next.

Xavier leans backward as he walks, like he's being blown by a fierce wind. He cracks his eyes half open and nods lazily when I ask if he's okay. If I didn't know him, I'd think he was either stoned out of his skull or the most premium kid on the planet.

"There's the jail," he mutters when we pass the little zombies lined up in rows.

"That's the elementary school," I say. "Ally's old school. Remember Ally?"

He gives four slight nods while glancing at me sideways. "Fruits and vegetables," he says. Then he squints like he's in pain.

I pat his back. "Whatever you say, man."

"I say I love you, Max."

Christ, he kills me. He sounds just like my dad.

When we reach the high school, Dallas marches over and says, "Zombies eat brains."

"I bet they taste good," I answer.

"It's nice to see you back at school, Xavier."

Xavier squints and nods. "You can't see me."

"Is he one of us?" Dallas whispers.

"Nah," I say. "He's just nuts."

Xavier hangs his head as if someone switched him off. Dallas twists around to look into his face. "You okay, man? You're drooling." We walk him to a picnic table and sit him down. He looks at the sky and smiles, then closes his eyes in ecstasy.

"What is he on?" Dallas asks.

I shrug. "Whatever he used to be on plus whatever they gave him."

"It doesn't seem so bad."

"Whispered words are never healthy," Pepper says.

I jolt and shudder. She's behind the bench, staring from me to Dallas with a look of absolute nothing on her face.

"That's why we never whisper," I say.

She squints. "You were whispering. I heard you."

"If you could hear us, then we obviously weren't whispering," Dallas says.

"You were in a movie I saw," Xavier mutters.

"It's nice to see you back at school, Xavier," Pepper says.

"Like all children, Xavier is lucky to go to school," I say. I jerk my head around like a robot. "Look at all these lucky children."

Dallas bends his arms robotically and says, "We are lucky...to be training...for our futures."

Pepper frowns. We might have gone too far.

"Xavier needs help getting to class," I say. "Dallas and I recognize the needs of all our classmates. Goodbye, Pepper."

We heave Xavier to his feet and steer him toward the door. He nods and mutters, "There will be consequences." I'm sure it's random but the timing scares me.

⁂

Xavier gets worse as the day goes on. Half the tenth graders are in one class now, over a hundred students, sitting at tiny desks shoved close together. It unsettles Xavier when students squeeze by him. He likes everyone in their place. He trembles and buzzes over each absence, staring at the vacant chairs in alarm. A few kids who were on psychotropics are off sick now. I haven't seen Tyler Wilkins since Halloween. "Maybe he turned into a butterfly," Dallas says.

Werewolf fills in for Mr. Reese in history. I hate him more than ever now that I can't express it. He doesn't seem to like us any better either. He tells us Montgomery is in the hospital having convulsions. "Shame," he says like he scuffed his shoe. "He was one of the better students."

Xavier gets up and sits in Montgomery's chair. Werewolf tells him to go back to his own seat. "There's another potential here," Xavier says.

Werewolf snorts. "Just get back in your seat."

Xavier docks his RIG into the desk port as if he didn't hear.

"Back in your seat!" Werewolf booms.

Xavier holds his head and moans.

Werewolf gets off his hairy ass. He leans in front of Xavier, lays both palms on the desk, and repeats, "Back. In. Your. Seat." He spits when he talks. It glistens on Xavier's face. I feel my blood start to boil.

Xavier mutters something incomprehensible.

Werewolf grabs his arm and tries to haul him up. "Get out of this chair, you idiot!" he shouts.

Xavier snaps to attention. He never liked to be touched.

He grabs Werewolf's middle finger and snaps it back. *Crack.* The sound of breaking bone echoes off the walls and pierces the surveillance camera. Werewolf emits a childish sobbing scream and holds his hand in the air like it's a foreign object.

A look of fury comes over Xavier, a look I've never seen him wear before. He stands up and roars—a shocking primal sound that spills into the hallway. He plows Werewolf in the face.

Werewolf's head swings over his shoulder and he staggers backward into Brennan's desk. His nose gushes blood, hot and red, spewing onto his beard and his clean white shirt, down to the floor tiles. Xavier steps through the splatter and punches Werewolf in the gut, breathing so hard he's almost smoking.

Brennan pushes his chair back into the desk behind him. Other students shake their heads, glance at the camera, chant the rules prohibiting violence.

Xavier strikes again with an uppercut. Werewolf lands on Brennan's desktop with his hairy neck exposed like a chicken on a chopping block. Xavier looks prepared to sever the head with his own bloody hands while the class looks on in annoyance. I almost want him to do it. I sit there and wait for it, but Brennan stands up between them.

Xavier turns his fury onto Brennan, who's ready for it. Brennan blocks a punch and knees Xavier in the groin, then gets him on the floor and pins his arm behind his back. "Easy, easy," he whispers.

Xavier curls up on the tiles and closes his eyes. He scratches his head like he's trying to claw something out of it and starts to sob, raw heaving cries of torment. His hair falls across his face like a veil streaked with blood. I can't take this. I'm on my feet. I don't know what I'm doing.

Werewolf sops his nose with a blue mitten stained purple. "Don't let go of his arms!" he shouts. He looks prepared to kick Xavier in the kidneys.

I intend to take him down, but Dallas blocks me and shouts, "Help! You don't belong here!"

Mr. Graham marches into the room with two security guards. They yank Xavier to his feet. He's limp now, muttering, a mess of snot and confusion. The principal stares at him in disgust.

Brennan brushes himself off and sits at his bloody desk.

"Would you like our statements, sir?" I shout at Mr. Graham.

"Don't do this," Dallas whispers.

"We are all witnesses to the disrespect that occurred in our classroom today!" I shout. "I would like to give you my statement."

"I don't want your statement," Mr. Graham says. "I have Mr. Warton and the recording."

"I want to give you my statement," I repeat. I push forward, but Dallas won't let me by without a fight.

Mr. Graham walks out the door, followed by the guards dragging Xavier.

I turn away from Dallas, squeeze between desks to the back of the room and up the middle aisle. I'm in front of the camera now. I know I should stop, I tell myself to stop, but I don't stop.

Werewolf eases his busted hand through his coat sleeve.

"Verbal and physical abuse are not appropriate responses, are they, sir?" I shout.

"What?" he asks angrily. He looks in my face and backs into his lecture projection. Words and images from history flicker across his face. His eyes glitter in the blue light.

Dallas hustles over. "Our teachers work hard every day to be role models. We owe them our respect," he says.

I don't glance at him. "Xavier Lavigne is a fifteen-year-old boy!" I shout at Werewolf. I want to rip his beard off with his smirk.

Dallas grabs my shoulder, shoves me to the wall, leans into me. "We are all lucky to go to a school with good role models. We would not be lucky if we had to go to school by ourselves."

He holds me there to keep me from digging my grave. He's risking his whole act like this, in front of Werewolf and the zombies and the surveillance camera. "We're all lucky," he repeats. He holds my gaze and nods, over and over, until I nod back.

Werewolf is disturbed and angry, but he doesn't accuse us of anything. He dissolves his lecture and squeezes behind Dallas, scampers to the doorway. He holds his broken hand over the place where his heart would be if he had one. "I don't expect to see you all here next term."

⁕

"He's suspended," Celeste says. "I'd rather you didn't come in. I don't know what'll set him off."

Xavier lies on his living room carpet, staring at the ceiling.

"Don't look so sad, Max. He'll be okay. He might just need a new patch." Celeste pats my arm. "We started an information campaign at the college about the new support program and how they should warn people on other meds to be extra-careful. We might do a petition."

I try to smile.

She looks over her shoulder at her baby brother. "Sunday's his birthday," she whispers.

At home, Mom sighs along with the news.

"The New Education Support Treatment will turn the tide in our failing education system," a government rep is saying. His words are straight from the Chemrose website, all about community improvement, cost savings, the best interests of the child.

"What are we going to do?" I ask. "This is every academic school in the country he's talking about."

Mom shrugs.

"I have three years left of school," I remind her. "Ally has twelve. Do you really think you can be there for every shot they give us?"

She bites her lip, shakes her head. "Maybe we should leave," she mutters.

"Of course we should leave. You're a geriatric nurse in a world full of old people. You can find work anywhere."

"But your schooling—"

"There are a thousand virtual high schools I could go to."

"But the quality, Max. I can't afford—"

"We can't stay here, Mom!"

She nods. "Okay. Maybe we can go back to Atlanta."

"Atlanta, where Aunt Sylvia was murdered?" I remember all the poor people on the dirty streets, the sad ones begging from strangers and lying half dead in alleys, the scary ones hovering in doorways, hungrily surveying the wealthy.

Mom rolls her eyes at me. "Either we stay or we go, Max. I can't change the world."

"All right. Let's go. A million people live in Atlanta, and hardly any of them are murdered. Right?"

"Right."

The news shows a labor riot in the American south, where illegal workers are protesting the new universal ID cards.

"Can we take Dallas with us?" I ask. "He's losing it here. He puts on an act all day and night." She frowns, so I poke at her guilt. "You either have to get him out of here or give him the shot. You can't leave him like this."

She holds her head in her hands. "Okay. We'll take Dallas. We'll take anyone who wants to come."

Ally plays inside the tent, singing to her teddy, "You find milk and I'll find flour, and we'll have pudding in half an hour."

<hr />

I blow off Saturday's coaching to do chin-ups in the park and run down the rich people's sidewalks.

I'm struck by the sight of a woman kneeling beside a two-year-old child and a bucket of chalk. They've covered twenty square feet of concrete with cloudy pastels—

scratches and scars from the kid, bold blocks and squiggles from the woman. I jog on the spot beside them. "That's glorious," I say. "You should color the whole world like that."

She smiles at me, sincere and well-wishing, and offers me pink and yellow chalk. "Draw something in front of your house." She has no idea they're going to zombify her kid once he gets to preschool, no idea she'll want them to. I leave them to their rainbows.

I end up at Pepper's house. I draw a pink heart on the concrete slab in front of her door. I write my initials inside it with a plus sign and a question mark. Then I ring the bell.

There's no answer.

I drop the yellow chalk in her mailbox and pretend she might fill in her own initials. There's a jingle in the box when the chalk hits bottom. My fingers find two keys on a metal wire. I close my fist around them.

For the sake of the camera, I ring the bell again. I wait for an answer that doesn't come, then reach into my pocket and whip out the keys like they were there all along. I hurry inside and shut the door.

I don't call Pepper's name because I know she's not here. I can tell by the smell and the static air. This is an empty house.

I tell myself I'll just get a drink of water and leave, but even as I'm thinking the words I know I'm going to search every inch of the place.

Even though it's on two floors, Pepper's house is almost as small as our apartment. There's a living room, kitchen and bathroom downstairs, two bedrooms and a utility room upstairs. There's not much to explore—no clothes on the drying rack, no dishes in the sink. A few dresses hang in Pepper's closet between dozens of empty hangers. There are some T-shirts in the drawers, but no socks or underwear. I've never thought about her panties before, much as I've thought about getting them off. But now that I'm searching her dresser, I wish I knew what they looked like.

I sit on her bed and feel her absence like a ghost. There's a thin layer of dust on her night table, with bare spots where picture frames might have stood.

She's gone. I lie back on the pillow and think those two words over and over.

Before I leave, I peek behind her bedroom door in hope of a flimsy nightgown I could fantasize with. Instead I find a thin strip of wood—sawn-off window trim—that holds the tiniest painting I ever made. It shows Pepper in a skimpy elf costume up on her toes beside a stack of presents, one leg high in the air behind her, her pointed shoe sparkling like a star. I sketched it at the Christmas production last year, worked on it through the holidays, gave it to her on New Year's Day.

I'm happy that she hung it here. Every time she closed her door, she was reminded of me. But then she packed her frames and panties and left my painting behind.

I lift it off its mount. It's not really stealing. She's never coming back for it.

***

Someone's crying in the tent on Sunday morning when I get back from cross-country. I pull apart the front flaps and find my mother on the couch bawling like a baby, her face twisted and stained, soggy tissues in her fist. She looks up at me and hides her face in her hands.

She won't tell me what's wrong. She shakes her head every time I ask, swats at me when I try to pry her fingers off her face.

"It's Xavier's sixteenth birthday," I say, but she just cries harder.

I head to the kitchen and butter some toast, sprinkle cinnamon and sugar overtop. I sit at the table and scroll through *Freakshow*'s "behind the scenes" clips. Zipperhead and his girlfriend just got engaged.

Eventually Mom comes out and sits beside me. I dissolve my screen and offer her my last triangle of toast. She shakes her head, clears her throat, takes my hand. She stares at the table and says, "Tyler Wilkins died last night from heart failure because of the shot I gave him."

The bread wads up on my tongue. I'm silent, disbelieving. I don't say, "You killed him." I don't say, "You didn't kill him." I don't say anything.

I feel all ripped up inside, as if Tyler was my friend. I try to remember him busting my ribs, slapping Ally's face, kicking Xavier, all the reeking moments he inflicted over the years, but every image gets pushed away by the memory of him storing my painting in his RIG and calling me an asshole because I thought I had him pegged.

I get up and go inside the tent. I can't sit down. I turn in circles and watch the walls blur by. I know exactly what I'm going to paint for the exhibit.

I'll paint children, dozens of them, real ones—Tyler and Pepper and Xavier, me and Dallas, Bay and Brennan,

Montgomery and Kayla, Saffron and Chicago, the baby on the sidewalk yesterday, Zachary and Melbourne from the park, Lucas from downstairs, the high school kids on skateboards, the throwaways on skates. I'll paint all of us doing what we used to—dancing and running and fighting and playing and laughing and being kids. I'll paint us on the walls inside the tent where I'm hiding now, in dazzling hues and luminance. I'll leave the walls outside dull gray, stenciled with a single word. I'll call the whole thing *Withstanding on a Perilous Planet*. And I'll give it to Xavier as a belated birthday present. I'll tell him it's a metaphor.

ELEVEN

There's a meeting at the high school to talk about concerns with the New Education Support Treatment, but only my mother has any.

"I expected you to be thankful for the treatment," Mr. Graham tells her. "Your son is an obvious troublemaker— and I don't mind using that word now that it's a thing of the past. Maxwell is bright enough to waste hours of class time with his antics yet still complete his work and earn As. But in exercising what you consider his freedom, he impacts on the freedom of others. He wasted their class time, too, and they needed that time to understand their work. His fun caused his classmates to fail."

Everyone turns to stare at Monster Max.

I have to admit, it's a good argument. I never thought goofing around might send someone to throwaway school. He should have told me that my first detention.

He blathers about the importance of home support strategies, which he's sure are lacking in my life. "Nesting makes the children receptive to the tools of learning, but it's up to us to shape them into excellent students."

Mom's hand shoots up. "So is it the treatment or the reinforcement that determines their behavior?"

The principal nods like she's finally catching on. "It's the reinforcement. The treatment makes them open to it."

"So they would behave in any way we promoted?"

Mr. Graham glances at a black-suited man on the stage behind him, then says, "In a manner of speaking."

Mom persists. "So we could train them to do almost anything?"

"No, you're misunderstanding." Mr. Graham smiles. "Let's move on now. We have more to discuss tonight than the concerns of just one parent."

He amazes the audience with pie charts of cost savings and bar graphs of academic achievements. "Chemrose practically donated the treatments," he says. "We barely had to pay half the cost." The audience claps while the black-suited man bows.

"How much was paid, exactly?" Mom asks.

Mr. Graham pretends he doesn't hear. Nearby parents glance our way and laugh. Their sons and daughters stand stiffly beside them, staring at the stage.

"This is the best thing we have ever done for our children," the principal says. "I know we'd do it even if the cost of education increased. It's in the interests of our students to keep their marks up so they can remain entitled to the privilege of coming here. Or to the trade schools. Jobs are coming and companies need workers who will work."

Clap, clap, clap, pause, clap, clap, clap. You'd think the adults had been dosed. "You don't want them disadvantaged in this competitive world," they all say through the coffee and donuts.

"I heard that the top student in each class doesn't get the treatment," a woman says beside me. "Is that true?" She's talking to Coach Emery, who shrugs as if it has nothing to do with him.

I catch Brennan's eye, but he quickly looks away.

"I'm sorry Nesting hasn't impressed you," a man says behind us. It's the black suit from the stage. He's tall and handsome with a wide face and close-cropped hair. He smiles and extends his hand to Mom. "I'm Bill Walters from Chemrose." I stare at him with more interest than a zombie ought to show.

"We sometimes have problems with subjects already taking stimulating medications," he says, like that's what's wrong with me. "The treatment works on the central nervous system and there's sometimes an adjustment period. The patch can be mildly sedating, but don't worry. The body will find its balance. Your son's attention will soon come into focus and his marks will improve. Nested children are extremely dedicated to their studies."

"But they lose initiative," Mom says.

He nods. "That's one of the benefits. Untreated students often initiate activities that aren't productive in the classroom." He lays his hand on my shoulder and looks at me like I'm terminally ill and there's no hope at all. "His body's chemistry is working out its harmony. I'm sure you'll see improvement soon. And keep in mind that this is a pilot project.

If the results prove that the treatment should be discontinued, we'll discontinue it immediately." He smiles and moves on through the crowd.

⚔

Everyone who goes to school is lucky, I read on the school notice board. *All of my classmates are my friends. There is nothing more important than completing my work.*

Mom reads over my shoulder. "We have to stop this," she whispers.

I snort. "It's a little late for that epiphany."

She stares off into some private distance. "I remember when we first conceived you, Max. The first match was a girl with a likelihood of breast cancer. The second was a boy with"—she shrugs—"nothing, really. He had nothing wrong with him. Increased chance of heart disease, I think it was. I couldn't choose between you."

I close my RIG and slide it in my pocket. "You don't have to tell me this."

"Your dad misunderstood. He said we could keep trying until we got one just right. But it wasn't that. I wanted all of you. I couldn't choose which ones to destroy. Just because they weren't perfect."

There's something about your mother telling you of the children she terminated that makes you want to be alone. "I'm going for a run."

I do chin-ups in the park until my hands are frozen stiff; then I pound the dark streets for an hour, north and south and north again, working my way closer to the core.

175

The houses grow larger every few streets inward, and soon I'm in my old luxurious neighborhood.

Lights blaze behind the curtains at Dallas's house. I stop on the road and catch my breath. A tall cedar hedge hides my old house from view. I want so badly to jog up the stone pathway, open the blue door and head up to my old room, to work in my sketchbook while Ally butts in every five minutes to show me a toy, and the soft voices of my parents float upstairs until finally Dad sticks his big blond head inside and says, "Time for bed, my friend."

I turn around and run back home to watch *Freakshow*. It's no fun without Dallas. The studio audience looks zombified. Zipperhead and Squid are the most human beings on the screen. I don't even care who wins.

A nurse comes to our door. She's in her forties, short and plump. She wears white pants, white shoes, white shirt, white coat, white gloves. Her hair is dyed platinum. Even her eyelashes are white.

She shows me an identity card. Her name is Lara Fleishman. She works for the city. "I have some questions to follow up your educational support treatment." She steps inside and frowns at the tent and the pissy stench of paint.

Mom calls us to the table.

"Maxwell Connors, age fifteen?" Lara asks me.

I nod. "Almost sixteen."

"Roll up your sleeve, please." She takes out a syringe and an empty vial.

"What are you doing?" Mom asks.

"Taking a blood sample."

Mom puts her hand on Lara's. "No."

Lara frowns at the black hand on her white glove. "But that's the main part of the follow-up. I *have* to take samples."

"No," Mom repeats.

"But I'm a nurse."

"So am I. Can I take your blood?"

"Of course not."

"You can't take theirs either."

Lara talks into her RIG, waits, sighs. "Okay. I'll just check their patches."

"I've done that already," Mom says. "They're fine. You're not touching my children."

Lara huffs. "Your negativity is harmful." She projects a document onto the table. "There's a short survey. Can I do that much?" She asks me twelve questions that sound innocent: *Do you have friends at school? What field do you want to work in? Who is your favorite teacher?*

Since I just read the notice board, I know the answers: *All of my classmates are my friends. I want to work in the field I excel in. Each teacher is suited to his subject.*

Ally takes the survey with the enthusiasm of a chatty corpse. When Lara asks, "Who is the top student in your class?" Ally says, "Every student does their best. No matter how small a part we play in the future, we're building our great country together." When Lara asks, "Do you work better alone or in teams?" Ally says, "It's good to be able to work independently, but too much time alone can lead to thoughts and feelings that bring trouble into our lives." These are the teachings I have to look forward to.

Lara closes her screen and turns to Mom. "You're having difficulty adjusting to the treatment." It's a statement, not a question. Lara has been briefed. "Your children haven't changed, Mrs. Connors. The treatment has no ability to physically change the child."

"All medications change the patient physically," Mom says. "That's how they work."

Lara smiles a tight so-that's-how-it-is smile. "We're manipulating them ever so slightly to give them the advantage of being better able to focus on their studies."

Mom doesn't return her smile. "I'm concerned about side effects."

"We all are! That's why we're monitoring the treatment in every area it's been piloted."

"How many areas is that?"

Lara shrugs. "I don't know that sort of thing. But I do know that every child being treated is being given a treat." She giggles. "They could hardly do anything the way they were, and it wasn't cost effective to sort them out."

Mom gasps, like she doesn't do the same thing herself every workday.

"It's not a bad thing!" Lara says. "At least seventy percent of the kids needed it, but one hundred percent benefit from it." She looks at Mom with sincerity. "Kids with behavior problems and learning disabilities used to rule the classroom. They brought our standards down so much that even the smartest students wouldn't learn until grade twelve what kids in other countries learn by grade eight."

Mom nods. "I heard that."

"You heard about school closures in places where they couldn't afford to pay the teachers?" Lara asks. "Bands of children had nowhere to turn but crime. But with Nesting, education is so cost-effective that the schools can reopen."

"Have they reopened?" Mom asks.

Lara shrugs. "I think so."

"With larger classes?"

"Yes, but kids thrive in larger classrooms because they scaffold each other."

"How is that possible when they have no initiative?"

"They monitor each other's progress along the program of study. They don't need initiative."

Mom shakes her head. "Our country can't survive without initiative."

Lara smiles. "Our *country* still has initiative. Those among us who use their initiative for the benefit of the community will always be allowed to have it."

Mom has no response to that.

Lara packs her things. "These kids seem healthy. Not like that poor boy down the hall. He needed a new patch. In this family, it's just *you* who has the problem." She stands up and stares at Mom with a bright white smile. "So we'll monitor the family unit for the next two months."

"Too bad about that ankle," Coach Emery says when I step out of the trailer in my gear, ready for the championship game. "Go plant yourself on the bench."

The Grizzlies descend from their bus in a long line of beige and brown. They drove ten hours to get here from New Harrisburg, Illinois. Their school is run by a different Chemrose governing board, but they're zombies, all the same. And they're lousy at football.

When our team scores, I stand up and clap, but my hands beat alone, like the only pulse on the field. A whistle blows and everyone joins in. *Clap, clap, clap, pause, clap, clap, clap.*

Ally shouts, "One, two, three. It's Dallas for me!" She stops before Mom has a chance to shush her.

Brennan plays too intensely for his own good. He swears at a Grizzly who takes him down a few yards from goal. His father pulls him aside for some whispered coaching.

Dallas is a better zombie than the real zombies. I get chills when I look at him. He keeps his mouth moving for my benefit, to look like he's eating brains. When I see him chewing, I know he's still himself. Anyone else would think he dislodged some food from between his teeth—repulsive maybe, but still within allowable zombie limits.

There's one Grizzly who might be a real kid. He leaps for his tackles and looks around the field more than anyone else. But the rest are machines of flesh and chemistry. After a while, I can't even watch them. I close my eyes until it's over.

Clap, clap, clap. We won.

I nudge Dallas in the ribs. "Good job. Wish I could have been with you."

He smiles and shouts, "Don't be silly, Maxwell! Some of us are on the field and some of us are on the bench, but we're all on the same team and our team did a fine job today. So good job to you too." Then he starts chewing brains. I swear he's going to make me laugh out loud some day and blow my cover.

"Please come celebrate at my house," he says. I hesitate, so he repeats, "Please."

Only three kids head over with the coach: me, Bay and Brennan. Three black kids. I don't know if that's significant.

Dallas's house is sparkling clean. The living room has been decorated green since I was last here. "Relaxing, isn't it?" Mrs. Richmond asks when she catches me holding a couch pillow up to a curtain. She wears a gray dress and carries a black RIG, messaging while she mingles.

"You have a nice home," Bay says from behind me.

Mrs. Richmond smiles. "Who won the game?"

Bay scrunches his massive brow. "We did, I think."

"Excellent." She wanders toward the adults, her eyes glued to her screen.

Bay follows her. He tugs Coach Emery's sleeve like a five-year-old giant. "We won the game, didn't we, Coach?"

The coach stares at him for a moment before answering. "That's right. We won."

Brennan leads Bay to a corner armchair and sits with him in a green silence.

Dallas joins me on the couch. "Feeble party," he whispers.

"We should fly," I whisper back.

"I wish." There's a sadness in his voice that eats at me.

"Good game though," I tell him. "I mean it. Good job."

He doesn't answer. We sit on the forest-green couch and hug the mint-green pillows. "Who do you think would win in a fight?" he whispers. "Bay as a zombie or Brennan as himself?"

"Shh." I nod toward the doorway. "Austin's home."

Dallas shakes his head. "He won't catch on. His class was done last week."

"So he's—?"

Dallas chews his brains.

Austin takes off his shoes and tucks them in a slot in the hall closet. He stores his hat on top and straightens his shirt before he enters the living room. His gaze roves around and stops on me. He smiles politely and approaches. "Hello, Maxwell. It's nice to see you again." No "Hey, faggot, come to ask me out?" No "Where's your daddy, little orphan?"

"Hi, Austin. How are you?"

"Very well, thanks. Did you win your game?"

I'm waiting for the punch, or at least the punch line, but there is none. "Yes, we did."

"I'm sorry I couldn't see it. I go to a homework club after school. We're helping each other prepare for next year."

"That's premium."

Austin smiles. "You two have fun." He kisses his mother on the cheek, laughs at a joke his father makes, picks up the empty bottles and exits.

"He's changed a bit," I say.

Dallas's eyes gleam. "Just a bit."

His father's voice carries across the room. "No more police visits for underground fighting. No more slutty girls sneaking over the back fence. No more constant arguments." He points at the couch and says, "And with the other one, there's no more detention or loud music or faggot Christmas productions."

His mom chimes in. "And they eat whatever I make for dinner with no complaints."

Coach Emery smiles politely. Dr. Richmond laughs until he chokes on his whisky.

Dallas hugs his pillow and stares at me. "So who do you think would win in a fight, Max? Us or the rest of the world?"

TWELVE

I hide in the tent with the *Freakshow* finale on my RIG and grow depressed watching Zipperhead haul his massive skull around the stage. I wonder what life was like for him growing up in Freaktown without surveillance cameras or Blackboard networks or nosy nurses.

Mom peeks around the front flaps. "Is Ally in here?"

"Don't touch that wall. It's still wet."

"Why aren't you doing your homework?" She grabs my RIG and dissolves the screen.

"I'm watching that!"

She kneels in front of me and takes my face in her hands. "You have to do your homework or you'll be revaccinated."

I shrug and stare at the messy sheets draped over the furniture.

"I know you're tired," she says.

"You don't know anything about it." I take my RIG from her hand and turn the show back on.

Ally pops up from behind the couch, wearing her earpiece and singing, "Pussycat ate the dumplings, Pussycat ate the dumplings. Mama stood by and cried, 'Oh fie! Why did you eat the dumplings?'" She giggles and claps.

"Get to bed," Mom tells her. "And don't sneak out again."

"You too," I tell Mom. A commercial comes on for a fertility drug, and I absentmindedly pick at my patch.

She puts her hand on mine. "Don't give up, Max."

I shove her hand away. "But I'd eat and sleep and take up hobbies."

"I won't let that happen."

"You let it happen for years." I look her in the eye and sing, "Mama stood by and cried, 'Oh fie!'"

She looks away from me to the faces I painted on the walls of my tent—Tyler, Xavier, Pepper. I turn up the volume on my RIG.

There's a knock at the door. We stare at each other, wide-eyed and paranoid. I peek through the tent window while she answers.

It's Dallas, vacant-eyed but chewing. "Hello, Mrs. Connors. How are you?"

Mom holds her hand over her mouth.

"It's okay, Mom. Shut the door."

Dallas smiles. "I'm good, aren't I?"

Mom nods. "You've always been good. Goodnight, boys. Do your homework."

Dallas sits beside me on the couch, and I stream the show on the big screen. He looks around the tent walls. "Wow. You're taking a risk."

"I take a risk every time I leave the house."

"I take a risk every time I stay home."

I give him that one. "How'd you escape?"

"I told my dad I was going to the Christmas Ball planning session. I couldn't miss the final *Freakshow*, and there's no way I could watch it with Austin. It stinks in here." He points to my wall of throwaways—the Asian kid skating for his life while Tyler and Washington leer over a railing. "Those were good days." He blows out a big breath. He looks exhausted. His hands shake. He holds them over his face and swears aimlessly.

"Have you lost weight?"

He shrugs. "I have diarrhea every day so I just stopped eating."

"You have to eat, man. Want some nachos?"

He looks at my paint-spattered plate and shudders.

"Want something else? We have apples and cheese."

"Maybe an apple."

He takes one bite of a Red Delicious and chews for forty seconds before he can swallow. "I'm tired, Max," he says. He lays the apple on my nacho plate. "I can't take this smell."

We close the flaps and sit in front of the tent on the carpet, four feet from the big screen. We scrunch our legs and lean back on our elbows, craning our necks. "This is better," Dallas says. He cracks a smile. "This is so much better than home. I can't even fall asleep anymore because I'm afraid my dad's got surveillance on me and I'll give myself away in a dream."

"You have to sleep, man."

He rolls his eyes. "Easy for you to say."

They show the gruesome freak tryouts for next season. I turn up the volume to mask my laughter in case Lucas is below us with a glass to his ceiling. I relax for the first time in days. "I'm so tense lately. I feel like ripping someone's head off."

Dallas nods. "I'm suffering withdrawal from fighting with Austin. I have too much adrenaline flooding through me now. I'll probably die of a heart attack before the zombies get me." He smiles briefly. "Which would you rather be? A brain-eating zombie or the kind at school?"

"Brain-eater."

"Me too."

The show comes back on. Because it's the final episode with this batch of freaks, they spotlight the last two contestants' families in Freaktown. They show the place before the leaks—lush forests and fertile fields, buxom women and rugged men, vague urban vistas of crowded sidewalks, money and success. Then they show the place now—buildings boarded up and crumbling down, soup kitchen lineups, blankets draped over lumpy bodies, kids with warped eyeballs and exposed jaw bones drooling over drugs.

"My father was there before the spill," Dallas says. "He has photos on his website."

"Has he gone back since?"

"No. Why would anyone go there?"

I shrug. "Criminals might. To get away from the IDs. Or maybe to get to Canada. There's still a border crossing there. I heard terrorists sneak into the country that way."

"I'd go south to get away from the IDs," Dallas says. "Just hop in a car and keep driving. Wouldn't you? It could take years before anyone found me. Don't you think?"

I nod. "I want to go back to Atlanta."

"I don't know much about Atlanta," he says. "Is it big enough to get lost in?"

"I think so."

There's a closeup of Zipperhead's scars and sorrows.

"I wonder if he was happier when his brother was still attached to him," Dallas says. "It's hard to believe there was a whole person there once and now there's just a scar." His face pulls tight and his eyes tear up. "I have to get out of here, Max. I can't do this anymore."

"Are you serious? Because my mom would take us. She already said she would."

Dallas wipes his nose. "Count me in." He stares at me hard, trembling with exhaustion. "Even if they get me. Pack me up and take me with you. Don't leave me here with them."

I envision Mom driving out of town and Dallas racing after us with a hundred zombies on his heels. "I won't leave you here."

He nods, over and over again. He only stops when they announce this season's winning freak. "Squid?" he whispers in surprise.

Zipperhead hangs his massive head to hide his tears. It's hard to see why he would bother to lift it up again.

I swear and moan. "Life isn't fair."

"I always knew that," Dallas says. "I just thought mine would be better."

Ally wakes me up the next morning. "Time for school."

I look at my watch. "Shit." I stayed up painting all night, and I'm a mess. I rush into some pants and smooth my hair as best I can. I walk as quickly as I dare down the hallway. "Do you have a lunch?" I whisper. She nods. Thank god Mom doesn't rely on me.

We arrive late in the lobby. I fake a limp. Seven kids are gathered to walk to the trade school. "I'm sorry," I tell them. "I tripped on my weak ankle and re-sprained it. I hope I haven't made you late for school."

Lucas bows his head. "We understand. Your mother works in the early mornings and you have no father, so you have to do things for yourself."

I nod. "I enjoy doing things for myself. But I can be slow."

He checks his watch. "It's fine. Let's go."

I limp all the way back to the apartment.

At school, I keep my nose to the grindstone as the minutes tick by. I don't feel safe until I'm back at home. I pull Mom inside the tent. "Dallas says he'll come with us to Atlanta. We have to go soon, though, before he loses it. They're still fighting the IDs down there, right?"

She shrugs. "I think so. No one asked for ours except at the airport."

"Good. Then we just have to get there without flying."

"They'd probably ask at the speed rail too," Mom says. "But maybe we could find a private car."

"Can we take him with us?"

189

"Who, Dallas? I guess so."

"You can't go back on this."

"All right. Yes. We can take him with us."

"Is it illegal to leave New Middletown?"

"No. I don't think so." She sighs and nods repeatedly. It's a habit everyone is picking up these days.

※

I walk Ally to the park in twilight. A few fat adults are heading home from work, all bundled up. A few skinny ones jog by in caps and T-shirts. Ally and I turn toward the park. "Hey, they put up a fence!" I say. It's not a real fence, just an orange plastic weave tacked onto temporary posts five feet high.

"Is it closed?" Ally asks.

"Looks like it. Wait. There's a sign." I read aloud, "*Public Notice. This playground is temporarily closed due to the—*" I shut my mouth.

"To what?" Ally asks. "Due to what?"

I shiver like a ghost walked through me. The swings tremble in the breeze.

Ally steps in front of me to read the sign. She sounds out the words. "*Due to the Rodent Central—*"

"Control," I correct.

"*Rodent Control Program,*" she continues. "*In response to the virtual—*"

"Viral."

"*Viral outbreak at New Middletown Manor Hegs—*"

"Heights."

She looks up and smiles. "That's where Mommy works."

"Let's go, Ally."

She doesn't budge. "It says the park is closed for six weeks. I can't stay away from Peanut for six weeks. She'll be hungry."

I stare at the black lumps scattered over the playground and I don't know what to tell my sister.

"That's the poison symbol," she says, pointing at the sign.

I nod. "That's right. We can't go in there because there's poison. Let's go home."

She won't leave. She stares at the lumps that aren't dirt. "They put poison in the park?" She frowns and squints. "Won't that hurt the squirrels?"

The scene suddenly makes sense to her. She utters a choking sound and tries to pull down the fence. "Somebody poisoned the squirrels!" she shouts. The plastic slices into her fingers.

I pull her off it, grip my arms around her waist and lift her off the ground. "No, Ally! You'll get the poison in your skin."

She's much stronger than I expect. It's like trying to hold a baboon. She writhes and kicks and screams. "Peanut! Peanut!" She throws her head back into my face and smashes my teeth with her skull. She kicks her legs up and over the fence and falls to the other side. She screams and stumbles across the poisoned ground.

"Quiet, Ally, please!" I look around frantically to make sure no one's watching.

She drops to her knees beside the nearest squirrel. She runs from carcass to carcass, touching them, turning them over, whimpering.

It takes me thirty seconds to climb the fence. The plastic stretches and sways beneath my feet. I flip and land on my shoulder. "Stop it!" I whisper when I reach her.

She's at the bottom of the oak tree, wailing like a siren, holding a dead squirrel in her hands. Snot hangs from her nose to her chin and her whole body shudders. I drop beside her, hug her, shush her.

The squirrel's eyes are open and glazed. Its mouth is twisted, a hardened cadmium ooze collected in the corners. Its belly is bloated, its front paws locked together like it tried to push something away. It didn't die easy. "Is that her?" I ask.

Ally looks at me desperately, and I know she can't tell one squirrel from another now. Whatever made Peanut recognizable is gone. "Yes," she says because she needs that much to hold on to. "It's Peanut. Poor Peanut." She leans her face in like she's going to kiss the thing, but I yank her head back. She can hate me, I don't care, but she's not going near that yellow ooze.

"She's poison, Ally. You can't keep touching her."

She pets the squirrel's head and cries.

"We have to get out of here." I pull her up beside me and she drops the squirrel. It falls straight and stiff from her hand to the ground and bounces on the dirt. She screams.

I hug her to my chest, hard enough to cover her mouth. "It's okay," I whisper. "Just leave her."

"No," she moans. "We have to bury her."

"No way. The ground's too hard."

"We have to!"

"Okay. We'll take her home first. I'll get her." I cup my hand under the dead squirrel. It's so soft and light, it feels hollow. I never realized how small Peanut was. Her whole body almost fits in my hand. The tail falls softly across my wrist.

"Is she dead?" Ally asks.

"Yeah. Yeah, she's dead. We'll find a box to bury her in tomorrow when it's light." I boost Ally over the fence and scramble after her. I tuck the squirrel in one arm like a football and keep my sister close with the other, trying to block her sorrow from the eyes and cameras that surround us.

⁎

Ally sleeps with a dried string of snot across her cheek, her hands bandaged, her hair flattened against her temple, her teddy bear stuffed in an armpit.

I walk to the lobby to tell Lucas that my sister is ill. I stop cold when I see Xavier waiting. Watching him beat up a teacher didn't unsettle me half as much as seeing him in a group of throwaways.

He stares at the ceiling, moves his head left and right like he's comparing acoustic tiles. His hair is pulled back. There are purple bags beneath his eyes and red nicks and scrapes along his jaw as if he shaved with his fingernails. He's lost weight. He's lost intensity. He's so dim he's almost a ghost.

"Hello, Max," Lucas says. "I'm pleased to see your ankle is better."

For a second I don't know what he's talking about. I look at my foot. "Oh. Yes. My mom's a nurse," I say, like she can cure sprains instantly. "I'm sorry to tell you that Ally's sick today with a bad cold so I'll be staying home with her."

"That's a shame," Lucas says. "Especially since your mom's a nurse."

I avoid his eyes. "Hello, Xavier," I say. "I have a belated birthday gift for you—I'm almost done it."

He smiles in my direction, unfocussed, unhealthy.

I turn around and head for the stairs.

"We'll see Ally tomorrow!" Lucas shouts. I don't answer.

I read my sister stories until she falls asleep. Then I sit in my tent under a blaze of colorful children. I spray-paint the exterior walls with one word repeated in capitals, wrapped around the corners without any breaks: *WITHSTANDWITH STANDWITHSTANDWITHSTAND.*

Celeste comes over the next morning to stay with Ally. Xavier clings to her hand with both of his. His hair hangs in wet waves and smells of strawberries.

"Is he sick?" I ask. "I mean, with a cold or something?"

She shakes her head. "He got in a fight at school and ran away. We're home-schooling him now. It's either that or an institution for the uneducable."

"Uneducable?" I've seen Xavier build robots and hack into government networks.

She walks her brother to the couch and helps him sit. He holds his neck at an odd angle and wears a pained expression that smoothes into emptiness when she turns on the big screen.

"Where's your tent?" she asks.

I point to a huge pile of canvas beside the door. "I have to take it in for the exhibit. I'm giving it to Xavier afterward."

"Really? Why?"

I shrug. "I don't know what else to do."

⁎

We run laps in the bitter sunshine during gym class. Coach Emery asks for volunteers to clean out the football trailer at lunch. Every student raises a hand. He chooses me, Dallas and Brennan.

The trailer is a reeking mess, with discarded clothes smelling up the corners and busted pads wedged under the benches. The walls are smeared with dirt and sweat and unidentifiable body fluids. The coach gives us a garbage can, a bag of rags, and three bottles of disinfectant. "Do a good job." He nods toward the surveillance camera in the corner. "I'll know if you don't."

They installed cameras in the change rooms a few years ago. There was some concern about privacy, but a damaged assault during a football game hushed it up. It's hard to imagine public safety without surveillance. So somebody sees you naked. If it keeps people from raping and murdering you, what's to argue? At least that's what I thought before the treatments.

I act like a zombie janitor in the trailer, partly because of the camera and partly because Dallas and I haven't had a real conversation with Brennan since the vaccinations and I'm scared this is a trap. When we've scrubbed the place clean,

Brennan checks the time and says to me, "Why don't you go outside and ask my father if anything else needs to be done?"

The coach is waiting for me around the back of the trailer. "Good work, Connors," he says loudly. He pulls me close and whispers, "I advise you to get out of town as soon as you can."

It's just not right to hear a football coach whisper. I squirm away.

"I'm serious," he says. "Arlington Richmond doesn't think you were properly vaccinated. He says there's something wrong with the way you laugh."

"I didn't know I laughed anymore."

"He recommended revaccinating you. Graham is hedging because overdoses are dangerous. He'll probably do it after the holidays."

He talks like that's just around the corner, but three weeks is an eternity these days.

"Suffice it to say that your teachers are going to keep a close watch on you until then," he says. "And you're not going to pass scrutiny. Feelings pass over your face all the time. You mutter to yourself when you think you're alone. Your eyes gleam from ten yards away."

"Should I wear contacts?"

"It's no joke, Connors." He takes my head in his hands and shakes it like he's trying to rattle a ball of truth into the right hole. "They'll never let your mother give you the next shot. They are suspicious. There won't be any warning. You understand me? You have to get out before the decision is made."

"We are getting out. But we need a car."

"So buy one from the carpark. I know your mother's not rich, but she must have something tucked away. A small car that works is cheaper than a van that doesn't."

"Are you going? Are you taking Brennan?"

"We're holding tight for now."

"Is it true that the top student in each class didn't get the treatment?" I ask.

He lowers his eyes and mumbles, "They don't know how permanent the effects might be. They know they're going to need some critical thinkers once you kids are in college so—"

"So they saved the cream of the crop," I finish.

"This is not a policy I agree with, Connors," he whispers.

"We're taking Dallas with us," I tell him.

I expect him to say that we're sentimental, that times are tough and we'll need our resources for ourselves, it's a dog-eat-zombie world. But he says, "Then you better head for Canada or Mexico. Because starting January first, every child in this country will need to show their ID whenever anyone asks for it, and there's no way that boy is going to be able to hide from his father."

※

I'm called to the office at two o'clock. My name blasts over the intercom. Dallas stiffens in the row beside me. I plan to make a run for it.

Mr. Reese looks up at the speaker and back to me with a worried frown. His face relaxes when he checks his watch. "It's time to take your work to the art exhibit, Max."

Two girls wait in the backseat of the principal's car, clutching black leather portfolio cases. I lean my rolled-up tent against the trunk.

"What on earth is that thing?" Mr. Graham asks me.

"It's my exhibit."

He stares at me, scowling, but eventually he opens the trunk. I sit in the front seat, empty-handed and open to scrutiny.

I stare out the passenger window as we drive south along the city spine. It's so efficient, New Middletown's core of office towers and hospital wards and agricultural warehouses. Nothing's ever wasted here, not a drop of water or a moment of time. It's beautiful in its way, and I know I'll miss it if I get the chance to leave, but for the first time in my life I feel like this is not my town.

Every moment I'm in this car, my tent seems more ridiculous. I can almost feel the weight of it behind us. It was a mistake, painting it the way I did. I should have submitted a small still life—fruit in a bowl or some naked beauty.

Mr. Graham drops us at the pedestrian conveyor closest to City Hall and drives away to park underground. I consider running home, but the tent's too heavy to carry far, and there's no way I'd leave it here. I step onto the conveyor and let it take me forward.

I raise my eyes to the shining columns of colored glass that reach into the sky. It's still the most premium building I've seen in my life. But I understand what that taxi driver meant when he called it cold as ice.

I drag my tent across the threshold.

A man rushes up and asks my name. "Connors. Yes. I expected a sculpture." He frowns at me and leads me to my station.

"Excuse me?" I ask the kid unfolding an easel across from me. "When you're done there could you give me a hand with this?"

"Yes. Certainly. I'd be pleased to."

He doesn't ask any questions, just follows my directions, holds the tent poles while I wrench the canvas overtop. I hang two flashlights from the ceiling and turn them on. The kid looks at the dim walls and says, "It's stuffy in here." He walks back to his still life—red tulips in a glass vase.

It's a long afternoon. People arrive at three thirty—parents, teachers, judges, citizens. They walk through the exhibit with polite curiosity, making small talk with the artists, nodding and smiling. I sweat beside my military surplus.

They stare at my tent, baffled. They open their mouths to speak but close them again before anything comes out, walk away shaking their heads.

I think I might get through this with embarrassment as my only damage, but at four fifteen a big black woman in a floral dress brushes open a tent flap and sticks her head inside my metaphor. "Oh my god," she whispers, catching a few ears. She grabs a flashlight and lights up the walls. She snaps photos, leaning in and backing up. She nods her head, smiles, frowns, gasps, mutters, "Amazing." Other adults peer through the windows or stick their necks through the front flaps but they don't enter. They take one glance and step away, like unwitting performance artists.

"Marvelous work," the flowery woman says when she emerges. She smiles and pats my shoulder. "You have an exciting career ahead of you."

The principal hurries over to shake her hand.

"I'm Rosemary Seawell," she says.

"From the *New Middletown Monitor*?" Mr. Graham asks.

She laughs. "No, sir. I'm up from Pittsburgh."

I want to call Xavier and tell him the free media is in town, but I don't know if he'd still care.

"Pittsburgh!" Mr. Graham scoffs. "Why would you cover an event like this?"

She smiles. "Great artists are discovered at events like this."

Mr. Graham stares at my work, revolted. "Stand with what?" he asks.

"Withstand," Rosemary corrects him. "Have you been inside?"

He cautiously nudges the tent flaps apart, but he doesn't pass through. He lingers in the doorway, canvas draped over his bald white girth.

"Use a flashlight," Rosemary says. She turns to me and smiles. "They're a nice touch."

Mr. Graham backs out without bothering. He walks up to me, stands far too close, and stares down into my eyes. "When did you make this, Connors?"

"I don't remember, sir."

"What does it mean?"

"I don't know, sir."

"It doesn't make any sense to me. Does it make sense to you, boy?"

"Nothing makes sense to me, sir."

He nods like that's a good answer. "Pack it up, and I'll take you home."

THIRTEEN

Mom fries hamburgers at the stove while I sit at the kitchen table and lose my appetite. I have four hours of homework to suffer through, simple but repetitive: conjugate a hundred Spanish verbs, describe the probability of a hundred random events. They like to drive a point home, these teachers of the new economy.

Ally sits across from me, her nose half an inch from the table, her tongue poking between her teeth. Lucas came by with her homework—a set of intricate black and white designs on paper with numbers in every white space. Each number corresponds to a color, and Ally has to fill in each space appropriately. She starts out well in blue and brown, but then she thinks of Peanut and starts to cry, smearing her work.

Mom sets ketchup and milk in front of us. "I have a patient named Connors whose grandson visits every few weeks. He lives in town. He's sixteen or seventeen, tall like Dallas, with black hair and blue eyes. I could get his ID for Dallas to use in Atlanta. We could say he's your half-brother, Daddy's child from another marriage."

"The fingerprints won't match," I say.

"They never check those unless you're arrested."

"The kid would report a lost ID. We'd get caught the first place we flashed it. You need to get his passport instead. He won't notice that's missing. If you can get his birth certificate, too, we could put Dad's name as his father."

"Good idea. We could use them to get Dallas a new ID in Atlanta."

I shoot down her dream. "We'll never get an ID with a stolen passport. But we might get into Canada with it."

"I don't want to leave the country, Max!" she shouts. "I don't even want to leave this city."

"We have no choice!"

"What on earth are we going to do in Canada? It's freezing there. If we have to live in a car, I'd rather park it in Atlanta."

Ally carefully picks up her pencils and takes her work to the living room. "I wish you'd put the tent back up!" she yells.

I take a breath and swallow all the sarcastic backtalk that rises up inside me. "At least you have a niece there. You don't have anybody left in Atlanta."

Mom swats the air. "I haven't seen Rebecca since she was your age. I don't even know her. And I don't know anything about Canada. Not anything good anyway. How am I supposed to get a job there? What makes you think they'll let us in?"

"They take anyone with a trade. Their economy's weak and their population is even older than ours. They need nurses. They'll probably pay us to move there." I smile, but she doesn't find it amusing. "They'll let you in, Mom, and you'll find work. We'll be fine. And we can hide Dallas there. We just have to leave before January first or they won't let him out."

"*We* can leave whenever we like."

"No, we can't! They'll give me another shot when the holiday's over. We have to leave by Christmas. You said you'd take Dallas, and you're not backing out. So get that kid's passport and birth certificate to use at the border."

She holds her hands over her face. "Oh my god, Max, what on earth are we heading into?"

The trade school calls after supper—Ally must return to school tomorrow or supply a doctor's note confirming her illness. When Mom tells her, Ally bursts into tears. She runs to the living room and stares out the window, crying for her dead squirrel.

"I don't want to send either of you to school tomorrow," Mom says.

I dissolve my homework with a sigh. "The police will take us if we don't go. It's been on the news. Zero tolerance for truancy." Another news story about a bear attack in the national forest gets me thinking about Mom's orchard memories. I lead her into the living room and ask nonchalantly, "Did you tell Ally about the squirrel I saw today when the principal drove me home?"

"What squirrel?" Ally asks through her tears.

"You know that squirrel we saw in the park? The dead one we thought was Peanut?"

"Yeah."

"I don't know if that was really Peanut. On my way home today I saw a squirrel heading toward the forest that looked exactly like her."

Her eyes widen and her mouth hangs open, disbelieving.

"I think she was following the roads out of town," I say. "Away from the poison."

Mom stares at me warily, waiting to see where this goes.

Ally wipes her nose. "You saw a real squirrel? You think it was Peanut?"

"It looked like her. And that one by the tree didn't look like her at all, did it?"

"No, it didn't."

"You know how smart Peanut was. She probably knew there was poison on the ground so she hid in her nest until it was safe to come down. Now she's running away to find a better home."

Ally sniffles and sighs. "Did you really see a squirrel?"

"Yeah. Not far from here. It looked just like Peanut. I told you that, didn't I, Mom?"

"Yes, dear. It slipped my mind."

Ally stares suspiciously at Mom, who avoids her eyes.

"So you know what that means," I say.

Ally shakes her head.

"It's really sad," I warn her.

She shrinks back.

"It means you'll probably never see Peanut again. She's so smart, she won't come back here because of the poison. She'll stay in the forest in an oak tree. You know what comes from oak trees?"

"Acorns," she whispers.

"She'll have time to collect them before it snows," Mom says.

Ally leans over the back of the chair, looks out the window down to the ground. "She's gone," she whispers. "Poor Peanut. She'll miss me." She stares down the back of the chair for a bit. Then she wiggles it away from the wall.

A spider has spun its web in the corner of the living room. It's plain, brown, half an inch long, scared of the light.

"Watch out," I say. "Spiders can bite if you bother them."

"What do you think he eats?" she asks.

"Flies."

"We never have flies. He must be hungry."

"Put the chair back, honey," Mom says. "You're scaring him."

Ally wiggles the chair back, but not as close to the wall as it was before. She leans over the upholstery and smiles. "I'm calling him Fred."

⚮

"You're a good brother," Mom tells me after Ally's in bed.

I shrug. "She wasn't going to make it through tomorrow without a lie."

"You make it through too, Max." She sits on the couch with her hands folded in her lap. "I'm sorry I yelled at you. I'm just scared."

"We'll be okay."

She pats my hand. "Sure we will. I looked up some things about Canada. Did you know that parts of it aren't much colder than here?"

I laugh. "That's the part we'll head to."

She smiles. "They have a nursing shortage. That's hopeful, right? And we can keep our citizenship so we could come back eventually."

"Great."

She nods. "I'm sorry I got so mad, Max. I'm supposed to lead you kids out of trouble, not the other way around."

"It's all right. So we're really going?"

"Yes. We're really going. I sent a message to Rebecca. We have a better chance of getting in if we have a place to stay."

"And we can go before Christmas?"

Mom nods. "We'll need a car."

"And a passport for Dallas."

"If he really wants to come."

"He really wants to come."

She sighs. "Okay. Hang on a little longer."

Ally can't stop smiling in the stairwell. She's imagining Peanut setting up house in the national forest, packing leaves and mud into a condo in the trees, making squirrel friends, storing acorns.

"You better get those giggles out," I whisper. "Remember how you have to act at school."

She relaxes her face and dims her eyes. We reach for the doorknob at the same time. She laughs, then turns it into a cough.

"Good girl. Who's going to get the door?"

She points back and forth between us and whispers, "One potato, two potato, three potato, four. Five potato, six potato, seven potato, more." She turns the doorknob.

Lucas and three other zombies await us. They wear bulky gray coats over their shapeless gray suits. There were more of them last week. They must be cleaning house at the trade school, herding kids into institutions for the uneducable. I wonder how many lower rungs there are on the ladder of childhood.

"Hello, Lucas," I say. "Nice to see you."

"Nice to see you too, Maxwell. And you, Alexandra. I hope you're feeling better."

"I'm much better, thank you." There's a smile playing behind her eyes, but I doubt the zombies can notice it.

"Goodbye, Ally," I say as she joins them. "Be good."

***

Dallas has a carefully disguised fit on the school grounds when I tell him we're going to Canada instead of Atlanta. "They're never going to let me across the border!" He keeps a straight face and an even tone but he still manages to convey that he's shouting. "They don't let minors leave the country without their parents' permission."

"We can get you a passport with the name Connors on it."

"Oh, that's royal. We look so much alike." He's so mad he has to turn away from me to regain control. "They'll catch us, Max," he says when he turns back. "They'll catch us and they'll send me back and my parents will find out that I'm not treated and they'll turn me into a fucking zombie."

"No. If we go to Atlanta—if we go anywhere in the States—any cop who wants to can ask for your ID and send you back home when they find out who you are. You can't change your fingerprints. You'll be at risk every day of your life until you're eighteen. But if you cross the border, it's just one risk and you're through."

"It's a big fucking risk, Max."

"No, it's not. We're going to cross at Freaktown. They let anybody through there."

"What are you basing that theory on?"

I shrug. "Rumors."

He nods for so long that I think it might be some kind of tremor. "It's another country, Max. They're going to examine my passport. We can't just glue my picture in it."

"Maybe you look like the kid."

"Maybe I don't."

"Then maybe we could take your real passport and forge a letter of permission from your parents."

"They'll call my home."

"Then we'll take the passport of someone a bit older who looks like you and you can come with us as an adult."

He clears his throat and says calmly, "Yes. Of course. We'll just make a wish in the passport fountain and all my problems will be solved."

"Then we'll—"

He walks away from me, into the school.

Dallas ignores me for two days. I finally catch him in the cafeteria, sitting alone with a buffer of empty seats between him and the zombies. "We're visiting my cousin on Christmas Eve," I tell him. I don't whisper because that's suspicious.

We've learned to hide our words in other words. "That's my birthday. I hope to do some shopping if the stores are open."

He plays with the turkey sandwich on his tray and doesn't respond. There's a tremor in his jaw and a twitch in one eye.

"It's the perfect place to shop because no one can find out what presents you're buying."

"It's a long way to go just to get out of town, Max."

"My cousin Rebecca went many years ago. She says the shopping is very good there."

He shakes his head. "I want to shop in Atlanta."

"It would be hard to find your parents a present in Atlanta."

He eats in silence while I list all the wonderful presents I want to buy.

"Christmas is two weeks away," he says at last. "I can't prepare myself in time."

"Yes, you can. And you know we deserve a break. You remember how Coach Emery said we did a good job cleaning the trailer."

"Yeah, but…"

I put down my spoon. "I thought you wanted to go Christmas shopping with us."

"It won't work, Max." He almost shouts the words.

A girl at the next table turns around and stares at us.

Dallas perfects his zombie face and says politely, "It's too sudden. I don't have enough money to go shopping with."

"Sudden? We've been saving up for six weeks."

He says nothing, sips his soda, moves his food around his plate.

The nosy girl turns back to her tray. Beside us, three ninth grade girls suck their soup in silence, eyes glued to their RIGs.

I sink into a whisper. "'How long do you think we can keep this up?' Those were your exact words three weeks ago. This is not sudden."

"Thank you, Max," Dallas says loudly. "It's nice of your family to invite me shopping. It's good to be with your family at Christmas. My family would like to be with me too. It's sad to be with someone else's family at Christmas, especially when you obviously don't belong with them because you're different races and couldn't possibly be related." Anybody listening might think he was a recall, but they wouldn't suspect he was talking about fleeing the country.

"I'm sorry," I say. "Of course it's better to be with your family. But if you need to shop and your family can't take you, then my family would be happy to adopt you as my half-brother. I know you'd like to come with us because you've said so many times."

Washington sits down a few seats away with two other goons-turned-zombies. "Hello, Max. Hello, Dallas. How are you?" he says.

I'm pissed off so I say, "We're fine, Washington. How's Tyler? Oh. I forgot. He's dead. You must be so sad."

He opens the lid of his sandwich box. "It's his memory that keeps me going."

Dallas looks down at his plate.

"You can't stay home while I go shopping," I say.

His jaw tightens and he sucks air through his straw.

I have to fight the urge to swat him. "Dallas, man, you're more desperate than I am," I whisper. "Once I'm gone there's nowhere you can relax. You won't make it."

The gurgle of the straw fades out with a sniffle. His jaw twitches and he blinks rapidly.

It's always a bad idea to needle your only friend until he cries in public, but it's especially bad when you're surrounded by zombie tattlers. Our escape from this sad school is so close— it's exactly the time fate would kick us in the throat for fun.

"I'm sorry," I say at normal volume. "We should never pressure our friends to do what we want to do." Then I mumble, "Just keep it together. We're surrounded."

He takes a few breaths, then looks up in perfect zombie mode except for the twitch in his eye. "I'm not sure I want to go that far."

"You don't mean that."

"Now that Christmas is so close, I might stay home and buy my gifts locally."

"There's not much selection."

"I love this country," he whispers.

Washington stares at us while he chews his sandwich.

"I know your parents love it too," I tell Dallas loudly. "I know they'd be very happy for you to shop locally for the rest of your life."

His head falls with the weight of that thought.

"How long can you last alone?" I whisper.

"I'm becoming good friends with Brennan. That's like trading up."

I nod to show I like his joke. "But what will you do when Brennan goes shopping? Think about it. My family would like to take you shopping with us and this may be your only chance."

"It's forever, Max," he whispers.

"*This* is forever," I say. "What do you think will happen to you? Look around."

Dallas turns his head slowly left and right. The zombies are staring at us curiously because we're the only people talking in the whole place.

⁂

I head to my hair appointment at 3:30.

"Hello, handsome," Kim says. "Didn't I just see you at Thanksgiving? You don't usually get a Christmas cut. I was surprised when you called."

"We're visiting my cousin this year. Mom wants me to look premium."

"You always look premium. Come to the sink."

It's unsettling to lean my head back into the porcelain bowl where she spits her toothpaste every morning, but the hot water and scalp massage feel glorious.

"Same as usual?" she asks as she towels me dry. "Not too short? Bit of a fade at the back?"

"Yes, please."

She sprays my hair with moisturizer. "You ready for Christmas?"

"No."

She holds up her scissors and smiles in the mirror. "I found my son an old set of tools, almost antique, so even if he already has enough wrenches, it's still a nice conversation piece." Like she needs more of those. "Old cars have different parts than the new ones, so old tools probably work better anyway," she adds.

"Who does he work for?" I ask.

She's surprised to hear me ask a question, since I usually don't even answer them. "He works for himself," she says with a mixture of pride and shame because her son has initiative but he's broke.

"Does he sell cars?"

She laughs. "Everyone sells cars out where I live."

"I mean cars that work. Cars you can drive across the state."

She shrugs. "He mostly takes them apart to make more living space. Once in a while he fixes an engine. Not a lot of people drive the old cars because the gas and permits are so expensive." She selects a section of my hair with her fingers.

"Permits?"

She nods. "You need a permit to drive them because they pollute so much."

I swear.

She cuts my hair in silence for a minute. "What's up with you, kid?"

I catch her eye in the mirror and she straightens up, her scissors held high. "My cousin lives far away," I say. "We have to drive to her house, and I thought maybe we could find an old car."

"Why don't you rent a car?"

I don't say anything.

"How far are you planning on driving?"

"Far."

She squints. "Will anyone be staying in your apartment while you're gone?"

I shake my head, pulling the hair out from between her fingers.

She finds that section again, looks back at the mirror, and asks, "How long will your place be empty? A few days? A few weeks? Months?"

I shrug.

"How big is it?"

"Two bedrooms, a big living room, a small kitchen." I try to think of a selling point. "It has a nice view."

She laughs and repeats, "It has a nice view. Well, that's good to know. How many months are paid in advance?"

"Whatever's required, I guess."

"Most places need a six-month deposit. That's why I live in a car."

"Then I guess the next six months are paid for."

Her eyes go dreamy in the mirror. "You're sure about this? You're not kidding? I know you're a joker. Don't joke about this, okay?"

"I'm not joking."

"In that case, I'm sure I can find you a car that works." She smiles and snips my hair faster than I've ever seen. "We'll find you a very nice car with a full tank of gasoline. I'll throw in an air freshener. And one of those little dogs on the dashboard that wags its head when you brake." She laughs a big hearty laugh. She pats my shoulder and repeats, "We'll find you a very nice car."

"I'll need it before Christmas Eve."

"That won't be a problem."

···

I take a detour to Pepper's old house on my way home.

My heart is gone from her doorstep. But I'm still carrying her keys.

It's unsettling inside, dark and hollow. I walk straight to her bedroom and close the door. I stare at the nail where my painting used to hang. I turn around and catch my dim reflection in a mirror: gray clothes and a black face. I could be anybody. I could be a zombie. With nice hair.

I don't know what I'm doing here. I rummage through her closet but find nothing new. I look under her bed and behind the dresser. I sniff the clothes in her hamper, bury my face in a jacket that smells like the chemistry lab. There's an earpiece in one pocket, a storage chip in the other. I plug it into my RIG.

I can't access the documents without a password, but photos scroll freely before my eyes. I moan out loud to see myself with tomato sauce on my chin, smiling. The next photo shows Dallas holding my pizza out of my reach. There are almost fifty shots of us—in the skate park, on the school grounds, on the football field. There's even a recording of our game against the Devils—not the one where I screamed but before that, when Dallas went wicked. I can't look at that.

There's a recording of Pepper's dance rehearsal, so premium it hurts to watch. She's so beautiful, the motion of her hips, the concentration on her face. She looks away and smiles, shining like a sun. The camera pans to the doorway where I stand with my eyes glued to her, grinning like a recall.

All the time I'd thought I was playing it cool. Yet there I am on camera with my eyes soft and dreamy and my tongue hanging out. There's no way she couldn't have known how I felt about her.

It's cold in her empty house. I pull my arms out of my sleeves and hug my naked chest. When the recording ends, I watch it again. I project it onto my hand as if I'm holding her, but that just makes me sad. "Goodbye, Pepper," I whisper.

I crack open the door of her bedroom, half expecting an ambush of cops and nurses in the hallway. But there's no one in the house or on the street. I lock the door behind me and drop the keys in the mailbox. I won't be coming back here.

Mom's crying when I get home. Ally's at the kitchen table coloring, and Mom's sobbing on the couch. I sit beside her, but not too close because it unnerves me when she cries. I break into her sadness as gently as I can. "Hey, Mom, I found us a car. From Kim, my hairdresser. Her son fixes cars. Supreme, huh?"

She looks at me and nods. Her eyes are red and her face looks ten years older than yesterday. "That's great news, honey." She tries to smile, but it's contorted with her sadness so it just looks pained. I recoil, and a sob bursts out of her. She puts her face in her hands and rocks back and forth.

"Did someone else die?" I ask. "Is Xavier okay?"

"He's fine."

"Did Dallas call? I know he says he doesn't want to go but he's just scared. He'll change his mind."

She shakes her head.

"Did Rebecca tell us not to come?"

"Stop, Max," she whispers. "It's nothing like that." She pats my knee and opens her mouth to speak but nothing comes out. She wipes her eyes and shakes her head.

"Are you sick?" I cringe as I say it.

She laughs. It takes me by surprise so I laugh too. Her eyes are shiny bright and she sounds like a girl my age. "No! I'm not sick." She laughs some more, then sighs and shakes her head at me.

"Good," I say. "Whatever it is, you shouldn't worry, because it won't matter in a couple of weeks. We've got our wheels. We're getting out of here."

She sucks in a big stuttering breath.

I figure it must be hormones. "I'm here if you want to talk about it," I say, though I'd rather eat my own waste than have a chat with Mom about her hormones. I rise. "It's good about the car, right?"

She nods.

"Anything to eat?"

She grabs my hand. "Stay here for a bit."

"Sure. I'll grab something and bring it over. We'll watch a movie or something. Okay?"

I don't wait for her answer.

I open the fridge and look for something to eat. "Hey, Ally, how are you doing?"

"Fine, thank you, Max. How are you?"

"I'm all right." I shift bottles of ketchup and pickles, as if a grilled chicken sandwich might be lurking behind them. "What did you have for supper?"

"We had soup with bread and cheese."

"Yeah, I guess that'll have to do." I lift the lid off the pot on the stove. There's a bit left, so I warm it up. "I had a great day today, Ally. How about you?"

"It was fine, thank you, Max."

"Did you leave the cream cheese out?" I find it behind the milk and pull them both onto the counter. I pour a glass, drink it, pour another. I sniff the cheese before I spread it on a bun because in this house, you never know. "You didn't mind going back to school?" I ask. "Everything went okay?"

"Everything is good at my school," Ally says. "Every child who goes to school is lucky."

"What did you say?" I turn around and set my plate across from her. But I don't sit down.

Ally's sitting very straight, with her head bowed toward her work. She looks intently at her page and fills in a numbered space slowly and carefully with a black pencil, her fingers moving back and forth in tiny overlapping lines.

"What did you just say, Ally?" I repeat.

She stops coloring when the space is entirely black. She sets her pencil down and looks up. Her eyes drift over the air before settling on me. "I don't remember what I just said." She scratches a stray hair off her cheek. "I'm having trouble focusing on my work. I'm too hot." She takes off her sweater and hangs it neatly on the back of her chair. She looks down at her page, picks up a blue pencil, colors another numbered space.

Her body barely moves, her coloring is so controlled. Her fingers jiggle. Her wrist shakes slightly. But her arm is almost still. Up at her shoulder there's no motion at all, just a dark arm at rest. I stare at the big beige patch that wasn't there this morning, and the knife slips from my hand. When the clatter of metal finally rings itself out, all I hear is my mother quietly crying in the living room.

FOURTEEN

"Whispering is wrong," Ally says. She stomps into the living room, dressed in pajamas, holding her teddy bear by the snout. I've been living with her for one week since her shot, and I can't stand her. "You should do your homework," she tells me.

We were right to call them zombies. They want to eat our brains.

I force a smile. "Time for bed, sleepyhead."

She looks at me like I'm defective. "We have to tell an adult when children don't follow the rules."

Mom rises from the couch beside me. "Max finished his homework, Ally. It's not your business to oversee your brother."

"Work is everybody's business."

We have to get out of this city.

Ally stares at the coffee table. She points her finger and calls the world to witness. "You used my coloring pencils! You're not allowed. They're for my work."

"I told Max he could use them," Mom says.

Ally marches over to my drawing: a sunny dandelion sprouts from a crack in the sidewalk where zombie children march to school, one huge shoe with an industrial gray sole about to come down hard on it. "That's not allowed!" She grabs the paper, knocking pencils to the floor, and folds it in her greasy hands.

I want to flick her across the room.

"That's enough, Ally!" Mom says. She stops a rolling pencil with her foot. "Pick these up."

"Okay." Ally groans and looks confused. "What do I do?"

"Pick up the pencils," Mom says. "We'll do it together." She claps her hands and chants, "One for the money, two for the show, three to get ready, four to go."

"That's silly," Ally says.

Mom takes a deep breath.

We pick up the colored pencils together. "You could be faster," Ally tells me. "We should always do our best."

I'm on my knees by the armchair when she walks past and my hand shoots out in front of her foot. She trips and falls. Immediately I feel like a beast—what kind of person trips the six-year-old zombie who used to be his little sister?—but I also feel intensely satisfied. "You should watch where you're going," I tell her.

"You should be respectful of those around you."

I give her the finger when her back is turned. I peek behind the chair and give the spider a thumbs-up.

It doesn't look like Fred has put much effort into his web, but he managed to catch a clothes moth. It struggles from its fate while Fred works up an appetite. I wish he'd just eat it.

Waiting kills me these days. Every moment is fat with hope and dread.

I lie on the floor beside the chair and try to make my mind go blank. Ally's shadow looms over me. I expect her to stomp my face. Instead she steps right over me onto Fred. His web peels off its anchors and sticks to her sock. She grinds the ball of her foot into the floor. Fred is a circle of black goo, his legs torn and scattered around his flattened corpse. Ally swats the web off her foot, catches the moth in the silk, and squashes it between her fingers.

"You have to kill bugs because they're dirty," she tells me.

I just lie there, nodding.

"We have to get out of here before she rats me out," I tell Mom. She's in the bathroom, brushing her teeth. I stir a packet of noodles into a cup of water in the kitchen. "We can't wait for the passport of some kid who might not show till New Year's Day."

Mom sticks her head around the corner. Her eyes are bright, her lips foamy. "Would you leave without Dallas?" she asks excitedly.

"That's not what I meant."

She wipes her face and walks over, rests a hand on my arm. "They're not going to let him go, Max, and taking him without permission is kidnapping."

I rip my arm away. "Man, you're such a liar! You're going back on this now?"

"No. I'm just worried. Our races won't play out well at the border."

She's right. No one would blink an eye at a white family taking a black kid out of the country. But there's no way the border guards will let someone as black as Mom smuggle a white ultimate away forever. "Did you tell Rebecca we're bringing him?" I ask.

"Yes. And if we stay with her, under her last name, Arlington might not find us for a while."

"You think he'll try to find us in Canada?"

"We're kidnapping his child, Max."

There's a knock at the door. We both jump. I figure the room is under surveillance and the word *kidnapping* alerted the cops.

"It's eight o'clock at night," Mom mutters as she goes to the door. I crouch behind her, tiptoeing in my own home.

In the hallway, Dallas waits with a backpack on one shoulder and his RIG in hand. "I'm informing the community about the benefits of our New Education Support Treatment," he says. He chews a bit, and I pull him inside.

Mom pats his arm. "Oh my god, you're good at that. We were just talking about you."

"I know. I had my ear pressed to the door."

"What if the camera saw you do that?" I snap.

He shrugs. "The zombies do it all the time. It's part of their training."

"Could you really hear us?" Mom asks.

"Just the odd word. I'm sorry about Ally."

"We should have left sooner," Mom says. "At least you two are still okay."

Dallas waits for her to shut her bedroom door before he heads toward the living-room couch. "I just came to give you this," he tells me. He unzips his pack and lifts out a blue-flowered pillowcase so full and heavy that the seams stretch tight. He sets it on my lap.

I peek inside—pearls, gold chains, earrings, coins, bundles of paper money. "Jesus, Dallas, is this real?"

He nods. "Austin's been stealing from our parents and their friends since he was little."

I jiggle the contents. "What's it for?"

"For the car, of course."

"I told you. We're trading the apartment for the car."

"Then it's for gas and food and somewhere to stay when you get there."

"When *we* get there."

He shrugs.

"Don't start that again," I say. "You can see your parents when you're an adult."

"It's not that. They don't even like me." He brushes his bangs from his eyes and tries to smile. "I just don't think I can go. What if it's all a spill-zone up there? Or what if there's no work and we end up living in the car? Can we even go to school there? What if they ship us back? Or what if we get killed in Freaktown?"

"It's a lot closer than Mexico. And safer." I try to lighten his mood by asking, "Who would you rather be killed by? A bunch of freaks or a bunch of Mexican drug lords?"

He scratches his head. "I've never been good at decisions."

"We'll be fine, Dallas. The timing is perfect. School's out on Friday. Mom has the weekend off. You can tell your parents you're Christmas shopping. No one will look for us all day. We'll be over the border before they know we're gone."

He nods, but his heart's not in it.

"Mom can probably get you that passport with the name Connors."

He snickers. "I'm a bit pale for your family."

"Then we'll hide you in the trunk," I snap.

"And what if they look?" he snaps back. "You've got this one chance, Max. You can't do anything illegal or they won't let you out."

"It's not illegal to leave."

"I heard that word."

"What word?"

"Kidnapping." He stands and brushes off his pants. "It won't be easy getting me out of here. Even you guys alone might have problems. Your Mom's a lot darker than you. They might think she's taking her kids away from her husband."

"We have his death certificate and all our documents."

"You can't take the chance of getting caught for kidnapping."

"We are not leaving you."

"I'll have another chance, Max. My family has money. I'm almost sixteen. By summer I could have my own car. I can drive myself across the border."

"Summer? Dallas, we've been doing this for eight weeks and we're barely hanging on. How are you ever going to make it through another six months?"

"I can do it. I'm good at it."

"You're falling apart! You'll have nothing left when I'm gone."

He shoulders his pack. "I can do it, Max. I still have my thoughts. I just can't say them out loud. I still have my feelings.

I just can't show them. I still have all the things that used to matter. They're inside me. They can't take that away."

I smack his arm. "Yes, they can! They can take anything away! They just took everything from Ally. They took it from Pepper and Xavier. And they sure took it from Tyler Wilkins, didn't they? If they get their hands on you, Dallas, you will line up and ask them to take those things away."

"Shh!" Mom peeks into the living room, half asleep. "Keep your voices down. Is everything all right?"

"Fine, Mrs. Connors. I'm just leaving." Dallas waits till she's gone, then whispers, "I'll be caught at the border. And I don't want to be caught, Max. I don't want to take that chance. I cannot take the stress of hoping for something that's not going to happen. I'd rather stay here and be hopeless. Then I might be able to hang on."

"To what?"

He doesn't answer. He just leaves.

Mom stomps back in, ready to give us hell for keeping her awake. She softens when she sees my face. "What's wrong?"

"Dallas is scared to come. He thinks he'll get caught."

She nods. "It's risky."

She holds up her hand to stop me from interrupting, but I interrupt anyway. "Maybe we should all stay," I say. "What if things are worse in Canada? Isn't that a theme through history—people go off in search of a better land but they end up in some nightmare and wish they'd never left in the first place?"

"There's also the theme of people going off in search of a better land and finding a better land."

"But if we're the only ones—"

"You're not." She takes my face in her hands. "There is a whole world out there full of normal children, Max. We think because we're trapped here that this is our only choice, but it's not. We'll be okay. Like you said, I'm a nurse. I can find work. We can go anywhere." She kisses my forehead. "We can't stay here for Dallas."

"You're leaving him?"

"No." She nods as she repeats the word. "No."

"I won't leave him, Mom. The teachers and his father? I won't leave him to that. We're taking Dallas or we're not going."

⁕

Montgomery limps into history class wearing a crisp white shirt under his gray uniform. His right arm hangs limp at his side, no rings or dangling bracelets. He holds his neck stiffly, head cocked to the right, the muscles of his face pulled tight, partially paralyzed. I've seen a few kids like that since the shots. I think it's temporary.

Mr. Reese looks up and follows Montgomery with sad dark eyes. Mr. Reese is a mess of sighs and pauses and coffee stains these days. The classroom tiles are spattered with French roast from the door to his desk. He arrives early every morning and projects his instructions so he doesn't have to hear his voice shake while he speaks. He used to be my favorite teacher and I guess he still is, but that's not saying much. Every time I look up, he's on the verge of tears, his eyes fixed on one of us, swimming in memories of better days. There's no outrage in his gaze. No petition, no protest, no hand up for clarification.

Just a dull resignation. Like my mother must have shown when she first started drugging her patients. Sad but self-interested, waiting on a bright side.

I can't think of a single adult that I admire.

"Please begin item one," Mr. Reese says quietly. "Keep your voices low, please." He does a lot of unnecessary begging.

We're supposed to pair up and ask review questions. I turn to Dallas, who sits in the row beside me. He looks away from me and taps Brennan's shoulder. "I need a partner," he says.

Brennan glances at me for a moment before he nods, rises, straddles the back of his seat. He and Dallas stare into their RIGs and murmur answers to each other. They look like they were born best friends—obvious ultimates, worlds away from me, rich and tall and smart.

Next thing I know, Mr. Reese is beside me, his bitter breath falling on my face. "Max, you seem to be the odd man out."

I almost laugh. "That is true, sir. That has always been true."

Mr. Reese frowns on me. "I'll do the review with you if you like. Come up to my desk."

I hate the murmur of voices in the room. I tug on my ears and fold the cartilage against my skull so all I can hear is a dull drowning rush. My face tingles and burns. It launches into spasms I can't control. My eyes blink and tear. My nose itches. My tongue travels inside my mouth, pushing over my teeth, under my lips, against my cheeks, poking around like something trapped and desperate.

"Are you all right?" Mr. Reese asks.

It feels like bugs are living in my eyebrows. My skin crawls with them, and I have a sudden compulsion to peel it off.

I rub my face, and the itch spreads up through my hair and down the back of my neck, across my shoulders, along my forearms, between my fingers. I can't stop clawing at myself.

Mr. Reese grabs my wrists with his pale sweaty hands. "Stop, Max, stop!"

I can't stand the smell of him. I yank myself out of his grip and jump to my feet. "Don't touch me!"

He reaches out like he wants to hug me.

I shove him away, and he slams into the wall. "Don't touch me!" I shriek.

I stumble between the crowded desks, out of the classroom, down the empty hallway. The only sounds are my heels hitting tile and my breath coming sharp. I pass lockers, cameras, corridors lined with photos of previous graduating classes. I walk by the receptionist and the guard and out through the doors of the school. My skin chills and trembles in the cold air, but I'm hot and throbbing inside. I need to run.

I tear away from the school into a maze of gray suburban streets. I run them hard, trying to focus on my breath and the soothing swing of my arms and legs. When I reach the Spartan my legs tremble, my gut rolls, my cheeks tingle. I double over and vomit on the dead grass beside the entrance. Milky puke burns through me and splatters onto my shoes. I retch again and again until my gut aches and my eyes stream and screaming gobs of phlegm are all that come out of me.

I hork and spit. I can't stand the smell of myself. I'm sour and rotten and shaking with cold. I straighten my spine and look around. I'm alone, brown and gray in a brown and gray landscape.

I break three branches off a cedar shrub and lay them over my vomit in a damaged attempt to cover the sight and smell of it. I wipe my hands on the soft creases of my pants and walk into the Spartan, up the stairs, down the stale hallway to my door.

I shower for twenty minutes and brush my teeth twice, then lie down in bed, naked under the covers. It feels too exposed, so I get up and dress. It's so quiet. I might be the only person in the whole building.

I empty the pockets of my uniform and stuff it in a laundry bag. I check my RIG.

Already there's a message from the principal about my outburst, a copy of an official letter to my mother. It informs her that I'm suspended for two days and that "any more unexceptable behavior will lead to expulsion." Seriously, that's how he spells it. A kid could choke to death on irony.

Mom hands me a large black wallet. "This is Cheyenne Connors, your new half-brother."

A sixteen-year-old boy with long black bangs and big blue eyes scowls from a passport. He's six-foot-two, one-hundred-and-seventy pounds. I know the kid—he's a footballer from New Middletown Southeast Secondary School, home of the Blue Mountain Devils.

"He doesn't look much like Dallas," I say.

Mom snatches the passport from my hands. "They're the same height, same weight. We can ask Celeste to make up Dallas's nose and mouth."

"And the birth certificate? Can we put Dad's name on it?"

"I don't have a birth certificate. It wasn't in his wallet. We'll have to take Daddy's passport and death certificate and be prepared to lie."

⋆

I'm in suspended isolation for the next two days. No one posts anything anymore—no journals, gossip, news, snapshots, nothing but school announcements. I don't want to return to classes but I hate being disconnected. Dallas won't answer my coded messages. We're supposed to leave on Saturday.

I'm unsettled in the apartment by myself. I hear noises in the hallway, creaks and murmurs when no one is out there. Yesterday a woman laughed so loud I thought she was in the kitchen. She stood across the hall rummaging in her handbag for a key. I watched her through the peephole. Middle-aged and sagging, with dyed blond hair and a black suit she must have bought when she was thinner. She spoke to a younger woman projected on the wall. "Oh my god, what a bugger!" she yelled, indifferent to the camera and my eyes. "No kidding. They're all the same."

I've looked and listened for her today. I don't know why.

I check out the *Freakshow* tryouts, but there's no one who interests me. I wish they'd bring back Zipperhead.

I do homework and lift weights until I'm bored senseless. I work up the nerve to visit Xavier.

He answers the door himself.

"Xavier? I almost didn't recognize you."

His hair is cut short. He wears white jeans and a blue shirt with a Western motif down the chest. He looks twenty years old, serious, handsome, clean-cut and well rested.

"Hey, Max!" Celeste calls from the living room. She sits on a couch covered in throw blankets, a RIG in her hand. "It's so nice to see you. I'm in a meeting, but come and keep us company."

Xavier steps aside to let me pass. He smells like cheap hand soap, a dusting of baby powder over lye. "It's good to see you," I tell him.

"Thank you." His eyes zoom in on me. He doesn't smile, doesn't sparkle.

"You know who I am, right?"

"Yes, of course. You're Maxwell Connors."

"Good. Royal. You're doing all right? You look healthier."

"Yes, thank you."

"You cut your hair."

"A man should wear short hair."

I smile. "You're sixteen, Xavier."

"Yes. I had a birthday recently."

I nod. "Mine's on Saturday."

He couldn't care less. "I need to do my homework now," he says. He leaves me on my own, sits at a little white desk in the corner, posture perfect on a tall pine chair.

"Xavier's going back to academic school after the holidays!" Celeste shouts over her RIG. "His body chemistry just needed time to harmonize. Thank god. We were so worried. But the new patch works great."

I lean on the sagging back of the couch and look over her shoulder. A color wheel and four faces float above her RIG. "What's your meeting?"

"College yearbook club." She points at me. "You could help with the design! You're such a good artist."

I straighten up, unsure if she's serious, unsure if she's been treated. She gabs to her friends about the color of stars and spirals in the yearbook sidebars. I stand there, awkward and ignored, hands in my pockets, smiling for no reason.

The room is furnished with odds and ends—glass coffee table, pine end tables, black plastic cabinet in the corner. An abstract art print hangs, black and pink, on one wall beside a huge brown Leonardo in an ornate frame. The place smells like bacon grease and disinfectant. It's crazy, like their family.

Xavier's eyes and fingers whip across his screen twice as fast as a normal person's.

"What are you working on?" I ask.

He stiffens, unhappy with my interruption. "It's a translation."

"He translated a whole book last week from English to Russian," Celeste boasts. "Now he's doing it in Spanish. It's his new obsession."

"What book?" I ask. "Can I see?"

Xavier sighs.

I hover over his shoulder. When he looks around, I hop to his other side just to bug him. I lean into his RIG. "I never knew you read poetry."

He shifts his chair away from me. "It's an English poem from a Sumerian text. I'm translating it into Spanish."

"*Gilgamesh?*"

He's surprised I know it. He looks from me to the screen and back.

I shrug. "How many Sumerian poems are there?"

"There are many Sumerian poems."

I laugh. "I didn't know that. But *Gilgamesh* is famous. Pepper rewrote it in Communications last year. What part are you at?"

"I'm half finished."

"What part in the story?"

"It's a poem."

"Is his friend dead yet? I liked his friend better than him." I read the English half of Xavier's screen. "Oh, this part. This is sad." Gilgamesh is in a tunnel, without a friend in the world, and he has to crawl for hours in total darkness to get to the other side. He's lonely and scared and he wants to give up. I sigh, shake my head, mutter, "I've been there."

"No you haven't," Xavier says. "It's from the Middle East."

I smile. "Yeah, but we've all been there."

He squirms on his chair. "No, we haven't."

"Don't agitate him!" Celeste hisses at me.

"Sorry. It's a metaphor."

Xavier shakes his head, furrows his brow, frowns at me with the exact expression Ally uses now, like I'm defective. "It's a poem," he snaps.

I don't like his haircut. I don't like his face with his new haircut. He looks like he was made in a factory. I don't know why he ever reminded me of anything else. "I have to go," I say.

He nods and turns back to his busy-work.

"Oh, hey," Celeste says, glancing away from her yearbook buddies. "Can you take your tent with you? I know it was a gift and everything, but Mom says we don't have room for it and it kind of smells."

I think for a second that she's joking. "You're giving me back my painting?"

"We really like it, Max, but we don't have anywhere to put it so it's kind of a waste."

I look at Xavier. "You don't want your birthday present?"

"It smells funny," he says without bothering to look at me.

Celeste laughs. "It really does."

I hope they're all zombified, the whole Lavigne family. I hate their dirty house and their shiny hair and their poor-but-authentic line of crap. Mostly I hate how much I miss Xavier. I don't bother smiling. "Sure, I'll take it."

As I drag my metaphor down the peeling hallway, I feel angrier but happier at the same time. I saved my tent from being stuffed in a closet full of thrift-store clothing and stacks of useless petitions, from a future folded in on itself until there's no memory of what it ever meant to anyone. To me. This tent is my work, the finest work of my life, and it belongs to me. Besides, I might have to live in it soon.

FIFTEEN

It's Friday, December 23, the last day of school before the holidays. Dallas is heading inside when I arrive at the high school. He holds his ID card under his chin and stares straight ahead. I take my place in line, quiet and cold like the world around me.

I sit behind him in Communications, still waiting my turn. Mr. Ames hands out holiday assignments on "persuasive nonfiction." Our syllabus used to list epic poetry for this term, but zombies don't care about fallen comrades. *Mail delivery from ancient to modern times* is a brain we can sink our teeth into.

"Yum," I say to Dallas as I read the list of topics.

He doesn't hear.

"Bring something of yourselves to this piece," Mr. Ames says. "Any questions?"

We stare blankly.

He sighs. "You children are not what you used to be."

I try Dallas again at lunch. I shuffle behind him in the lineup and say, "My mother watched a movie about zombies last night. They ate people's brains."

He doesn't look at me. His eyes follow the cheesy macaroni spreading across his plate in a yellow ooze. His eyelids are purple with fatigue, black against the bridge of his nose.

I tap his shoulder. "Did you see that movie?"

He turns to me like he just realized I exist. No smile behind his eyes. No chewing. No clue. "I used to watch movies," he says. "I don't watch them anymore. I don't know why." He grabs his tray and sits at the nearest empty chair between two strangers.

Brennan nudges my spine. "Shake it off," he whispers without moving his lips.

I'm not aware of ordering lunch. I'm sitting at the end of a long table beside Brennan, staring at a tray of food I don't want to eat—mushy vegetable soup, cold bread, bitter grapes.

Across the room, Dallas chews and chews but never seems to swallow. Eventually he rises and stacks his plates on the trolley. His jacket stretches tight across his shoulders but his pants barely hang on to his ass. He's skinnier than he was three days ago.

"Stop staring," Brennan whispers. He has a natural talent for ventriloquism. "Eat your food."

I suck a spoonful of gelatin back and forth between my teeth until it liquefies with a red squeak.

History is excruciating. We study industrial catastrophes through the ages. We leave out the suffering and death, skip who's to blame and focus on the bouncing-back techniques, every nose to a grindstone, getting the job done right.

Mr. Reese doesn't participate. He shows a documentary, assigns a reading, points to questions on the screen, goes about his duties like a secretary to his former self. I hate him and all that he withstands. I hate him like I hate my mother, whom I love and wish I didn't hate but I can't help it. I hate every adult who feels bad about what they're doing and does it anyway, sighing with every breath, clinging to the notion that they're good people in bad times. I hate them for not standing up for me. I hate them for not helping me stand up for myself. I hate them for not teaching me to care about all the people they mowed down before they got around to us. I hope they choke on all their coffee-talk and tissues.

Mr. Reese squeezes down the aisles, inspecting our progress. I stick my foot out, and he stumbles, shocked and outraged but too scared to tell. I continue my work.

I'm no good at history anymore. I can't separate the past from the future.

I harass Dallas at the lockers before gym class, stand too close and whisper, "Did you know that zombies eat brains?"

"No." He reaches around me for his water bottle.

I'm right behind him at the gymnasium doors.

Coach Emery lays a hand on my shoulder and keeps it there. "You look tired, Connors. Do you need to sit on a bench?"

I realize I'm staring after Dallas like a kid watching his daddy leave the daycare. I take a deep breath and relax the muscles of my face.

"There's more to health than exercise," the coach says. "Did you get a proper sleep?"

"Yes, sir."

"You're all right to participate?"

"Yes, sir."

He pats my shoulder. "Good boy. You don't want to be sick for the holidays."

"No, sir."

We start with laps. I can't tell if I'm imagining things or if Dallas speeds up whenever I close in on him.

"Stay as a group! This is not a race!" Coach Emery shouts.

We form small circles for basketball drills, passing and stealing the ball. Dallas stands directly across from me, next to Brennan. His T-shirt drapes over his ribs. The veins of his arms snake along his pale flesh like a topographical map. His eyes drift over me as they follow the ball. I fumble on purpose, but he doesn't react.

"Pick it up and try again," the coach says.

I slam it straight at Dallas. Brennan ducks in reflex. Dallas catches the ball half an inch from his nose without flinching and bounces it over to Bay.

"Careful how you throw!" Coach Emery shouts. "You must remain aware of your situation and those around you."

Every time I get the ball I slam it at Dallas. He never tires of it.

Coach Emery finally grabs the ball from my hands and shouts in my face, "Spit that gum out of your mouth, Connors! You know there's no chewing gum in my gym!"

"I don't have any gum, sir."

He frowns. "What the hell are you chewing then?"

"I don't know, sir."

He puts his hand on my forehead, like I might be coming down with something. "Go sit on the bench."

I sit out the rest of class. I close my eyes, take shallow breaths, listen to the ball bounce off the gym floor. *Boom, boom, boom.*

The coach kicks my foot as he walks by, and I realize I'm muttering to myself and pulling all the hairs from my thighs.

I sit on my hands, stare at the ropes that hang off the far wall, multiply numbers in my head. Two times two is four times two is eight times two is sixteen, and on and on until the trillions jumble in my head and I have to start over and over and finally the bell rings.

Panic grips me in the shower. I can't accept the fact that Dallas has been treated just before we leave. I cannot live with that.

I adjust the water temperature. The drops hit me like a thousand needles, freezing then scalding then freezing. The stench of chlorine fills my nose and lungs. I hear murmuring beneath the hiss of water and slap of feet. I jerk my head around, ready for a trap, but all I see are silent boys draped in towels, walking away to dress or waiting their turn in the water.

I watch Dallas from the corner of my eye, not caring if I come off gay. He faces the showerhead, moves slowly but efficiently like all the others. He rinses and towels off and walks away without looking at me once.

"Get dressed, Connors! You're lagging behind!" Coach Emery shouts from the door. I haven't even soaped yet, but I don't bother. I shut off the taps and cover myself.

The coach stops Dallas from leaving the room. "Somebody," he announces to the half-naked class, "I'm not saying who, but somebody left a water bottle on the football field, and you all know how I like a clean field. I want two volunteers to walk the yards and check for litter." He points at Dallas, then across the room at me. "I want to see you two march like soldiers up and down that field. Pick up any garbage you find. Make sure you check around the trailer. The rest of you are free to go. Merry Christmas."

I dress hurriedly, not caring that my socks are inside out. As I tie my shoes, I notice that my hands are trembling.

Brennan drops his shoes on the floor at my feet and sits beside me on the bench. He lowers his head and whispers, "Don't ask any questions till you're away from the cameras." He wriggles his foot into his shoe and leans down to tie it tight. "Don't give yourself away to him, just in case. Let us know what you find out."

He stands up and passes me a swift sympathetic glance. As he reaches down for his dirty sweats, he adds, "Then get out, Max. With or without him."

When Brennan leaves, I'm all that's left in the change room. I like it here. It's smelly but it smells like kids. Whatever the treatment did to them, it didn't improve their stink.

Coach Emery sticks his head around the corner. "Time is ticking."

<hr />

Dallas and I drop our packs at the trailer and walk to the field in silence. I should have worn my coat, but it's stuffed in my bag and I'm not thinking straight. I button my uniform, turn up my collar, shove my hands in my pockets. Dallas walks tall beside me, zipped and hooded. I can barely see his face.

The field is an expanse of dead grass fringed with skeletal trees in the west. They reach into a monotonous sky of the palest gray. The sun is a bright disk behind the clouds, already sinking at three thirty in the afternoon.

It's strange to walk this field in shoes instead of cleats. The ground is hard beneath me, the blades of grass stiff and slippery.

"We should separate and begin at opposite ends," Dallas says.

"No. We should walk together."

"It's more efficient to separate."

"Four eyes are better than two."

"No," he says. "Two eyes—"

"We're walking together."

Sixty thousand is a lot of square feet when you're walking it with a zombie. Fifty paces take us to the sideline, where we square off and head back like we're mowing a lawn. The school looks formidable in the winter light, six units of ambition stretching into the distance, a place where futures are decided behind black glass.

The students are probably walking out the front doors now, or already gone home for the holidays. The teachers are still here—I see their bikes and Mr. Graham's car in the lot— but they don't show any sign of life. It feels like we're alone.

We reach the sideline, square off, head west again. Dallas lowers his eyes but keeps his chin up, so it looks like he's staring down his nose. I imitate him, but he doesn't notice. He doesn't care.

"What did you do after the library last night?" I ask.

"Small talk distracts us from our work."

I want to swat him. "What did you do?" I repeat.

He stops and stares at me like I'm defective. Then he furrows his brow. "I don't remember." He shivers and walks on, staring down his nose.

"Did you watch a show? Did you do homework? Did you take any medicine?"

"You should look at the football field, not at me."

"There's nothing on the football field! I can see the whole thing from here. It's clean. There is no one left in our school who would even think of throwing garbage on this field." I stumble into him on purpose, banging his shoulder. "No one except you and me."

He stops walking. "I would never throw garbage on the football field. That's wrong! Why would you throw garbage on the football field? We're lucky to have a football field. We should take care of what we have."

I want to take his head off. I want to rip out his larynx. I want to knee his testicles into a useless pulp. My cheeks burn as I stare up into his eyes. God, I wish I was taller. I could kick his ass when we were small. He tapped out every time. Now he could hold me off at arm's length while he picked his nose.

There's outrage in his expression, but it's the outrage of Lucas and Ally and all the other tattler zombies.

I can't stand to think of him telling on me. He never told when I broke his dad's headlight last summer, or when I loosened the lid on Coach Emery's thermos in grade nine so he scalded himself and had to go to the hospital. He never told when I ran away after Dad died and hid in our empty house overnight, or when I forgot Ally in the yard when she was two and we found her in the core an hour later. He never told on a single wrong thing I did in the past fifteen years. But now we're almost grown and he'd turn me in for a piece of garbage.

The fact that there is no one in this world who cares about me except my mother is just too much truth to bear. My face starts to tingle like I'm going to cry or throw up. I can't talk anymore. The field is under surveillance and my tongue is too heavy to move.

For ten more minutes we walk in silence side by side, searching the field and bleachers for garbage nobody believes is there. I pretend the kid beside me is someone else, some new kid whose name I don't know.

"It's clean," Dallas announces when we reach the end of the bleachers.

I have to bite my tongue to keep from crying, I'm so exhausted. My blood washes warm against my teeth.

"Now we'll check the trailer," he says.

I don't go inside with him. I stare at the ground because I don't want my grief-stricken face on camera. When I reach the back of the trailer, out of view, I start to shake. I bite my lips and wipe my nose and groan and hyperventilate and stomp the ground and do everything I can to keep from crying like a baby. I bang my face on the trailer wall and I like the feel of it, firm but with a little give, so I do it harder and harder, in the dead center of my forehead, and it feels like nirvana is just one knock away. But it's not a typical zombie move, so when I see Dallas at the corner, watching me in confusion, I know I'm wrecked. He's going to rat me out.

"What the hell do you want?" I say, sniffing my weakness up my nose.

He stares blankly, silhouetted by the winter sun.

"Come here," I tell him.

"I am here."

"Closer."

He hesitates, but then he takes one step, out of view of the cameras.

I grab on to his winter coat and slam him against the trailer.

"Ow!" he says. "Stop this. I want you to stop."

"I don't care what you want."

He frowns and tries to pry my fingers off his clothing.

"We're supposed to meet tomorrow at my apartment," I say. "You'll tell your father you're at the library, but you'll come to my place instead. You told me to come and get you if you don't show up. Do you remember that?"

He pulls on my thumb but otherwise ignores me.

I shake him, rattling his shoulders into the wall. "Do you remember that?"

"I remember that, but it was wrong. It's wrong to force someone to do something they don't want to do." He gives up on my hands. He unzips his coat and pulls his arms out of it, leaving it empty in my grasp.

He's walking away, and I can't accept that. I plow into his back and tackle him to the ground. He tries to roll me off, but I slam my knee into his spine and force his head into the dirt, my elbow jammed in his temple.

"You come over tomorrow morning," I say. "Or I'll come to your house and haul you out of it."

He lies there, unresisting.

"You hear me?"

No response.

I worry that I might have hurt him. If he takes medications I don't know about, I might have rattled his brain into a seizure.

"Dallas? Dallas, are you all right?" I get off him, turn him over, stare into his vacant eyes.

He blinks. He sits up and wipes the dead grass and dirt off his cheek. He rises to his feet and brushes off his uniform.

"Are you all right?" I repeat.

"I'm fine." He picks up his coat and turns to leave.

"No!" I shout, pulling him back. "No way! You're not leaving till you promise to come over in the morning."

He shakes his head. "I have work to do in the morning."

"No, you don't." I grab the gray lapels of his uniform and pull him closer. "I'm taking you with me."

He brushes at my fingers. "That would be wrong."

"I'm not leaving you here!" I scream those words, and I can't stop screaming them. I shove him hard into the wall, over and over, stabbing my knuckles into his ribs. "I'm not leaving you here! I'm not leaving you here!"

"Stop!" He peels my hands off him and holds them in his fists. "There is something wrong with you. You need to see a doctor."

Suddenly I'm fighting tears again. All my tension—hours and days and weeks of it—starts to leak out of me. "I'm not leaving you here," I whisper and choke. "I'm the only person who cares who you are. I'm the only friend you've got."

He smiles and lets go of my hands. "All our schoolmates are my friends."

I smack his head.

His eyes darken and he gathers himself, tight and tense. "I have to go." His voice rumbles deep and low. It's an awful sound because it's almost real and my hope rises to the bait.

"Dallas?" I try to catch his eye, but he stares at my hands where they cling to him.

He clenches his jaw. "Let go of me." He leans into me, wraps his hands around mine, crushes my fingers.

I wince but I can take it. "Dallas? Is that you?"

He wrenches my hands from his uniform and pushes me away.

"No!" I hurl him around and slam him into the wall. I shove my forearm into his throat and press on his windpipe. "Where do you have to go? Are you going to tell a teacher?"

He doesn't move, doesn't look me in the eye, doesn't answer. But he's shaking. He's angry, he's losing it, I can feel him start to burn.

"If you were one of them, you'd tell a teacher," I say.

He breathes deeply, blinks, says, "I don't want to hurt you. You're too damaged already. We should be kind to those less fortunate than ourselves."

I step back and slap him across the face. His head swings against the wall and my handprint blooms pink on his pale cheek. "You are not one of them!"

He shakes his head and snorts. "You're having mental health troubles. You need to see a doctor." There's nothing in his eyes, no sparkle, no hidden message. He's angry because I'm in his way. I'm disobedient. I'm history.

"You're not one of them!" I shout. "You're not! You're not!" I slap his face over and over until I'm out of energy and his cheek is flaming red and I'm just sort of patting him and bawling my eyes out, begging, "You can't be, man. You can't be one of them. You can't be."

"What have we here?" Mr. Graham stands at the corner of the trailer, smiling at me, round and shiny as a big white ball.

SIXTEEN

I shiver with cold and fear. I'm finished.

Dallas straightens up, takes my hands off his uniform, places them at my sides. "Max is unwell, sir. He needs to go home."

The principal smiles. "I have just the thing to make him better." He moves fast for a fat man. He's at my side in a flash, hugely tall and wide, wrenching my arms behind my back.

Dallas stands just inches away, looking down on my struggle, doing absolutely nothing. "Pass me your necktie, Richmond," Mr. Graham tells him, and he does.

The principal ties my wrists behind my back and pats my shoulder. "Now, Connors, stay calm."

"Max needs to go home to his mother," Dallas says. "She's a nurse."

Mr. Graham snickers. "I don't want to send Maxwell home just yet. I might lose him over the holidays, and I don't want that. Once he masters his antisocial tendencies, he'll do the school proud." He moves in front of me and pats Dallas. "Good boy, Richmond. Your father told me to keep an eye on you two."

Dallas stiffens, blinks rapidly, clenches his jaw.

I arch my back and stretch my arms in hope of getting my hands around my legs and up in front of me, but they get stuck on my ass. Mr. Graham laughs at me. He grips my arm tightly. "Come back to my office now, Connors. I'll drive you home from school today." He looks at Dallas and smiles. "You're free to go. Merry Christmas."

He pushes me ahead of him, away from the trailer. I have a brief view of the school and the frozen grounds. I see Mr. Reese walking across the parking lot. He has a coffee cup in one hand, briefcase in the other. He's the only person in sight.

"Wait!" Dallas shouts. "There's something in the trailer you should see, sir."

Mr. Graham pauses, turns, yanks me back out of view. "What?"

Dallas blinks rapidly. "There's something in the trailer, sir. You need to see it."

"Can't it wait? It's Christmas."

"No, sir, it can't wait."

Mr. Graham huffs, scowls, rolls his eyes. "All right. Go get it."

Dallas nods. He picks up his coat and turns the corner.

I hear scraping and thumping from inside the trailer. I think about tearing free and running for it, but I'm reluctant to try. Part of me wants to see how it all ends. I don't feel like it's really me tied up, about to be zombified. I feel like I'm beyond this moment, above it all, looking down on the last kid on Earth.

Mr. Graham frowns at my misery. "It's much better this way, son. They've done studies to back that up. You'll be glad once you experience it." He pats my shoulder, but I shrug him off. He runs his hand over his fat face. "Believe me, you will never want to go back to the way you are now. And you won't have to. Other parts of the country can't afford to keep up the treatments, but we're privileged here, Connors. The future is in our hands."

I hear Dallas stomp down the trailer stairs. I regret not running away. I reconsider it—there could be another teacher on his way home, Mr. Ames or Coach Emery—but I don't bother. I don't do anything except stand in the shadows and wait. The skin on my face is tight where my tears have dried. I can't believe I made such an ass of myself. I'll be sixteen years old tomorrow and I still cry in public.

Dallas waits at the corner of the trailer. He wears his football face, stands taller and stronger than I've seen him all day.

"Where is it?" Mr. Graham asks.

"I can't get it because it's on the wall." Dallas's voice is different. Deliberate.

Mr. Graham snorts. "Thank you, son, but I am not interested in graffiti. It's the Christmas holidays. It can wait."

"It's not graffiti, sir. It's a list of names."

"Whatever, son. I'm not interested. I have to get Connors fixed up and get him home before his mother comes running over in a fury." He turns away with a tight grip on my arm.

"It's important, sir!" Dallas shouts. His jaw twitches and he blinks too fast. "I saw Max's name on the wall while I was cleaning the trailer. I moved the bench and found a list of students who missed the vaccinations."

Mr. Graham turns around and rubs his belly. "Really? Who's on the list?"

"I don't remember, sir. It's on the wall."

He's lying. I know he's lying.

The principal weighs the benefits of such a list against the hassle of climbing three steps. Dallas holds his gaze with too much interest for a zombie. "All right," Mr. Graham says. "Lead the way."

He pushes me ahead of him, up the steps and inside the trailer after Dallas. He sniffs the stale sweat and makes a face. "How do you all fit in here? You change in this trailer? The whole team? With the pads in the way? How do you keep from falling over each other?"

I barely hear him. I'm staring at the trailer's security camera. Dallas's coat is covering it—not hanging from it but wrapped around it tightly and fastened with tape. My skin crawls, thinking of all that could happen in a room like this when no one's watching.

Dallas waits in the far corner, so tall that he has to hunch. He stares at me, his eyes deep in his thoughts, his face twitching, his jaw moving up and down in a chewing motion. He has a weight belt wrapped tight around his right fist.

"No," I whisper. "No way."

"So where's the list?" Mr. Graham asks.

Dallas points to the wall beside him. "It's right here, sir, behind this bench."

"No, it's not," I say. "I erased it earlier when we cleaned the trailer. I saw that Dallas found it so I erased it."

"No, you didn't. It's still there," Dallas says. "It's just hard to read."

"Mr. Graham, there's nothing there. Let's just go." I strain against my bonds. "Just get out of here."

"How can you care about people who care nothing about you?" Dallas asks.

"I care about *you*," I tell him. "Where are you going to go after this? You're not thinking straight. You haven't slept or eaten for days. You're all messed up."

Mr. Graham eyes me suspiciously and shuts the trailer door. He looks at Dallas, raises his hands, rolls his eyes. "Move the bench so I can see."

"No. This can't happen," I say. "I'll take the shot. I'll take the shot and Mom will take us somewhere safe until it wears off."

Mr. Graham snorts like I'm a babbling recall. "I want to see that list."

Dallas leans over, grabs the bottom of the bench with his left hand and tugs it out from the wall. He rises, points and waits.

Mr. Graham shoves my shoulder down. I realize I'm bouncing on the balls of my feet, edgy with nerves and the fear that my best friend is about to kill our principal. "Keep an eye on him," he says to Dallas.

"Yes, sir." Dallas's eyes track Mr. Graham as he walks to the bench.

"No!" I shout.

Mr. Graham leans over, hands on the bench, looking for the writing on the wall. "I don't see anything." His belly grazes the wood, his head hangs there like an offering.

Dallas raises his fist, ready to slam the weight belt into Mr. Graham's skull.

I dive for him. I pitch forward and ram my head into Dallas's hollow belly as fast and hard as I can. He smashes into the wall and slams his weighted fist into my back. I jerk to my knees. We fall, knocking the principal off his feet. Mr. Graham collapses in the crowded corner. His arms give way beneath him, his cheek hits the bench. *Oomph, crack, crash.*

Dallas lifts me off him like a weight bar and hurls me aside with a strength that doesn't come from calories. I fall into a pile of ripped pads and cracked helmets, smashing my elbow and my ass.

Dallas rises to his feet. He straddles Mr. Graham's broad back, lifts him by the suit collar, and slams his head into the bench. *Crunch.*

"No!" I shriek. "Stop!"

Mr. Graham isn't moving. Dallas presses a hand on his back while he leans over to pick up the weight belt from the floor.

"Untie me!" I yell. "My arm's twisted. It's going to break!" I grimace and moan.

He doesn't even look. "In a second."

I kick at his feet. "Now, man! There's something wrong with my elbow. I think it's going to break."

He rolls his eyes and swears. He keeps his legs around Mr. Graham, holding him in place with his head on the bench, and gestures impatiently at me.

I rise and offer the wrists behind my back. "What are you doing, Dallas?" I whisper.

He shoves my shoulder down, yanks my arms up until I scream, and frees his necktie from my hands.

"Thanks, man." I grab his arm and fake a smile. "Let's go."

He doesn't smile back, doesn't even seem to recognize me. He turns away and wraps the tie around Mr. Graham's throat.

"No!" I claw at him and pull him off the principal. He tumbles onto his shoulder and swears. He knees me in the gut and slams his palm into my temple. I roll away from him, my head ringing in pain. He kicks at me furiously, knocking the bench onto its side. Mr. Graham thumps to the floor. *Thud.*

Dallas whips his head toward the sound. He sees a job half finished.

I grab the necktie and throw it across the room. Dallas reaches for the weight belt. I throw myself on it and trap it beneath my knee. He tugs, sighs, looks at me like this silliness won't be tolerated.

"You can't do this," I say. I grab his lapels, lean into his face, speak softly, reasonably. "Dallas? Dallas, you can't do this, man. Look what you're doing."

He stares at me like he hates me.

"You can't walk away from something like this. You do this and that's it, man, you go to jail, you don't go anywhere else."

He runs his tongue over his teeth, waiting for my lecture to end.

I slap his face. "Do you hear me? Get control of yourself. Look what you're doing. Look where we are. Remember all the kids who used to be in this trailer? Remember our friends? We are all that's left, man. We have to get out of here, Dallas. You're not thinking straight."

He leans away from me, looks around the trailer, stares up at his coat wrapped over the security camera. He furrows his brow, scratches his elbow, lifts up the sleeve of his uniform and tugs down a roll of duct tape he had jammed around his forearm.

"Oh, Jesus, no. That's the principal, Dallas. This is assault. You stop now, you're fine. It was an accident. He got hurt when I tackled you. The bench fell on his head. Leave it like this. You're going to get us both executed!"

He pushes me away from him, sits on his ass, sucks in his cheeks. He nods. His eyes soften. He glances at Mr. Graham and asks, "Is he alive?"

I get on my knees and feel for a pulse. "He's fine." The principal's mouth is bleeding. A huge bruise blooms across his torn cheek and a cartoon lump rises on his forehead. "He'll have some swelling. He should have his head checked." I lean back and try to think of a plan. "We should put him in recovery position," I say, not moving an inch, just staring at Mr. Graham prone at our feet.

Dallas starts to curse, an aimless barrage of swear words that seem to soothe him. "You shouldn't have hit me. I would have told on you if I'd really been treated."

"I didn't care."

He rubs his cheek. "What's with the slapping? Could you not hit me properly?"

"Are you okay now? You were far gone, man. You weren't really going to kill him, were you?"

He snorts, stretches his neck, stares at the ceiling. "It seemed like a good idea at the time."

"We have to get out of here. We have to leave tonight."

He smiles sadly. "I'm not coming with you, Max. I don't want to get caught. Your mom will go to jail for kidnapping. You'll be treated and so will I. I'm not taking that chance."

He waves a hand toward Mr. Graham. "Now they'll be after you for this too."

"This was an accident. Sort of."

"I can stay here and tell them that."

"I can't leave you here."

He laughs as he grabs my hand, which I realize I've wrapped around his lapel again. "Honestly, I'm not that way, Max. Give it up."

I'm not smiling this time. "You're coming with us or we're not going."

"They won't let you take me out of the country."

"My cousin said other families are leaving with no problem. Lots of them."

"Families, Max. We are not a family. I can't pass for your brother." He puts his hand on my shoulder, all mature now. "We're cinnamon and garlic, remember?"

I do remember, and the solution to our problem hits me so hard, it's a flash in my brain that actually hurts. I grab his hand with both of mine and laugh.

He pushes me away. "Stop it! Enough with the touching."

I jump to my feet, smiling. "You got it, Dallas! What you just said. That's exactly right."

"About what?"

"Salt and pepper."

"We're going to wear our Halloween costumes to Canada? Is that your distraction strategy? 'We're not runaways, officer— we're shakers?'"

"No! But they'll let us cross. They will." Energy pulses through me. I could run a five-minute mile. "We have to get out of here." I run my hands over the principal, check his airways and circulation. "We have to find a teacher to take him to the hospital. Can you go out there and be a zombie again?"

Dallas shakes his head. "I'm never going out there again." He picks up everything he can reach from where he sits—weight belts, jump ropes, helmets—and piles them on his legs. "Can you pass me that shield? Thanks." He leans back and props a long red pad over his torso and head. "I'm going to melt into the walls now. Someone will scrape me off in the spring." He starts to giggle.

"You need to eat, man. Come on. We have to get help."

There's a knock at the trailer door.

I scream. Dallas snickers. He peeks out from behind his shield. "Maybe we can hide him." He points at Mr. Graham—face down on the trailer floor, huge and immobile, his legs and arms splayed, covering half the open ground between us and the door—and he starts to laugh, big and goofy, from the gut. He swats at the air, hunches over the debris around him, gasps for breath.

I get up and walk to the door.

"Who is it?" Dallas calls out in a girlish voice; then he laughs hysterically, listing to one side and kicking his feet. His face pulls into a grimace as he runs out of breath. His mouth gapes, but he's silent except for his heels banging the floor and his laughter clicking quietly in the back of his throat.

"It's Coach Emery! Open up!"

I obey. The coach glares from the trailer steps. "Why is this door closed?"

"Mr. Graham closed it."

"Mr. Graham? What on earth was—?" He walks inside and falls silent. He stares at the principal, sprawled on the floor, and Dallas, curled up and quivering.

"Hey, Coach," Dallas squeaks and heads into hysterics again, slapping his knee.

The coach rushes to Mr. Graham's side, checks his pulse, turns him over and gasps at his bloody face.

"He hit his head," I say. "Dallas and I were fighting and we pushed him into the wall accidentally and he fell into the bench. He's been unconscious for a few minutes. He needs a doctor."

Coach Emery looks up at the security camera.

"We panicked," I say.

"What's wrong with Richmond?"

"He's exhausted."

"Not treated?"

"No, sir."

"And Mr. Graham knows that?"

"I don't think so, sir. He knows I'm not but I don't think he suspects Dallas isn't." I tell the coach what happened and how it's conceivable that the principal's injuries are accidental.

"You need to leave now," he says.

I nod. "We have a plan."

"I don't want to know it." The coach looks at Mr. Graham and shakes his head. "You can't leave the country if there are charges against you."

"It was an accident, sir."

Dallas sighs and wipes his eyes. "I did it."

"It was an accident," I repeat.

The coach looks from one of us to the other. "I should never have sent you out here."

"It's not—"

He silences me with a hand, reassesses the situation—me, Dallas, the disabled camera, our disabled principal—and comes up with a game plan. "Can you pull yourself together?" he asks Dallas.

Dallas shakes himself like a dog and stands up, tall and vacant.

"All right," the coach says. "You and I will go into the school and get security."

"No. We have to get out of here," I say. "We have a plan."

"Shut up, Connors," Coach Emery says. "This is the plan. You're leaving tonight."

"I'm not going without Dallas."

"He'll meet up with you."

"He won't. I'm taking him now or he'll chicken out."

Coach Emery swears. "All right. Both of you go then. I'll get Mr. Graham to a hospital. I'll say I walked in and saw you two fighting and you accidentally knocked him into the bench." He looks at Dallas. "I'll tell your father you went somewhere. Where would you go if you were treated?"

He shrugs. "The library, maybe. Or Christmas shopping."

"That'll do for an hour or two. But where would you go for the next few years? Do you have any friends in other cities? Anything you ever wanted to do, like join the military?"

Dallas shrugs.

"If you disappear tonight, your father will go straight to the Connors," the coach says. "He'll go wherever they go and take you back unless he has another trail to follow."

"I guess I always wanted to be an actor," Dallas says.

Coach Emery nods. "Good. Write your parents to say you're going to California to work in the trade that best suits your skills. Then get rid of your RIG so they can't trace you. And find a way not to be there when they come knocking on Connors's door." He looks at Mr. Graham. "How long has he been unconscious?"

"Several minutes," I say. "We didn't mean to hurt him, sir."

"I did," Dallas says. He looks at Graham with disgust.

"Thank you for doing this, Coach," I say.

"Just go. I'll give you five minutes before I take him out. You have to leave town tonight. Right away." He starts tugging the tape off Dallas's coat. "Do you want to take this?" he asks me.

"It's mine," Dallas says.

The coach looks at him in surprise. Everyone always blames me for everything.

"It's the only thing I own now," Dallas says. He grabs his coat, and we turn our backs on the camera, walk outside into the sights of another camera.

"Good luck wherever you're going," Coach Emery says.

Little Jack Horner
Sat in a corner
Eating his Christmas pie.
He put in his thumb
And pulled out a plum
And said, "What a good boy am I!"

Eighteenth-century nursery rhyme

PART THREE
REJECTION

SEVENTEEN

At six o'clock I leave Dallas at my kitchen table with Celeste and head for Kim's Trims. It's dark and the temperature's dropping, but sweat drips down my ribcage beneath my coat. I walk quickly, careful not to draw attention. The library closes at eight, and after that Dr. Richmond will come looking for his son.

Halfway down Fairfield Road I get a message from Coach Emery. Mr. Graham is awake, confused, suspicious. The police are accessing the school surveillance data to corroborate the coach's testimony that the principal's injuries were accidental.

I break into a run. This is how it happens in Xavier's old movies. The hero embarks on his escape and there's the bad guy waiting for him, snickering, right behind him all along. Dallas was right—living with hope is like rubbing up against a cheese grater. It keeps taking slices off you until there's so little left you just crumble.

Kim is alone with the lights dimmed when I enter her shop. "All set?" she asks.

"Do you have the keys?"

She shows me a picture of a fat green car. "It's a station wagon, two thousand and twelve, legally registered."

"Two thousand and twelve? That's ancient. It still runs?"

"It runs fine. The tank is full, and there's two cans in the trunk in case you run out."

"Is that possible? It doesn't tell you if it's about to run out of fuel?" I picture us stranded on the highway at midnight, hunkered in the backseat under our leather coats, staring through tinted glass at some flat moonlit landscape writhing with drug-crazed freaks and freebies.

Kim laughs at my expression. "It doesn't speak, so you have to watch the dials. It's perfectly safe. Your mom knows how to drive it."

"You spoke to my mom?"

She nods. "She came in for a cut. I did what I could. You got lucky on hair."

I run my hand over my head self-consciously. "So where's the car?"

She holds up her RIG and projects a map of the city. She zooms in on the southwest quadrant, then slides the safe streets of New Middletown out of view to display the makeshift world beyond the walls, a sprawling shanty town I've been warned to stay away from my entire life. "You know the car park where I live? Just past that, on the south side—don't go north to the old strip mall, you don't want to take any valuables that way—but south of the carpark, along the old two-lane highway, you'll find my son with your car."

She shows me a picture of a white man in his twenties. "This is Churchill. He'll be there all evening."

"He's just standing there?"

She rolls her eyes. "It's a car full of gasoline. What do you expect him to do? He has a second key in case he has to move it."

"Why would he have to move it?"

"Don't worry, kid. He won't. I told him you'd be there at seven." She checks her watch. "Is that still your plan?"

"Yeah. Thanks. I have to run. Are you coming back with me to see the apartment?"

She shakes her head. "I'm going out to celebrate. But I'll take your keys."

"There's a code for the stairwell—"

"Got it." She stares at my keys like they'll open the gates to heaven. "I'm so excited I can't tell you, kid. Don't change your mind."

"I won't."

She smiles. "You're a good boy, Max. I'll miss you."

I can't say the same, but you never know what you'll miss about your life after it's gone.

Back at home, my dad is sitting at the kitchen table.

"Told you I was top of my class," Celeste says.

Dallas smiles. He beams. He radiates joy that pierces through all the makeup Celeste has packed on his face.

I can barely speak I'm so impressed. "I can't recognize you."

"That's the idea."

"How'd you get so blond?"

"It's a wig," Celeste says. "A woman's wig, but I cut it into shape. Do you like it?"

"Yeah. I should have gone to you for haircuts all these years."

"He's right, Celeste," Dallas says. "You could have been doing us regularly."

"That's just damaged now that you're middle-aged," I tell him.

"Keep it down," Mom calls from the living room.

"Ally's upset," Dallas whispers.

"You have to work on your voice," I tell him. "You sound too young."

"My daughter's confused by my return to life," he says, deep and smiling.

I can't smile back. I should be happy because this plan is sure to work, but it saddens me to see my father at the table. I want to tell him what I've been up to for the past three years.

Mom comes in and kisses my cheek. "You'll get used to it." She stares at the face of her dead husband and sighs. "Well, no you won't. Just get your bags."

"What's with Ally?" I ask, peeking into the living room. "Is she asleep?"

"Just resting."

"Your mom had to give her a sedative," Celeste whispers. "She freaked out when she saw her dad. I don't know why— you said it was her Christmas wish to be with him one more time, right?"

"Right," I say. "That's why we're doing it." I wish we could tell Celeste the truth, but it's better this way. If the police interview her, she might say we played a sadistic prank on my sister, but at least she won't say where we've gone.

"She doesn't seem happy about it," Celeste says. "Maybe I should take it off and try again Christmas morning."

"No!" I shout with Mom and Dallas.

"It's the best present we can give her," Mom says. "Besides, we'll be in Atlanta on Christmas morning."

My eyes return to Dallas. My father smiles at me. I shudder. "Are we ready?"

He pulls a stained towel from his shirt collar, brushes off his hands, rises tall and pale beside my mother.

"You look forty years old," I tell him.

"Forty-six," he says. "I like to keep fit."

"Was Dad really this tall?"

"Almost," Mom says.

"Why am I so short?"

Dallas laughs. "You got my artistic genes, son."

"Let's go," Mom says. "Thank you, Celeste. Thank you so much." She practically pushes Celeste out the door. She checks that our passports, IDs, immunization records and birth certificates are in her handbag. She keeps her money and the jewelry Dallas stole from his brother in a suitcase with files of papers for Rebecca. "Get rid of your RIG," she tells Dallas. "We all should."

I groan and fret. "Can't we just take the batteries out?"

We all stare at our RIGs with no idea how they work.

"I'll ask Xavier," I say.

"I'm throwing mine out," Dallas says. "But first I have to write my father and tell him I'm headed for Dallas."

"I thought you were going to California," I say.

"No. That coast is toast and zombies don't aspire to acting careers. I'll fulfill my destiny in Dallas."

"Because of your name?"

"It's something a zombie would do, don't you think?"

"They do whatever they're told."

He shrugs. "Mr. Graham said, 'Go home, Dallas.' I could have misheard."

"We're supposed to be zombies, man. Not morons."

"Have you got a better idea?"

I admit that I don't.

I head down the hallway. "I need to say goodbye to Xavier," I tell Celeste. Xavier sits at his white desk, fingering his projection and muttering. "He's doing really well," Celeste tells me. "He'll be ready for school in January."

I nod. "I'm sure he'll be fine eventually."

That's what Mom says about everything now: *It'll be fine eventually.* She has nightmares about the kids in detention that day she gave the shots. She says Tyler is haunting her, and I think she's right. That's what I'd do if I were him.

"Xavier?" I say. "Can you help me with something?"

He stiffens and turns to me, annoyed. He's still shockingly handsome but he looks all wrong, like a businessman instead of an angel.

"I need to take the batteries out of my RIG so no one can find it for a while."

"You shouldn't do that. People may need to find you."

"Sure, but I'm playing hide-and-seek with somebody who cheats and I want to make sure I'm not sending any signals out so they don't find me. How do I do that?"

He frowns but holds out his hand. I pass him my RIG as well as Mom's and Ally's. He doesn't question them. He just says, "I need some tools." He opens a kitchen drawer, takes out a toolkit, removes the backplate from each RIG. He stares at the interior workings with his tongue between his teeth. He removes six silver squares with a pair of tweezers and replaces the plates. He drops the tiny pieces in my hand. "No one can cheat on you now."

"Thanks." I stare at him despondently, knowing this is the last time I'll ever see him. He smells of lemons, but I don't find it reassuring. "I always liked knowing you, Xavier. I hope you make a new friend when you go back to school."

"All our schoolmates are our friends."

"Not really, man. Most of them would like to see you fail. But I always liked you. You were always my friend."

He nods. "We ran cross-country together."

"That's right, man. We ran together." I would shake his hand but mine are full, so I press my left shoulder into his in a clumsy armless hug. I turn my head toward his neck, look over his shoulder through the space where his hair ought to hang, and watch Celeste stream an ancient movie onto the big screen. "I miss running with you, Xavier," I whisper.

"I haven't been feeling well," he says.

"Yeah. Me neither."

Dallas shoulders my backpack and nudges me down the hallway. "We can't be late, son."

Mom locks our door for the last time. I never have to smell this dirty carpet again, never have to wonder what made the smears on the wall. "Get going, boys," she says.

"Daddy isn't a boy," Ally says. "He's a man."

"That's right, honey." Mom waves us on ahead.

Lucas enters the building just as our taxi pulls up. "Hello, Maxwell. How are you?" He stares at Dallas with his head cocked, like a confused but excited dog.

"I'm fine, Lucas," I say. "How are you?"

"Fine. Are you going away?"

"Yes. We're spending Christmas in Atlanta. We'll be back on Monday."

Lucas stares at Dallas while I speak. He turns to Ally, like he knows she's the only one who'll give a straight answer. "Who is this?"

"That's my daddy," Ally says.

Lucas squints at me. "Your father died before you moved here. You told me that." He looks from me to my mom, then back to Dallas. Dallas doesn't move, doesn't say a word, doesn't act like anybody's father.

"They lied," Ally says. "Daddy's not dead."

I push Dallas ahead of me through the lobby door.

Lucas watches us through the glass. I turn around before I get in the cab and wave goodbye.

"Hello, again," the driver says. "Nice to see you."

Mom looks at him in confusion, clutching her handbag tightly. "Hello?" she says.

He peers into the backseat. Ally is tucked behind his chair, staring at the seat fabric. Dallas sits tall and tense in the middle. I sit behind Mom, with a clear view of the driver, and for some reason I'm happy to see him again. "Abdal-Salam, right?" I say.

He smiles. "You have a good memory."

"It's on your ID," I tell him.

He nods. "To the airport shuttle?"

"No!" Mom almost shouts. "To the southwest carpark, please," she adds politely.

The driver raises his eyebrows at me, then pulls away from the Spartan. We all stare sadly out the windows at the streets we're leaving behind. They're gray and empty. People are holed up in their houses, glued to their RIGs, indifferent to our departure.

The driver holds his tongue for as long as he can stand it, but finally he asks, "Are you moving to the carpark?"

Mom ignores him.

He shifts his rearview mirror to catch my eye in it.

"No," I say.

"You selling things there?"

"No."

He nods, watches the road a bit, looks back at the mirror. "Buying things?"

"You should take the underpass here," I tell him.

He drives underground and speeds us west across the city, and I'm thankful that I don't have to see the beautiful cold core of my world disappear behind us. We come back up to ground level and head toward the city walls.

We show our IDs at the gates. The guard barely glances at us before he hands them back and nods us through. We're outside the city at last, and the reality of this journey hits me like a cold shower. I'm chilled and sweaty and scared to death.

"You want me to wait for you and take you back home?" the driver asks.

"No, thanks," I tell him.

"I don't have any calls to go to. I could wait," he says.

"Thanks, but we don't know how long we're going to be."

I don't like being dropped off outside the walls in the dark. I wish we were carrying weapons instead of luggage. I wish the taxi would take us straight to the car, but Mom doesn't want the driver to know where we're going or who we're meeting in case Dr. Richmond tracks us down.

We unload our luggage outside the carpark fence. Abdal takes his payment and looks around in confusion.

"You should go," I tell him.

He shrugs. "Good luck, architect."

We watch him drive away.

"Seven thirty," Mom says. "We're late."

Live music and laughter rise from the carpark. Dallas runs toward it so fast I think he's leaving us, but he stops at a recycling bin just outside the fence. He stands under a streetlight in Mr. Lavigne's suit and black woolen coat, his hair feathery blond, his face bent to his screen. He looks so much like my father I can barely breathe. He turns to us with a smile and holds up a finger, telling us he'll be a moment. Mom takes a sharp breath and looks away.

I look down at the black bin and shiver. Fear crawls along my spine. Over the usual notice of pickup times and fines and acceptable deposits, someone has written the word, WITHSTAND.

Dallas fiddles with his RIG, scratches inside his ears while he reads, fiddles some more, removes his storage chip, then drops the RIG in the recycling bin.

"Everything okay?" I ask when he returns.

He moves away from Ally. "My dad says I can't go to Dallas because I have to finish school. He says I need to come home because something's wrong with my patch."

"That's it?"

"Coach Emery says we should hustle."

"Hustle?"

"His exact word was 'Run.'"

I glance at the garbage can containing Dallas's RIG. I expect police cars and helicopters to swarm in on it.

"Go!" Mom shouts.

It's a five-minute hustle down the road to the car. Our baggage is heavier than it looks. I drop the tent four times. Everyone thinks I'm a recall for taking it, but no one says a word, not even Ally. We have our jackets unzipped and our mitts in our pockets by the time we arrive. "Thank god," Mom mutters.

Churchill sits on a lawn chair beside the only car on the road. A lantern and thermos wait at his feet. His butt is perched on the edge of the seat and his head rests on the back bar. He could be sleeping. He wears a black ski cap pulled down over his eyes. He has tattoos up and down his neck and rings in his ears and nose. Not what I expected. I thought he'd be like his mom, all chipper and zesty. He looks like he spends most of life lying down.

The car is shiny like it's just been washed, but it's hideous—huge, old and fat, like a giant toad on wheels.

"We had a car like this when I was a kid," Mom says.

Churchill lifts his head a smidgeon, pushes back his cap, smiles. His teeth are not what you'd call white. "You the people with the apartment?" He holds the lantern up, looks at each of us, settles the light on me. "Nice hair," he says, which is more of a compliment to his mother than to me. He nods a few times, then slowly removes his ass from the lawn chair.

He's my height, I'm pleased to see. He holds out his hand for me to shake, pumps mine a few times before pulling back and shaking Dallas's. "Thank you, sir, for making this trade. You will not be disappointed with this car. Here's your bill of sale and permit, which I believe are under your wife's name. Registration and insurance are in the driver's visor."

He turns to Mom. "You couldn't find a better car, ma'am. It's in mint condition. What it lacks in efficiency, it makes up in cargo space. It'll take you wherever you want to go." He turns to Dallas again and adds, "So don't hurry back." He sticks his hand in his jeans and pulls out a key dangling from a metal ring. "You want to try it out?"

Mom holds out her hand. "I'll drive."

He drops the key in her palm. "You're the lucky one."

She steps behind the car and opens up the back.

"Now I understand why people live in cars," I say, peering inside. It's not a proper trunk, more of a gaping maw that could sleep two. Mom shoves two jugs of gasoline to one side and says, "Put your bags in here, kids. Hang on to what you want to keep for the ride."

"There's ten gallons of gas there," Churchill says. "Funnel's in the can."

"Thank you," Mom says. When we've stuffed in our bags, she unrolls a vinyl sheet that stretches from the backseat over the contents of the cargo space.

"That's the flimsiest storage system I've ever seen," I say.

Mom is entirely unconcerned that our luggage will fly into our skulls when she taps the brake. She smiles and pats my arm. "It's a station wagon, Max. They're perfectly safe."

It's roomy, I'll give it that much. Even with the tent on top of our bags, the view out the rear window is clear.

"You don't have much stuff," Churchill says. "You're sure you're not coming back soon?"

Mom opens the back door for Ally. "Get in, honey. You too, guys." She stops Dallas from climbing in beside me. "You should sit in the front, dear."

He looks confused, then he laughs. He pulls in his chin and lowers his voice. "Are you kids sure you'll be all right back there on your own?"

"Yes, Daddy," Ally says.

Dallas raises his brow to me.

"We'll be fine, Dad."

He lowers himself into the seat in front of me. He fiddles with a lever by his feet, then slides his chair into my knees. "Lovely night for a drive," he says.

Mom turns to Churchill and says something I can't hear through the glass. She pulls her house key out of her bag, smiles and pats his arm.

He folds up his lawn chair while Mom starts the car. It ignites right away, doesn't catch fire, sounds all right.

Churchill bangs on Dallas's window. Dallas presses a button and the glass slides down. "Take it easy," Churchill says, like that's sage advice. He points to the glove box and adds, "I put my number in there, and the numbers of some other mechanics in the region if you need them."

"Will we need them?" Mom asks.

He shakes his head. "It rides like a dream. But just in case."

Dallas closes the window so fast that Churchill has to cock his head to pull it free.

"That's not nice, Daddy," Ally says.

Dallas laughs. I laugh with him. Mom shakes her head. Churchill just stands there looking confused as we leave him behind.

It's a two-and-a-half-hour drive north to the border, but time passes slowly when you're terrified and disconnected.

We encounter toll booths every twenty minutes, and I'm thrilled to see them. Not Dallas—he breathes out a sigh after we pass each one. I know we might be caught for kidnapping, but if the police catch us, the worst they'll do is turn me into a zombie. I'm more afraid of being eaten or sold by the locals. Cameras and guards have always been there to protect me, or so I thought. In their absence, I fidget and groan in the backseat until Mom has to shush me.

Most of the houses we pass are dark, but the odd one is lit like a billboard. I figure those homeowners are waiting to ambush any cars that break down. A few cars pass us on the highway, headlights blazing like demon eyeballs. I expect each one to slam its brakes, skid to a stop and tear up the highway after us, scythes and pitchforks hanging out the windows.

That doesn't happen. No one notices us at all.

"Will you stop with the groaning?" Dallas mutters.

"You're keeping your sister awake," Mom adds.

I am never going to make it in a town without walls.

"Why can't we cross the border at Buffalo?" Dallas asks when we start heading east.

"Too risky," Mom says. "Rebecca says Freaktown is the safest border crossing left."

Dallas and I groan in unison.

As we approach Syracuse, the toll-booth operators smile at us. "Christmas shopping?" they ask.

After Syracuse, the highway leads to nowhere but Freaktown and the border, and the guards are not so friendly. "Where are you headed?" a butchy white woman asks at the last toll. She surveys our salt-and-pepper family with a scowl.

"We're going to a funeral," Mom says.

Hopefully it won't be our own.

EIGHTEEN

We hit Freaktown sooner than expected. I thought we'd
see blackened forests or glowing craters or shanties on the
outskirts, but there's an ordinary town ahead, flat and dated,
at the end of an empty highway. There's an official welcome
sign that says the population is 120,000, but it's at least thirty
years old. It's been painted over with the words, *Welcome to
Freaktown,* in six-foot letters. I shiver when the headlights
reveal the sign. Not because I'm scared of Freaktown, although
that's true enough, but because the bottom of the sign is
scrawled with the word, *WITHSTAND*. We're driving slowly.
The sign does not blur by. I am not imagining things. The
word *WITHSTAND* stares me in the face in my darkest hour.
It's like God is talking to me. I don't like it.

The highway turns into Freaktown's main street, the only
route to the bridge north. The road is broken and bumpy but
not much worse than where we've come from. There's no other

way to go forward. "Maybe we should wait till morning," I suggest.

"Don't be silly," Mom says. She turns down the high beams, dials up the heat, checks that the doors are locked. We breathe shallow and cringe into our seats.

Abandoned fast-food restaurants fringe us on both sides: Denny's, MacDonald's, Kentucky Fried Chicken, Taco Bell, Dunkin' Donuts, Arby's, Jack in the Box, Pizza Hut, A&W, Baskin Robbins, Quiznos, Domino's, Hardee's, Dairy Queen, Roly Poly, Church's Chicken, Burger King, dozens of them side by side with gas stations, empty for twenty-five poisoned years. Bits of siding, lights and drainage pipes are torn off the exteriors, and if we had the balls to stop and look inside, we wouldn't find appliances. But the shells are intact, happy and colorful after all these years under a brutal sun.

I've studied North American history but I've never imagined anything quite like this. This is a landscape paved in grease and gasoline, prosperity and peace. A world where everybody had a car and a doctor and a right to an education, where entire lifetimes were spent in weekend shopping sprees and drives to the beach just to look at the waves. It boggles my mind, the number of people with cash required to make this street exist. "What do they eat here now?" I ask. "Do you think there'll be roadblocks?"

"Shut up," Dallas says. "You'll scare your sister."

"She's asleep."

"Shut up anyway."

"They're not going to eat us, honey," Mom says, but really she doesn't have a clue.

After the last fast-food restaurant, the road climbs a hill. Mom slows at the crest, expecting to descend into total darkness. But the town below us flickers with light. Smoke rises from chimneys, windows sparkle in a rainbow of colors.

"Oh my god," Mom whispers. "I forgot it's Christmas." She eases the car down the slope.

Freaktown does not look like the *Freakshow* footage. It's just a rundown town, probably rundown long before the disaster. The main street is lined with three-story stone and brick buildings with stores on the bottom and apartments on top, nineteenth-century styling—patterned brickwork around the windows, recessed entrances, wooden awnings. The original signboards have been painted over in several languages to read, *Doctor, Appliances, Food, Housing, Trade, Clinic.* Most of the glass in the display windows is still in place, and where the windows are broken, they're boarded up and painted to look like vistas—forests, oceans, fields of wheat, white gabled houses with rabbits in the yard. This is not what reality programming led me to expect. You need a fully functional brain to transform a broken window into a view.

"What's their power source?" Dallas asks.

Mom shrugs. "Solar?"

"It could be fish oil for all we know," I mutter. "Do they have guns?"

The streets are wide and clear. We're the only car moving. A few ancient vehicles are parked at the curb as if someone might hop in them to deliver pizza at any moment. No one does. You'd think it was three in the morning instead of ten thirty at night. There are no joggers, no partiers, no criminals, no one.

"Where are all the freaks?" Dallas asks.

"We must be in the wrong part of town," Mom says.

"Wrong for those who want to find freaks?" I ask. "Or wrong for those who want to stay alive much longer?"

Mom ignores me. Dallas rolls his eyes like he really is my father. I don't like sitting in the backseat.

"There's something going on ahead," Mom whispers.

We're in the heart of town now. The alleys are strung with colored lights, doorways hung with wreaths of vines and dried apples, stumps of old telephone poles topped with straw dolls shaped into angels and steel wires bent into stars.

People emerge from a building up ahead, dozens of them, maybe hundreds. They pour out of massive double doors onto the sidewalk, pushing strollers and wheelchairs into the street fifty yards ahead of us.

"Were they waiting for us?" I ask.

"It's a church," Dallas says. I don't know if that's an answer.

They keep coming out, some on crutches, some carrying babies, some with their arms draped around others. They look more united than any people I have ever seen. They fan out along the road and turn to us, caught in our headlights.

Mom idles in front of the church. I stick my face to the window.

Two men in long ministerial robes follow their congregation outside. They stop when they see us, their hands lifted halfway up to their neighbors' shoulders and held there as if they're waving. Beside them is a nativity scene made of painted wood and a white sign that lists the hours of Christmas sermons in English, Spanish, Mandarin.

Blankets cover the strollers and wheelchairs and some of the people on their feet. Others wear bulky coats with scarves wrapped around their heads. It's hard to tell who's normal and who's freakish. They don't look like *Freakshow* contestants. They just look poor and sick.

They stare at us like they're scared, like they've been caught in headlights before. They don't scream or surround the car. They don't beg or steal our stuff. They just stare in silence. And then they step aside. An old woman close to the car waves her arm with a graceful flourish and everyone clears a path for us to travel.

Mom drives so slowly that I make eye contact with people as we pass them. A mother bends over her stroller and raises the enormous head of her deformed child, murmuring soft words and pointing at our car. A girl Ally's age with bulging eyes lifts her straw angel to my window and makes it dance. I give her a thumbs-up and she smiles. I smile back at her and wave. Suddenly everyone I pass smiles and waves at me, and I hear a hundred shouts of "Merry Christmas!"

"It's just a town," I mutter as we leave the crowd behind with their rundown storefronts and heaps of garbage and recycled decorations. "I don't think the world is exactly what we've been told."

⸺⸳⸻

Ally wakes up when we get to the border, like there's a tracking device in her patch and she's alerted to the fact that she's leaving zombie territory.

We glance at her nervously. She looks around but says nothing, asks nothing.

There isn't one other car at the border. I was expecting long lines of people pacing beside their vehicles, babies crying and moms hushing toddlers, old people asking what's going on, police ushering suspicious drivers inside for strip searches. But there's just an empty road blocked off by metal gates with two armed guards standing directly in front of them, staring at our car. A squat brown building to our left houses more police officers, computer networks, jail cells.

"All right, everyone," Mom says as she pulls into the light. "Someone will ask us questions now. Just answer them calmly."

Dallas bounces his leg up and down, twists in his seat, scratches at his wig. Mom lays a hand on his shoulder. "Just do what you've been doing for the past two months. You're Patrick Connors. You're taking your family out of the country. Understand?"

He takes a deep breath and stills. He flips down his visor and catches my eye in the mirror. I watch with amazement as my father's face says, "Here we go."

There's a knock at Mom's window. She rolls it down.

"Good evening, ma'am." The guard has a thick accent I can't place, some part of the world where the income is low. He takes us in with big brown eyes fringed in lashes so thick he looks like he's wearing mascara.

"Good evening," Mom says.

"Passports please."

She passes him all four. "We have these too," she says, holding up our ID cards. He looks at the cards curiously. "These are first issue," he says. "We just got ours up here. They're a little different."

"Really?" Mom asks.

He nods. "You'll get the new ones when you renew, I expect." He hands back the cards and looks through our passports so thoroughly I assume we're the only car that's passed his way today and he's short on reading material. He opens each one and stares from the picture to the person three times, reads the description and stares back at the person, then flips through the passport to see where each person has been, which in all our cases is nowhere.

"Do you understand that you're about to leave the country?" he asks.

"Yes," Mom says.

"Where are you headed?"

"We're going to visit my niece." Mom clears her throat and forces a casual tone. "We have some papers for her from her mother. She died. My sister, I mean. Not my niece."

The guard's eyes move while Mom speaks, passing over each of us. "Do you understand that this is a one-way border at the present time?" he asks as he stares at Dallas.

"I do," Mom says.

"And the only means of returning to this country is via your embassy through a reintegration process that takes ten to twelve weeks?"

"Okay."

"And you are responsible for your food and lodging during the entire ten-to-twelve-week waiting period?"

"That's fine."

He taps our passports against his palm and says, "I have to run these against a criminal database and then you're free to go. You have your car registration?"

Mom tugs the paper from her visor and hands it to him, still folded.

"Thank you." He disappears into the building.

"I think he's a zombie," I whisper. "Did you see his eyes?"

"It's hard to tell with adults," Dallas says. "But he didn't search the car."

"No one cares if you take problems out of a country," Mom says. "It's smuggling them in that's hard."

"Do we have to do this again on the other side?" I ask.

She nods. "Just past those gates is another set of gates."

"And past them?"

"We'll see when we get there."

The guard is back and he's brought two friends, a tall black man with a pencil mustache and a stocky white woman with cropped blond hair. They stand with their hands clasped behind their backs while the mascara man approaches. "Mrs. Connors? Mr. Connors? We have reason to believe you're harboring a minor who is not your child."

Mom stares at him, dumfounded.

"You must mean Dallas Richmond," Dallas says.

"Yes, sir. Is he in this vehicle?"

"No. Our son wanted to bring him, but he didn't want to come."

"Do you know his whereabouts?"

"I believe he went to Texas."

"Step out of the car, please."

They don't take us into a room and shine lights in our faces, ask questions, check our stress levels. They stand us up at the side of the road, cold and isolated. It feels like they're going to shoot us.

The tall guard and the woman search the car—under it, on top of it, inside it. They remove our bags and open each one, shift the contents around with gloved hands. They unroll my tent, pat it down, roll it back up. They flip down the backseats of the car and lift up the floor of the trunk to reveal a spare tire no one knew was there. They even check under the hood, as if we might have a six-foot kid curled around the engine.

The mascara man asks us about Dallas.

"I told him he'd have to leave with his own parents," Mom says.

"He didn't want to come," Dallas adds. "It was our son who wanted to bring him."

"He said Coach Emery told him to try out for the Dallas football team," I say. "He's been confused since his vaccination."

"He's a very troubled young man," Dallas says. "I hope you find him because I honestly don't know what he'll do out there on his own."

The guard steps in front of Ally, leans over to look her in the eye. He smiles and bats his lashes. "Do you know where Dallas Richmond is, sweetie?"

We hold our breath and try not to stare too hard.

She shakes her head. "He left when Daddy got home."

"What time was that?" the guard asks.

"Six o'clock."

"Do you know where he went?"

"He disappeared."

"Did he say he would meet you somewhere soon?"

"No. He just disappeared."

He nods, glances at his colleagues who are checking our tires, turns back to us and nods again. He heads into the office building while the others place our belongings back in the trunk. The vinyl cover won't stretch over top this time. My tent sticks up too high. They try to ram it down.

"Just leave it," Mom says. "It's fine."

The mascara man returns with his orders. "The boy's father suspects he'll follow you on foot. It's imperative that you understand this boy is a minor and he is not allowed to leave the country without his legal guardians. He will not get across this bridge or any other border crossing. You understand that if you're waiting for him he will not be leaving and you will not see him again."

"Yes, we understand," Mom says.

"He's not coming this way," Dallas says. "He's going south, to Dallas."

The guard sighs. "You're free to go." He passes Mom the car registration and passports. She checks to make sure they're all there. "Keep them handy," he says. "You're going to need them in a minute. You'll also need your birth certificates and immunization records. Do you have those?"

Mom nods. "We have everything."

The guard shrugs. "Once they pass you on, I can't let you back in."

"That's what we're hoping," I say.

The metal gates swing closed behind us. We drive slowly across a thousand feet of two-lane suspension bridge that hasn't been repaired for decades. The headlights barely penetrate the fog. Although I know how overbuilt old bridges are—it'll be centuries before the bolts rust out—it smells like decay, and I can't help fearing that the steel deck might collapse beneath us.

Mom rolls down her window as if it'll help her see. The bridge is lined with streetlights that burned out ages ago and no one from either side of the border is willing to replace. The air is cold and wet with the scents of the poisoned river and the damp concrete suicide barriers. I wish it were daytime so I could step out and look at the world we're heading into.

My fear doesn't lessen when we reach the border crossing near the end of the bridge. There's a tiny building not much bigger than a toll booth with a swinging metal arm barring the road. No spotlights glare at us, no armed guards survey us. It's unsettling because it implies a serious lack of financing in this country. There's no room to turn around and we're still a hundred feet in the air, so if they don't let us in I can't see what they'll do with us except throw us over and steal the car.

Three guards are crammed into the one little booth, visible through a window that takes up half of one wall. They're smoking cigarettes and drinking from thermoses and talking like they're friends. It's jarring because since the vaccinations I haven't seen anyone talk like this, just shooting the breeze, laughing, passing time. It's not the sort of behavior I expected from border guards. They're all in their thirties, all white men with short hair under blue caps. They wear blue uniforms with silver badges like police officers. But they don't act like police. They act like we're not even here. They smile at each other and speak loudly, happily, like they're in the stands of a ball game. One cuffs another on the shoulder and the third rolls his eyes.

"Should I honk?" Mom asks.

"Are you crazy?" I say.

"Just wait," Dallas says. "This might be some kind of test."

"It smells funny," Ally says.

I reach out and pat her head, but she gives me a look like I'm defective, so I curl back into myself and stare out the window.

One of the guards sticks his head out and shouts, "Just a second!" He ducks out of view. Spotlights flicker and blaze around us. We're momentarily blinded. I feel like we've been ambushed by trigger-happy soldiers. The guard steps out of the booth with a metal rod that he stuffs in a holster. He takes off his cap and smoothes back his hair. It shines red in the bright light. He puts the cap back on and smiles. "You're the first car we've seen since morning." He holds out his hand. "Passports please."

Mom hands them off.

He nods. "Connors. Yeah. Hang on."

He goes back into the building and says something to his colleagues who nod and get busy on their RIGs.

"I've never seen such happy police officers in my life," I say. "You think they're drugged with something better than our guys get?"

Dallas shrugs. "They're not very intimidating."

They're all smiling inside, like there's nowhere they'd rather be in the world than stuck in isolation on this decaying bridge in the dead of night. One of the guards waves at us through the window while he talks on a RIG.

"They knew our name," Mom says. "Why would they know our name?"

The redhead returns, smiles, says, "You've got some friends coming. They've been waiting all week, hoping you'd get here for Christmas." He checks his watch and smiles. "You're cutting it close." He points past the spotlights to some vast unknown. "They're not allowed any nearer, but you'll see them in a minute if all goes well."

Mom nods.

"Karenna Connors?" he asks. "Where were you born?"

Dallas fidgets in the passenger seat while Mom answers a long list of questions. I hope he memorized Dad's vital statistics or we're screwed.

"Last place of employment?" the guard asks.

"New Middletown Manor Heights," Mom says.

The man's face creases like a foul smell hit his nostrils, and he pulls away from the window.

"It's a geriatric center," Mom explains.

"I know what it is." He stares at her with a whole new face, one that makes it easy to see he's a cop. "Are you a doctor there? A janitor? What?"

"I'm a nurse."

"A nurse." He looks at her so coldly I have to suppose that his mother was killed by a nurse in his infancy. "What about you?" he asks Dallas. "What do you do for a living?"

"I was a doctor." Dallas coughs, lowers his voice, explains, "I've been unemployed for three years but before that I was a doctor."

"And where did you work?"

"New Middletown Manor Heights."

"You were a doctor at that place?"

"Yes."

The guard nods, turns to the building, waves his colleagues out, turns back to us. "You know what we call the places you call geriatric centers? We call them totalitarian medical facilities. You know what we call what goes on there? Unethical experiments on helpless populations. And you know what we call the doctors and nurses who work there? We call you monsters."

Mom's mouth hangs open in disbelief.

"We're going to search your vehicle now." He says it like there's no doubt they'll find contraband because they are never letting us into their country. "Get out. Get your children out."

So once again we're standing on the side of a lonely road afraid of being shot. The redhead keeps his eye on us, his hand on his holster, while the other two open the trunk. He likes to talk, this guy. He talks at Mom and Dallas, glances at me and Ally every now and then and shakes his head like it's always the kids who suffer. He feels inside our pockets, drops our coats on the road, pats down our shivering bodies, tells us how it is.

"You think you're all closed up down there, watching everybody. You never stop to think that maybe somebody's watching you. We know what goes on in your cities and your hospitals. Nobody's buying your story about self-protection and how you're leading the way for the rest of the world." And on and on he preaches from his moral high ground while his buddies throw the contents of our bags onto the dirty bridge.

"That's why we're leaving," Mom says. "We don't like what's going on at home."

The redhead laughs at her. "Took you a while."

Dallas stands tall and clears his throat. "I quit my job because of it, years ago." He looks indignant and ashamed at the same time, a disgusted doctor, man against society. "And now we're leaving the country, risking everything we have, risking our children's futures because we don't want to be part of it anymore."

The guard looks him up and down, sees a middle-aged rich bastard on the run.

"We don't allow any companies, public or private, to test or prescribe medications on their employees or students or clients or soldiers or prisoners or anybody else without permission. Do you understand? This is not the world you're used to, doctor. This is not the world that you belong in."

At the car, the taller guard whistles. He's holding open the blue pillowcase that was stuffed in Mom's suitcase. He pulls out a handful of coins, gold chains and pearls dangling from his fist. The redhead whistles too. All three of them look at us like we're filth, like we peeled these jewels from helpless old invalids before we experimented on them.

The tall guard puts the pillowcase to one side, closes Mom's suitcase and sets it down with the others.

"Put that back in!" I shout.

"Max," Mom whispers.

I look at her—she's scared, cold, confused and guilty. I shake my head, turn back to the guard beside the car.

"You can't have that. My friend gave that to me to help us get away. I won't let you take it."

He laughs. "All right, kid. You can stop me." He and his short buddy haul my tent in front of the car and start unrolling it.

"Put it back!" I shout.

The redhead chuckles, steps in front of me, his hand on his holster.

"You can't take our stuff," I tell him.

"Max, stop," Mom says.

"No." I step forward. The guard steps forward. We're one foot apart, staring in each other's eyes. He smiles like he can't wait.

"You talk about my parents like you know who they are," I say. "But here you three are in your own little world with no cameras watching you, and you think you can do whatever you want to us. I bet you look forward to people like us trying to cross, don't you? You can take our stuff if you want to, call us names, lecture us, make us stand here in the cold while my little sister's teeth chatter."

He takes a step back, cocks his head, lets me finish.

"What do you know about our lives? Who are you to judge us?" I shout. "What is the difference between what you're doing right now and what people in power have done where we're coming from? What exactly is the difference? I want to know."

He says nothing. He's not smiling now, just looking at me, biting his tongue.

"You're no different than any other adult I ever met in my life."

He nods, raises his eyebrows, nods some more. "They sure didn't drug you, did they?" He laughs out loud, one harsh snort, and nods some more until my adrenaline drains and I'm shaking with nerves and cold.

"Pick your coats up," he says.

"Gavin!" the taller guard shouts from in front of the car. "You're never going to believe this!"

They've set my tent up in the road, the whole thing, poles up, flaps down. I don't know how they did it so fast. They must be regular campers.

The spotlights blaze down on it. It's gray and ugly on the damp cold road. *WITHSTAND* glares black and fierce across the wrinkled canvas walls, and all my people live safe inside it in the dark. All I can think is, Man, that is some magnificent work of art, some flash of brilliance passed through me when I made that.

The front flaps open and the short guard peeks out, holding a flashlight, smiling. "This is it," he tells the redhead. "I think this is actually it."

Mom helps Ally button her coat. She sniffs back her tears. "I don't know what to do," she says. She looks at Dallas. "I'm so sorry. I don't know where to go."

He shrugs. "There must be other places. Places where the ID cards aren't used yet."

"We can go back to Freaktown," I say. "I bet they'd let us live there. They must need nurses. We can work, too, me and Dallas. We could teach languages and math, whatever they need. We could start a football team and make a life there. For a while anyway. We could do something real, something to change what's happening at home."

Dallas looks at me like I'm crazy. Mom smiles sadly. Ally says, "Dallas disappeared."

"I'm not going back to New Middletown," I tell them. "There is a world out here that is nothing like anything I've ever seen, and I want to be in it."

Mom sighs. She'd go along with anything, she's so tired.

I look to Dallas. He shrugs. "I just want to go to school, Max. I don't care where. I want to be an engineer. I want to build things. That's what I'm good at."

"You're a doctor," Ally says. "You save people's lives."

Dallas looks down at her and pats her head. "Poor kid. You're going to be so messed up by the time this is over."

"Where should we go?" I ask him.

"Anywhere. Anywhere but home."

The redhead swaggers over to our huddle. "Where'd you get that tent?" he asks.

I hate this guy. I hate his smile, I hate his freckles, I hate his voice, I hate the way he holds his hips. "It's my tent. You can't have it."

"It's your tent?"

"It's my tent."

"But where did you get it?"

"It's mine, man. I got it from my living room. What do you want?" He looks over at the tent. The stenciled word, *WITHSTAND,* jogs down the wall and into my heart. I take a deep breath, shake my head, "No way. You are not taking that tent from me."

He sucks in his lips and steps in front of Ally, leans over to look her in the eye. "Do you know who made that tent?"

"Mommy found it in the surplus store and Max painted it."

"Who's Max?"

"Max is my brother."

He looks over at me, back to Ally. "Your brother painted that tent? This boy right here? He painted that tent?"

She nods. "For the art exhibit. He didn't win. His principal drove him home and he saw Peanut in the forest."

He straightens up and turns to me. The other two guards walk over, smiling. "I can't believe it," the short one says.

"You painted this tent?" the redhead asks me.

"You're not taking it."

"What's inside it?" he asks. "If you painted it you should know."

"My life is inside it, and you're not taking it from me."

He laughs again, the harsh snort, and looks at his buddies. All three of them start shrugging and laughing and shaking their heads—not like they're savoring the moment before they kill us, but like they're genuinely happy.

The redhead puts his hand on my shoulder and shakes me a little. I step back out of reach. He laughs. "This tent is all over the world, kid." He holds his hands up like he's lifting a globe. "It's everywhere. Everywhere."

I shake my head, unnerved by his smile and touch. "It's been in my apartment since the exhibit."

"No, you don't understand. It's all over the news, kid. It's a symbol."

"It was on an international broadcast a few weeks ago," the taller guard says. "Some reporter in Pittsburgh wrote a story about it, and it spread like wildfire. It symbolizes resistance against corporate control, how people are uniting in secret and biding their time before they take their country back."

"It's been picked up everywhere," the redhead says. "This tent is everywhere. And that word, *withstand*, you can't go anywhere without seeing it."

"It gives people hope," the short one tells me. "That there are still people who care, even in places like New Middletown, that there are people who are ready to lead it somewhere better."

I don't like the way they look at me. It's that same feeling I had in the skate park when Washington and Tyler harassed the Asian kid. It's like they expect too much of me, like I should be special and heroic. But I honestly don't have anything to say. I just want my tent back.

"It's amazing you're here," the redhead says. "You obviously don't know the influence you've had. This word is on army barracks and factory walls and prisons and malls and everywhere people are hiding themselves." He takes off his cap, finger combs his hair, laughs.

"What are you going to do with us?" Mom asks.

He smiles at her and bows his head. "I'm going to ask you to take our picture in front of this tent and then I'm going to let you go meet your friends."

"And our stuff?" Dallas asks.

"You can have your stuff."

"And my tent?" I ask.

He shakes me by the shoulder again, smiles and says, "You can have your tent."

My cousin Rebecca embraces me, full and hard like I'm her long lost brother. She's older than I expected, well past thirty. She's dark, like Mom, but tall and regal. "Happy Birthday," she tells me. "I'm so glad you made it."

"Oh my god," Mom says. "It's past midnight. Happy Birthday, Max." She hugs me hard and long, shuddering in my arms.

"Hey hey, don't cry, Mom," I say. I hold her away from me and look in her eyes. "You got us here, right? We're okay. Don't cry."

She sniffles and nods, steps back toward Rebecca.

I turn to Dallas, who's watching us sadly. I open my arms wide. "What? No birthday hug, Dad?"

He smiles and slams my shoulder softly. "Happy Birthday, Max. Glad we made it." He looks around the wet dark nowhere and nods nervously, like he's wondering what the hell we do now.

Rebecca holds out her hand to him. "How do you do?" she asks. He's about to explain who he is, but Mom shakes her head and points to Ally, then back to the border station. He nods and says to Rebecca, "Nice to meet you."

She kisses Ally on the forehead and cheeks. She goes so far as to pick her up, but she puts her down quickly when the zombie becomes evident. She turns to Mom, hugs her again. "I forgot how much you look like Mom," she says.

While they talk about Aunt Sylvia, Rebecca's mother, the passenger door of Rebecca's car opens up and a girl steps out and leans on the hood.

"Is that—?" I say. "That looks like—" I can't say it. I can't let myself hope it.

Rebecca looks over her shoulder and smiles. "You're not the first family here from New Middletown. I hope you don't mind that I brought her. She wanted to come." She waves the girl over.

Dallas and I moan at the same time. My heart flutters in my chest.

Pepper walks over, smiling shyly. She looks beautiful. A little skinny, and shorter than I remembered. Either I've had a growth spurt or I never realized how tiny she is. She stuffs her hands in her pockets like she's afraid to reach out with them. Her eyes shine.

"Oh my god," Dallas says.

"You're normal," I add.

"Hey." She looks down at her feet and back at me. "I'm sorry I couldn't tell you. My parents made me promise. I almost told you that last day with Xavier. I could have sworn you were normal, but I couldn't take the chance, you know?" Maybe she's worried that I'll say, "No, I don't know. You shouldn't have left me." But I don't say that.

"How did you know we were coming?" I ask.

"There's a big push up here to get people out. There are support groups in almost every city. People pass on names in case anybody can help sponsor someone. Dad told me you were named a couple of weeks ago. We found Rebecca right away and we've just been waiting for you." She smiles radiantly and I love her for it. I haven't seen a girl really smile since the shots.

"I can't believe you're here," I say.

"Same here." She takes her hands out of her pockets and opens her arms. We hug awkwardly. She pulls away, but not too far, and asks, "What about Dallas?"

I realize that she thinks it's my dead father hovering at my shoulder all this time. I shake my head slowly and say, "Dallas didn't make it."

Dallas cuffs me.

Pepper cringes. "Poor Dallas."

"You always had a crush on him, didn't you?" Dallas asks.

Pepper gives my dad a very weird look.

"Don't be embarrassed," he says. "A lot of girls have crushes on him." He smiles, beams so brightly you can just make him out beneath his disguise.

Pepper steps back, her hand to her mouth.

"Not bad, huh?" Dallas says in own voice.

She laughs and hugs him, a big warm hug not at all like the awkward one she gave me.

"Did you?" I ask, totally miffed. "Did you really have a crush on Dallas?"

She laughs some more and hugs me, too, big and warm. Dallas joins in to make it a group hug, the dirty dog.

When we break apart, I see Mom watching us and smiling. Ally stands at her side looking angry, like we've misbehaved and she wishes there was someone she could tattle to.

Dallas clears his throat and tells Pepper, "Call me Patrick Connors. Just till I get cleaned up."

Rebecca asks Pepper, "Would you like to ride with them on the way back?"

"Yes. Sure," Pepper says.

"You'll follow me home?" Rebecca asks Mom.

"Yes. Whenever you're ready. Pepper, why don't you sit up front with me?" Mom asks. "Ally can't ride with an airbag, and the boys will fight over who sits with you."

"Daddy is a man, not a boy," Ally says.

"That's right, honey," Mom says.

Pepper does a happy little dance step, like she likes being fought over. Then she hops into the passenger seat beside Mom. "I can tell you about your new life. It'll take some getting used to."

"We can withstand anything," I say.

Dallas climbs in the backseat first, leaving me and Ally outside the car. "Do you want to sit in the middle?" I ask.

"I'll sit wherever you tell me," Ally says.

My happiness drains a bit.

"It'll be okay, Max," Mom says. "Just give it time. Get in."

I nod. Ally's still waiting to be told what to do.

I use one of her rhymes, even though she doesn't care about those anymore. I use my favorite. It doesn't leave everything up to chance, like Ally always thought her rhymes did. But it doesn't make what happens the inevitable outcome of where you start either. It puts the result in the hands of the person choosing.

If I count every word of the rhyme as I say it, it will end with Ally. But if I count every syllable, it will end with me. How it turns out is my decision.

I want her to get in the car first, so I can sit behind Pepper and touch her hair and make Dallas jealous. So I don't count the syllables. I just count the words, and I hope they're true. I say, "One, two, three, four, five, six, seven. All good children go to heaven."

ACKNOWLEDGMENTS

Thanks to my editor, Sarah Harvey, for enthusiastic support and constructive criticism. Thanks to Dave Desjardins and the Aylmer English Writers' Group for commenting on early chapters. Special thanks to Tim Wynne-Jones for agreeing to be my first reader. As always, thanks to my children, Sawyer and Daimon, for inspiration through naughtiness and good hearts, and to my husband, Geoff, for paying the mortgage and being so proud of me.

I should also acknowledge Ira Levin and Dav Pilkey, but I swear I did not intend to write this as *George and Harold Meet Teen Zombie Nerds in Stepford*. It just came out that way.

CATHERINE AUSTEN worked in the conservation movement before becoming a freelance writer. She lives in Quebec with her husband, Geoff, and their children, Sawyer and Daimon. Her first novel with Orca was *Walking Backward*. To learn more about Catherine and her books, go to catherineausten.com.